White Road

HARRY WHITEHEAD

CLARET PRESS

Copyright © Harry Whitehead, 2025
The moral right of the author has been asserted.

ISBN paperback: 978-1-910461-80-8
ISBN ebook: 978-1-910461-81-5

A CIP catalogue record for this book is available from the British Library.

This paperback can be ordered from all bookstores as well as from Amazon, and the ebook is available on online platforms such as Amazon and iBooks.

The author gratefully acknowledges the T.S. Eliot Estate for permission to quote a line from 'The Wasteland', in his *Collected Poems 1909-1962* (Faber and Faber Ltd.)

Cover and Interior Design by Petya Tsankova

www.claretpress.com

Claret Press

For Nila and Brân

When I look ahead up the white road
There is always another one walking beside you
...who is that on the other side of you?

T.S. Eliot, from 'The Waste Land'

CONTENTS

THE KNOT

Carrie Essler
The Hamlet of Tuktoyaktuk
Southern shore of the Beaufort Sea, Canada
October – Tomorrow

Carrie Essler sprinted along the concrete jetty. She halted at the end beside a mooring cleat as big as an anvil, squatted on her haunches, tried to catch her breath. The freezing air had scoured her windpipe, the hairs in her nostrils frozen, prickly and tickling. She made a fist, soft-punched the cleat. Something in its pig-iron obstinacy calmed her more than the eight miles she'd run.

She pulled herself up, sat on the cleat. A breeze blew in from the southwest, lifting the ice-dust from the frozen sea-surface into spectral eddies. She was shivering already, the sweat on her face beginning to frost. Never sweat in the Arctic, it'll suck the life right out of you when it freezes.

A Chinook helicopter dropped from the clouds in the north-east. It banked out across the sea and then straightened on final approach. She sighed, checked her watch.

'Typical,' she said.

Carrie jogged back along the empty jetty that thrust out into the Beaufort Sea like some engineer's hard-on. She ran past the offshore supply boat moored there for the winter. The deep thwock of the chopper's twin rotors cut through the wind's low hiss.

'Be nice...be nice...be nice...' she muttered over and over as she ran past warehouses and portacabin offices, then along by the corporate and dormitory buildings that lined the airport runway. She swung in through a gap by the charter helicopter hangar. Skidded to a halt on the slippery tarmac beside an Inuvialuit man in a Canadian Coast Guard parka.

3

'Ma'am,' he said.

She nodded, put her hands on her knees, panting.

'You been out where polar bears'll get you again.' He wore a conciliatory smile, but his quiet voice was serious.

'Here's hoping, Mike,' she replied.

He wasn't to be put off so easily. 'They come in off the sea. More now the pack ice stays away in the north.' He shook his head, as if weary with the entire world and everyone in it, then stepped forwards to wave the Chinook down.

Huge whorls of dust enveloped Carrie as it landed. Red and white with the livery of the Canadian Coast Guard, its deafening engines made her duck away. 'Be nice...' As the rotors slowed, she saw the pilot through the cockpit window.

'Oh, marvellous,' she said aloud.

The Chinook's rear ramp dropped. She walked over to stand beside it. A short, round man bumbled down the incline, way too much gold braid on the jacket beneath his overcoat. Above her head, the twin rotors came to a stop.

Carrie made a show of saluting.

'I see you dressed for the occasion,' Assistant Commissioner Grady said, looking her up and down, his lips thin. Carrie wore Lycra skin-tights in hippy-trippy colours that, she conceded, looked a little curious with her Arctic boots, Coast Guard fleece and ancient yellow bobble hat.

'You showed up early, sir.'

'Jogger now, are you?'

She breathed in hard through her nostrils, tried to quell the hatred, the anger. 'Swimming's out, this time of year,' she managed.

Grady made a visible effort to smile. 'It's good to see you, Carrie.' She didn't return his smile.

'So we're part of your whistle-stop tour of the provinces then?' she said.

'I'm here to see PentOil off its drill site. That's it.'

'I heard. Flying out to the rig with the corporate vampires tomorrow. Very cosy, if I might say so, sir.'

'I'm hoping you'll join us.'

'Not a chance, sir!' She was thinking about the Chinook's pilot.

Grady closed his eyes, raised his face to the heavens. His breath came steaming from his nostrils. He took a moment to look around. Carrie followed his gaze. The runway contained just a lonely Twin Otter, heavily sheeted against the weather. A few lights glinted from Tuktoyaktuk village, half a mile away. The odd window shone in the two-storey airport block beside them. Light bloomed from the control tower above the modest original airport building that predated the arrival of corporate money.

'If the Arctic did tumbleweeds...'

'Things closing down for the winter,' said Grady.

'Been a thrill a minute all summer, though, sir.'

He exhaled heavily. 'I gave you a promotion.'

'You gave me punishment detail. I'm a rescue swimmer, not some gormless border guard.'

'You never liked Canada,' he said, 'even when you and Don were still together.'

'Well, I surely am loving it now. Yes, siree. What a blast.'

'That's not how it was.'

'How it was, is you packed me off to the arse-end of nowhere for screwing around on your wee Coast Guard poster boy.'

For a second he looked like he was actually going to punch

her. Here we go, she thought, just try it, boss! Me lamping a senior officer's one way out of this coal hole. But Grady only squeezed his hands tightly together.

'Lord Almighty,' he said, 'then just go home!'

'That's it? Ship me back to Bonny Scotland where I come from? Immigrants out, rah, rah, rah?'

Grady looked at her with a kind of patronising comprehension that really did make her want to clock him one. 'But you're coming with us tomorrow,' he said.

And now Carrie saw Don himself, standing at the top of the ramp, six foot three of, yes, poster-boy military zeal. As he strode down to stand beside her, his co-pilot and loadmaster following, she ran her fingers through her hair. Felt it crunch where the sweat had turned to frost. A dog's hackles rising.

'Donny,' she said.

'How are you, Carrie?' He didn't smile.

'I'll show you to your rooms.' She marched away across the tarmac, not waiting for them to follow.

—

Pressed up against the outer wall of an airport building, Tuktoyaktuk's only bar had once been a steel goods container. One side had been cut away and a prefab lean-to with a corrugated tin roof added. There was no sign. The owner hadn't bothered; everyone knew what it was.

Carrie shouldered open the weather-beaten door and ducked inside, snowflakes billowing in after her. She pulled off her parka, hung it on a peg. A twin-bar electric heater glowed hopelessly on the ceiling. Caribou antlers drooped above the bar beneath dismal strip-lights. A rowdy group of rig workers waiting for a flight home drowned out the portable stereo on the counter. One of them wolf-whistled and the rest sniggered like the arse-wipe schoolboys they were. Everyone knew about her. Everyone was male. No one was going to shut up, ever. That, Assistant Commissioner Grady, was how it was.

'Carrie Essler,' a voice called from a nearby table in a mock Humphrey Bogart accent, 'Arctic counter terror squad. She's got it licked.' He waggled his tongue to more laughter.

Carrie glared at Donny's co-pilot. 'Yeah, fek off, Lightsy,' she told him quietly, her Scottish accent coming through as it tended to at such moments. 'I'll drive that bottle through yer face.'

Voices said, 'Ooh,' but Lightsy didn't reply. He knew better.

She nodded to Jeannie, the old woman tending bar. A tall Inuvialuit man perched on a stool at the counter. He was grinning nastily at Carrie, obviously enjoying the spectacle.

'Oh not you too, fuck's sake,' she said.

'Oh yeah,' he replied.

She sat opposite a chubby little guy with a ratty, entirely Arctic-inappropriate trilby perched on the back of his head. A half-empty bottle of bourbon and two tumblers awaited, one of them empty. She poured herself a slug and tipped it in gratitude.

Jim Ross was reading a thick, technical document. He peered over the top. 'Who's the wise guy?' he said, tilting his head towards Lightsy's table, his trilby remaining on his head as if glued there.

'My ex-husband's co-pilot. They came in with Grady. Flying you and your company morons out to the rig tomorrow.'

Ross mouthed a silent O. When she didn't speak, he said, 'Your jilted ex, plus Grady, the man who banished you up here for it. Gotta hurt.'

Carrie poured another slug, glared at the glistening rime frost in the ceiling corners.

'Guess you don't want to talk about it,' said Ross.

'Quit the oil business. Get into mind reading.'

'Quit the Coast Guard. Get your sense of humour back.'

She raised her glass. Touché.

Ross said, 'You not coming with us, then?'

She made a disparaging sound, swirled her drink.

Ross looked like he was waiting for more, but she damn well wasn't going to offer it.

'How about the Inuit guy, then?' Ross said, nodding towards the man on the stool, who was watching the little TV now. 'What you do to him?'

Carrie pushed her chair back on its two rear legs, stared up at the ceiling. 'Ah Christ,' she said, 'he's the only one who probably does owe me an earful. I was vetting him earlier. Told him he didn't look Inuit.'

'Wow, not good.'

'Gets better. Then I told him he was a Russian spy.'

Ross put his papers on the table. 'You told him *what*?'

'I know. He studied at Far Eastern University in Vladivostok. And he's a way of looking at you straight, not like the Inuit way, right? Maybe. I was in a bad mood, Donny and Grady. What can I tell you? Anyway, he's one of your crew. Name's Joe Amaruq.'

'I've seen him around. But a Russian spy?'

'Leave it, will you?'

Ross whistled and went back to muttering over his papers. What was this place turning her into? Her fingers traced the tabletop pattern she knew so well. A Carrick bend knot. Had a sailor chiselled it? Some Siberian oil worker etching an old gangland crest?

She'd first tied a Carrick bend when she was about ten. She remembered it exactly. Ten miles out of Stonehaven into the North Sea, Aberdeen just a suggestion further up the coast. Her father's Fulmar Thirty-Two heeled over, riding a stiff breeze from the south-east, her brother Stephen at the helm. Dad showed her the Carrick bend knot, then once again, irritated already, his eyes darting from the racing stratocumulus to the telltales flapping on the sails. While he barked orders to her other two brothers, she'd muttered 'Carrie-*Carrick*-Carrie-*Carrick*' as she tied and retied the knot. The little girl so far away – in time and now in space as well.

Back in the present, she rubbed her temples. Getting maudlin. Time to leave.

Abruptly, the ambient bar racket diminished. Carrie looked round to see everyone watching the TV screen. It showed climate activists unfurling a banner around the leg of an offshore oil rig. *BRING THEM DOWN*.

'Bring down a monkey wrench on their fucking heads,' a rig worker said to general assent.

The images cut to an oil refinery aflame. Carrie read ... *Saudi Arabia...*

'You see why we need you up here, doing your job?' Ross said.

'Oh, leave off. A few numpties going lah-di-dah on an oil rig. What, now they're all on route to Tuktoyaktuk?' She snorted, slugged her bourbon.

But Ross was still staring at the screen, as if, in its cathode heart, there might lie some answer.

Carrie tugged gently at his greying goatee. 'You're not the weasel you think you are, Jim.' She winced to herself. It sounded harsher than she'd intended.

He glared at her, and Carrie saw the bloodlines zigzagging across his sclera. Then he squeezed his fingers over the closed document until they turned white. 'Oil's the devil's...' he began, slurring. She laughed, an explosion of sound that silenced the whole bar, this woman laughing while the men watched their working world ablaze. 'I just... No disasters.'

'Now there's a word.'

He filled his cheeks with air, waved a hand around hopelessly. 'My name...' Rapped his knuckles hard on the documents. He glanced at her, warily now.

Carrie looked in confusion at the documents and then lifted her eyes to his. 'You've signed something dodgy about your oil rig?'

'It's a drillship. And I'm drunk. And everything rides on tomorrow.' He began to rise, but she leaned over and pushed him back down.

'No you don't, sunshine,' she said kindly. 'Come on, what's going on? Grady being here to kick your sorry arse off your drill site tomorrow? Not like you aren't two weeks past your license cut off, after all. Even I've given you grief over that, and I don't give two shits. You and your rust-bucket Russky oil-rig, drillship, blah blah blah.'

'It's Azerbaijani.'

'But we all know the money's Russian, whatever sanctions-busting, mumbo-jumbo license finagling you cooked up to make it happen.'

Ross stared down at the table, seemingly lost in thought. She wondered if he might run his fingers over the Carrick knot too. Instead, he looked up, said, 'Okay, here's how it is. We had to stay on. No choice. The US-owner's bank loans come due next Monday. If we don't show a result, we're done.'

'Bankrupt.'

'Bingo.'

'But that's the US company.'

'Who own me. Then there's the ship...' He stopped, eyed her warily, flicked a hand angrily in the air. 'On which note...'

As he pushed himself to his feet, his walking stick clattered to the ground. She reached down and picked it up.

'Come on,' she said.

As they headed for the door, Lightsy grinned like he knew all her secrets. She mouthed the words *Piss Off*. Joe Amaruq lifted a newspaper from the counter and made a show of hiding behind it.

'Funny,' she told him, though it kind of was.

Outside, snow fell thick and silent in the orange glow from the lamps on the buildings. Ross hobbled along. His walking stick kept sliding out from under him. Carrie gripped his upper arm. They pushed their way in through the main door to the accommodation block. The heat was almost as much of a shock as the cold. She scrabbled her parka loose, hung on to Ross as they stumbled past the conference room and climbed the stairs to the second floor.

Ross said, 'I know you're all about leaping out of helicopters...'

'Not for three years I haven't.'

'But don't you ever want to curl up on a sofa? Cats and box sets?'

'No.'

'I guess my dream of our future life together needs some work.'

She made a rude sound.

They trudged along the corridor to his room. Outside the

door, Ross slid a hand round her back. His lips parted as he leaned in close. Playing stupid though he was, still Carrie dug two fingers up under the rear corner of his jaw.

'Sweet Jesus!' Ross said.

'Something going on with your drillship, Jim?' She surprised herself with the seriousness of her tone.

But he just made a dismissive gesture with his hands. So she gave it up, kissed him on the cheek, then strode off towards her own vile billet.

'I'm filing for assault,' he called after her affectionately.

She showed him the finger over her shoulder – as a matter of form – but wondered what it could be that he was so obviously hiding.

Jay Skelton

The Drillship 'Belyy Medved', Beaufort Sea

Jay zipped up his boiler suit, bumped his elbow on an upper bunk. Too much company, too little space. Two bunks, one man on duty, one off. This was a Russian drillship in all but flag-of-convenience: four-man crew accommodation, solitude an impossible luxury.

Still, just this once, for a few moments, he did have the cabin to himself. He fished in the back of his locker, brought out the little tin, flipped it open. Inside, the heat-seeking missile.

He snapped the box shut, put it deep in a pocket of his boiler suit.

'Do it,' he told himself in the mirror. Breathed a long breath. Opened the door.

Lights in rusting metal cages ran along the bunkroom corridor's ceiling. Through a bulkhead hatchway, spinning the wheel-handle. *Always Close the Hatch Behind You.* Another corridor, the machine shop visible on one side through a scratched floor-to-ceiling Perspex window. Two men in face-protectors were re-filing a giant screw joint. The machine tools whined and ground. Sparks flying.

He turned left, following the black walkway with yellow safety lines. Signs along the walls in Russian and English and more-recently-added Azeri. *Always Follow the Yellow Lines.* He passed three men on their way back to the accommodation area. Blackened hands and faces. He kept his head down. No hellos. Not today.

Through another bulkhead hatch into an open area. Engines yowled in the cavernous space. Steel pounded steel. He pulled the ear defenders down off his hard hat. *Always Wear Ear Protection.* The stink of lubricating oil and scorched metal filled his nostrils. Everywhere, rust bubbled through paint.

He turned right to the barrier around the moonpool, the huge rectangular hole right through the centre of the ship. He stared down, though he hadn't meant to stop.

The sea's surface sucked and heaved below, surging up then dropping away in great gushing roars. Freezing sea spume wet his face. A fat steel tube, the riser, plunged from the drill floor above into the moonpool, connecting the ship to the well on the sea-bed below.

They were coming to test the well's integrity today. The bossmen. Well, Jay was ready for them.

Dimly, he heard the ocean beating against the outer hull, felt the entire drillship's uneasy motion in the sea: even this vessel, bigger than an aircraft carrier. Nature was knocking to come in.

He passed under a crane, a huge bent, steel finger, striped

with veins of rust. High above, the flare boom was swung way out over the ship. It burned gas in a spray of yellow fire against the low, slate-grey cloud cover. The wind battered him so he had to cling to the railing. Could the helicopter even land today? That, at least, was beyond his control.

He headed inside the bridge superstructure and made his way to the radio room.

'Morning, Chuck,' he said, drawing off his gear and stowing it in the wardrobe.

Chuck yawned, took his headset off. 'I'll have your day gig, you twitching Limey, if I got to toss you overboard to get it.'

'Boil your redneck head in gumbo,' Jay managed, relieved his voice didn't crack.

As Chuck ran him through the daily agenda, Jay paid just enough attention to make the appropriate sounds and nods.

Alone, he went over his checklist on autopilot, then he gazed out of the stern-facing glass. In the ship's centre, the derrick rose more than two hundred feet above the main deck, a vast steel pyramid, and Jay and his scurrying co-workers like insects supporting a leviathan.

His hand touched the box hidden in his pocket. An image from a Lichtenstein poster came into his mind. *VAROOM! BAAM!*

He wiped his sweaty hands on his thighs then went online, via satellite, to the private email account. In the Drafts folder was a new draft message, addressee and subject line empty. It contained a single word:

Don't.

Don't. Do Not. Not. Ton. Don. Do...

Jay shook his head. He deleted the email, went to Trash, emptied it.

Do. Do not…

He drew out the little box from his pocket. Opened it. Placed what was inside on the desk.

'Do,' he said.

Carrie

Carrie heard the whine of aircraft engines through her second-floor window. She tugged at the zipper on her orange survival suit. It stuck. She swore. At last, she slid the zip open, clambered inside and velcro-ed various flaps into place.

The engine whine was louder.

What had she forgotten? Never mind. Go!

She hurried downstairs, ungainly in the suit, rushed along corridors to the helicopter departure lounge. Only a member of the ground crew stood inside the door that led out onto the tarmac. Everyone was already aboard. The Chinook's engines growled, its blades a whirling blur.

'I gotta check your equipment, ma'am.' The crewman stepped in front of Carrie as she headed for the door.

'And I gotta check if there's somewhere even further north I can have you posted,' Carrie said.

He raised both hands, palms outward, but smiling. She strode past him and into the dull, cloudy morning. She saw Don's face in the cockpit window. He looked at her, tapped his wrist where a watch would be and smiled that infuriating smile of his. She made a show of stopping, gazing round, before sauntering towards the rear of the chopper.

The Chinook's loadmaster waited inside. She flopped into a seat. He helped strap her into the harness.

The Chinook lurched, fell back, then abruptly lifted into the air. She did miss the thrill. Still, you don't chit-chat in a

Chinook. The twin rotors could be felt as much in the stomach as they could be heard through the ear defenders. It felt like they were being hit by anti-aircraft fire, the wind brutal at five hundred feet, just beneath the clouds. She peered out of a tiny porthole behind her shoulder. The shore ice's scuffed surface gave way to black, as yet unfrozen, ocean. She could feel the cold trying to claw its way into her suit. Little crystals of ice had formed on her tear ducts. She pulled her hood up, considered zipping the plastic face visor into place.

Ross sat opposite, clutching his walking cane in front of him, as if it were a ceremonial mace. She could imagine how white his knuckles must look under his gloves. It was a chopper crash had busted up his leg in the first place.

Joe Amaruq, the Inuvialuit crewman from the bar last night, sat to one side of Ross. Carrie offered him a wary nod but he looked away, clearly still pissed at her for the grilling she'd given him during the crew-vetting process. One more male with a reason to hate her. Get in line.

Grady, the cause of her really just wonderful good mood this morning, sat on the Inuvialuit guy's other side. Avoiding Grady's glare, she looked at the person sitting on the other side of Jim Ross: the great man himself, PentOil's Chief Executive Officer, Alexander Falcon Willetts III. Only Americans had names like that.

She'd been prepared to dislike him even before he arrived. And he hadn't disappointed.

When he'd swanned out of his corporate jet earlier, Ross'd introduced her as the person with 'overall command of this facility.' Willetts had winked at Grady as he offered Carrie a limp hand, his colourless eyes beneath a widow's peak as cold as winter.

'I took you for the, ah, personal aide to our good Commissioner,' he drawled in his Southern twang. All the men – and they were all men – smiled. All but Ross. Even Grady – her noble leader – hadn't called out the sexist bampot. Instead, he'd insisted she join them on their little boy's-own joyride.

'Consider it an order, Essler,' Grady muttered to her as Willetts and he moved on.

'Donny put you up to this, right?'

'Just be on the damned flight.'

—

So here she was, splatting across the Arctic, wondering if she'd permanently blown her chances of getting out of this wasteland with her career intact. Across the Chinook's hold, she watched Ross trying to shout an explanation of the new survival suit's design to Willetts: the inflatable lifejacket, whistle, compressed air canister in case the helicopter ditched and rolled, the LED torch in the glove, the Arctic-capable thermal lining. Ross was pointing now to the EPLT attached to Willetts' chest – the 'Emergency Personal Location Transmitter' that let the world know where you were, given trouble.

Carrie grinned at Ross's efforts. It was hopeless: Willetts couldn't hear a word. Anyway, what had been yanking on Ross's chain last night in the bar? He'd been twitchy for days now. Well, weeks. It was more than just the tension of being forced off-site, of the company loans or whatever. Something about the drill-ship. Oh well, seemed she'd get a look at it herself, now.

Something else nagged as she watched them, however. Something about the EPLT. That little, flashing, green battery light on its front. They blinked at her from every man's chest. She looked down.

She'd forgotten to put hers on.

She'd been in such a hurry, rattled, she had to admit, by Donny's presence. Had anyone noticed? Would Grady see? Her toes curled inside her Arctic boots. It could hardly be more humiliating. She was supposed to be in charge, however hard that had proven these past months.

The Chinook banked, kept banking. She realised it was circling. Leavitt, the loadmaster, came down the hold, clinging to the ceiling rails. He leaned in close, lifted one of her ear protectors.

'Chief asks you come look,' he bellowed. She nodded and he unfastened her harness. 'Careful.' He took hold of her arm in one massive paw and, as turbulence clattered the helicopter, virtually carried her along the hold to the side door with its larger window. He removed her noise protectors, placed a headset over her ears as she sat in the window seat, and secured the waist belt.

'This is Essler,' she barked into the mouthpiece.

Donny's voice came strangely soft yet clear against the general roar. 'On the water. Three o'clock.'

Through the window, the sea was nickel-grey, lined with paler veins of foam that curled away towards the horizon. The wind snatched the wave-tops into milky puffs of spindrift. A solitary shape glowed white against the seascape. Leavitt handed her some binoculars. She focused.

A yacht. Here, at this time of year! Single-masted, probably a forty-two footer. It was certainly a stable boat, upright despite being side on to the wind. Storm sails had been rigged, a slim orange staysail and a trysail. That, at least, showed right seamanship. However, they flapped without control. She couldn't see anyone on deck.

She zoomed the high-mag binoculars across the boat's length, then stopped. For a moment, her mind could not compute what she saw. She took her eyes from the viewfinders. Heard Don speaking her name. Didn't answer. Couldn't answer. Then looked again, had to roam left, right, before she found the image.

Across its teakwood boards, the entire forward deck contained the design of a carrick bend knot.

'Carrie,' Don was saying, 'you're the yachtie. That look right to you?'

As she tried to think, her fingers traced the etched Carrick bend on the bar-room table back at Tuk.

'How far are we from the drillship?' she said at last.

'Fifteen miles, south-south-east. He shouldn't be here, this far north, right?'

'No. Maybe. Not so late in the season.' Carrick bend knot. Coincidence? It just could not be a coincidence. But what did that mean? It was only rig workers who used the Tuktoyaktuk bar. The odd local.

'Got to be that eco-warrior nutjob,' Don went on. 'The one's been blogging about oilmen destroying the Arctic, right?'

Yes, there'd been a boat following the oil rigs this year. Earth First! types. A report had passed across her desk, but so what? she'd thought. A light yacht with one or two people aboard hardly constituted a threat. Let them do their thing, say their piece. But now...

'We need to get down there,' she said.

'No chance. I've a blood-load aboard needs delivering.'

'Don, this is an emergency. And...something's wrong.' The Carrick bend knot. 'We have to get down there.'

'Forget it, Carrie. Look at that sea.'

'Exactly. Look at it!'

'There's a storm coming.'

'We're the Coast Guard, for chrissakes.'

'I need to talk to Grady.'

'Forget Grady. It's me holds operational command here.'

There was silence. Then Don said, 'Put Leavitt on.'

She handed over the headset. Leavitt listened. His eyebrows went up. Then he returned the headset.

'Carrie,' Don said, 'I really don't want to say this, but you're the rescue swimmer.'

She'd have insisted anyway.

—

'I can't put you on deck,' Don told Carrie. 'Not how it's rolling like that. You go in the suds, then I'll tow you close as you're not in rescue gear.'

The Chinook descended. The sloop came closer, the Carrick bend visible to the naked eye. The helicopter slewed suddenly, righted itself. She heard Don curse.

'Look, Carrie, I know we've got our...you and me...but this storm's due. And it's worse than expected. The wind could build to force 10 inside the next three hours. Going be tight.'

'Well, chop chop then.'

Leavitt strapped the drop harness on her. 'Do what I say. Go where I say,' he shouted in her face. She saw the bottom hatch door open on the cabin floor. A freezing wind came in. He was shouting the routine. Her pulse quickened. She noticed Grady standing behind the two pilots at the open cockpit. He clung to their seatbacks, staring at Carrie without expression.

'You know all this, right?' Leavitt shouted in her ear.

'Kid stuff.'

She could feel her own hands clammy with sweat. He slipped her into the drop-rope harness, yanked the helmet over her balaclava. Through the lid's phones, she heard a mass of instructions being voiced by Don and his co-pilot. Leavitt secured her to the winch overhead. Pulled a goggle-visor over her face.

He said a few words into his mouthpiece, gazed down through the floor hatch. He shouted at her, 'Like a swimming pool.'

'Got to practice my backstroke some time,' she yelled back. It was the best she could come up with.

Leavitt squeezed her shoulder, anyway, hard enough she winced.

She put her toes to the yellow band round the open hatch's edges. Sixty feet below, the ocean was a maelstrom of hazing foam where the twin blades confused the surface. In the copter, everyone was staring from that gaping hole to her. Ross, struggling in his straps, tried to wave her over. None of them had radio headsets, so none knew what was going on. Willetts, though: what was that look on his face? Almost a smirk. Like he knew something. Like he knew what this was about. She shook the thought away. Focus!

'For the record, Carrie,' Don said in her helmet earpiece, 'this is a shitty idea.'

'They shouldn't be here, not this close to the drill site, not this time of year.'

'Okay, Leavitt. Clear.'

She felt the winch lift her on her toes.

'Out and over,' Leavitt shouted. He pushed her so she hung above the hatch, feet dangling. He held her still with one hand, the other at the winch control. 'I'll drop you fast for ten metres, get you clear of the bird. Then slow, but not too slow, to the surface. Don't worry about the cold. You could be an hour in the water in these suits. Ready?'

'Oh do get on with it,' she said.

She plummeted through the Chinook's belly.

The shock of the plunge stopped her breath. As she slowed, the wind caught her, spun her too fast to see anything clearly. A blur of greys and sea mist from the rotors, tiny freezing bites on her face where the wind got into the gap between goggles and helmet. She thought of her firearm back at base, just as she hit the water.

'Okay?' Leavitt asked through her helmet-phones.

She raised both arms, thumbs up, forgetting for the moment to speak. She hadn't been in the drink for more than three years. Not since moving to Canada. Man but she'd missed it. Freaky fun. Not that she'd trained explicitly for Arctic conditions. There's a hell of a difference between the North Atlantic and the Arctic Ocean. So super freaky fun. She bobbed on the rotor-flattened ocean, the harness inflatables keeping her back arched and chest on the surface. The spray made it impossible to see. The Chinook's belly rose as Don took her higher, the winch paying out to keep her in position.

'You okay?' Leavitt asked.

'Shall we get this show on the road?'

She heard the co-pilot say, 'Cool bitch, isn't s...' before the radio clicked off. It came on again a second later.

Don said, 'Here we go.'

Leavitt and Don communicated in a technical jargon so familiar it comforted her. She should get a recording made, play it while doing yoga. The helicopter drew her along through the water.

'Fifteen metres from the boat, Carrie.'

She kicked herself round until she faced the right direction. Through crazy, roiling spindrift from the rotors, she saw the sloop's mast roll through more than a hundred degrees as a wave flowed under the hull. Carrie lifted and dropped as well. She was viewing the boat's stern with a ladder up.

'Ten metres,' Leavitt said. She looked up, could just see his face, peering through the hatch, above and slightly ahead. 'Closing, five metres.' he said. 'You good?'

'Yeah, yeah.'

Carrie got a hand on a ladder rung. The boat dropped into a trough. Her harness tugged her up and away. She clung on to the rung, hanging horizontally out of the water.

'Shit,' she said, 'I'm going to release.'

'No, no, no,' said Leavitt. 'Do not –'

She ripped the release handle on her chest, felt the pull from the drop-rope suddenly gone. It surprised her so that her clumsy, thickly-gloved right hand slipped from the rung. She scrabbled, missed, missed again. Felt the current begin to drag her away. Panic-fear, sea spray in her face, goggles blurring, clearing, blurring again, heavy in the survival suit. Then the copter jargon in her ears pulled her back into focus. She kicked hard. Reached, scrabbled, caught hold of the ladder, felt the muscles in her hand almost spasm, so tightly did they clench.

Leavitt's voice in her ear, cursing. 'I say again: do...you... have...the...ladder?'

She caught hold with both hands. 'Got it.' Sucked in deeper breaths. Keep moving! She tried to get her foot on a bottom rung, but the ballooned suit wouldn't let her bend her leg enough to reach it. Instead, she pulled her body up, hand over hand. The water that touched her face burned with cold. Her knee brushed the ladder, then her foot slid on.

A larger wave broke over her from the side. The sloop rolled. She was lifted from the water, thrown against the hull, her helmet clanging against the upper ladder. It left her head ringing.

'The hell was that?' Don said.

The boat rolled back. She heaved herself up onto the transom platform. Lay on her back.

'She's on,' Leavitt said. 'God damnit, Carrie.'

She just breathed for a moment. The Chinook's great hulk hovered over her like a dragon. The twin rotors made a blur of the grey cloudscape, the engines' thunder masking the roar of the tide, the wind's hiss, anything else that might be heard... Which brought her attention back to the situation at hand. Carrick bend.

No one on deck.

She rolled quickly onto her side and squatted, gazing round. Closer up, the sloop was big money, more like a fifty-footer. Exquisitely finished, everything had been subtly softened, normally sharp lines rounded off. The cockpit before her contained all the electronic gizmos she knew and then some. She recognised a high-end, automated sailing system. She checked the sails: the orange staysail and trysail; a cautious approach to heavy weather.

'Don, there's a dinghy hoist astern that looks as if it's been deployed.'

'You saying she's abandoned?'

'You don't abandon three quarters of a million bucks-worth of boat. Not without a distress call first.'

She stood, kept her knees loose, conscious she'd no sea legs as yet. She'd not been aboard a boat for more than a year. Her attention was drawn to the open cockpit hatch. That showed dangerously poor practice in such seas. Bowed as much beneath the Chinook's looming hulk as by its downdraft, she clambered across the wildly rolling aft deck and dropped down into the cockpit. She kneeled, lifted her goggles onto her helmet, peered in through the open hatchway. A gorgeous teak and pale leather interior, hallway leading forwards into darkness. No lighting, only what tepid daylight came through the high cabin windows and the hatchway.

As she stepped onto the companionway ladder, she saw him. A man lay at the ladder's bottom on his back. He wore yellow foul-weather gear. His legs trailed up the steps, one straight, the other with the foot wedged between rungs. His head was bent at an odd angle. Carrie peered again into the darkness of the forward hallway.

'Anyone else here?' she called, her voice muffled through the helmet.

'What's that?' said Don in her ear.

'Got a body. Male. Looks like he tripped down the hatchway and broke his neck.'

'No one else?'

'Doesn't seem like it. Should be, so large a boat. Got to check.'

'Dead bodies we can pick up later. Two minutes.'

She stepped down into the interior, peered into the gloom, felt somehow exposed, waiting for the cocking click of a firearm...You don't sail a vessel this large on your own, however many automated systems it had. You needed a captain and mate, minimum.

'This is the Coast Guard,' she called. 'Is anyone else aboard?' She thought of the empty dinghy hoist. She heard water slopping in the bilges, wondered how much had come in. Enough, and the boat wouldn't handle. Had she been hulled, somehow, or was it merely the open hatch?

Then she saw the man's chest rising and falling, visible even through his suit.

'Don, he's alive. The man's alive.'

'Oh, good God. Status?'

Carrie kneeled beside the man. She opened the zips along the back of her forearms and freed her hands. Put fingers to his throat, felt the blood pounding, timed his pulse with her watch. Very gently, she felt along behind his neck.

'He's unconscious, fracture to the neck at C6, I think. Heart rate one eighty. Looks fevered. My hands are so cold I can't tell properly.'

'Can you take command of the boat, Carrie? Keep him alive till I get the drillship's support vessels to you?'

Kneeling there, she peered again into the hallway darkness, thought about the Carrick bend knot. Too bizarre a coincidence.

'Can you handle this, or do we winch you back in?' That settled it.

'I can, Don,' she said.

'Get the engine running, the radio up. Check in on the half hour, you got that?'

'On the half hour.'

'Your direction should be two-nine-five. I say again: two-nine-five. I remind you: winds building to probable force ten, south-westerly, maximum three hours. Carrie, it's going to get lively down there.'

'Go tell your mother.'

'Out.'

Jay

Jay stared down at the tiny bomb, the missile, on his desk. He flipped it with the straight forefingers of each hand, one to the other, across the desktop, like the old Atari Pong game.

'Do...Don't...Do...Don't,' he said in a robotic voice.

Then the radio clicked. 'Drillship *Belyy Medved*, this is Coast Guard helicopter Charlie Tango Golf Three Zero, carrying crew from Tuktoyaktuk. How do you read me?'

'Charlie Tango Golf Three Zero,' Jay replied automatically, 'I read you good, with signal strength four. We're expecting you.'

Jay certainly was.

'I'm inbound one seven zero degrees from your port stern, two miles out. Do I have permission to land?'

'Charlie Tango Golf Zero Three, you have permission to land.'

'Thank you, *Belyy Medved*. I'll circle the ship once and approach from zero two zero degrees for landing.'

A knot had formed in Jay's sternum so intense he had to double over in his chair. He cleared his throat to inform the Coast Guard pilot he'd be transferring him to helipad control.

But then the chopper radioed again. 'All marine vessels on station, be advised: we assisted a disabled vessel thirteen point seven nautical miles south-south-east, bearing one six nine degrees. Vessel is a private yacht of approximately fifty feet in length. We lowered a Coast Guard operative to the vessel. Operative has taken control but requires assistance. One man aboard is unconscious with serious injuries. Request: is the MV Tug *Raven* able to offer such assistance?'

Jay listened as the tug master explained he wasn't permitted to move more than one nautical mile from the drillship.

Jay breathed one long breath in, one out. He could hardly keep from screaming into the radio mic, 'What serious injuries? Who?'

The master of the drillship's other support vessel, *Bon Marie,* came on the radio. They could be ready to depart in twenty minutes.

'Charlie Tango Golf Three Zero,' the *Bon Marie*'s master said. 'It's those polar bear huggers, right? Blogger, or something?'

'Looks that way.'

'Should let the bastards drown.'

'Be advised, we don't countenance that kind of language on the airwaves,' the copter pilot said, if in a friendly enough manner.

Jay dropped back into his seat, opened the comms. But he couldn't think of any way to ask for further information without sounding suspicious. So he watched.

Out the window a big copter appeared. Even so huge a machine as the Chinook veered and dipped on approach, battered by the growing gale. There was a storm warning, Jay remembered. He brought up the information on the computer. Storm ten, out of the south-west, though it looked like it would back into the south during the night. The yacht was supposed to have moved off by now. What were they doing so close? That one message from earlier: 'Don't!'

He could just abort...

The email message had been clear: 'Don't!'

Okay. Abort. Until he knew more...

Carrie

Carrie lifted off her helmet. The air frosted the sweat in her hair like fingernails clutching at her skull. Outside, the Chinook's engines augmented and then diminished. She heard the ocean plock against the hull. Heard the wind saw at the ropes, clatter the sails. Heard the man's ragged breath. Then the boat rolled sharply to starboard, flinging Carrie across the cabin. As it levelled, she pulled herself gingerly up. The man's wedged foot was keeping him in place, though his torso and head shifted dangerously. Each movement could potentially kill him. But he'd have to wait.

Back on deck, the wind was coming harder. She took hold of the wheel, feeling for the sense of rudder.

But the wheel wouldn't move.

The consoles and instruments were all blank, the sail trimming dials unresponsive. She punched switches but nothing reacted. No electrics. Surely the steering mechanism didn't only function electronically? Had the automatic steering been on when the electrics went down? Would she have to take apart the steering pedestal, see if the bearings were clogged, the linkages jammed?

There was no time to make sense of it. Another wave. She clung to the wheel as the deck tipped to fifty degrees before just as quickly righting itself. The flying spume struck her like a giant, slapping hand. She had to gain control of the rudder somehow, attempt to heave-to.

She noticed a three-foot piece of wood, slid tight into some webbing in the cockpit's corner. Half the wood's length was sheathed in metal casing. The emergency tiller. An outsize spanner had been thrust in beside it. Behind her, the cover had been removed from the top of the rudder stock, a grand affair on so large a boat. Had the injured man been trying to fit the tiller when he fell down the cabin ladder?

The rudder stock was locked hard to starboard. As the

next wave began to roll the sloop, she snatched up the spanner and worked to loosen the connecting nut. It came away. She clasped it tight in her thick glove. But then a breaker smashed into the hull, threw a wall of water over her. She was hurled against the cockpit wall and, as her hands opened to snatch at a stay, both spanner and nut disappeared over the side.

She had no breath to curse. Instead, in the wave trough moment of calm, she dived across the cockpit, snatched the emergency tiller and jammed its metal-lined, square hole over the rudder stock. It rested there, loose, but in place. Good. She should now be able to steer the bloody thing. Careful to keep it straight so it wouldn't slip off, she heaved on the tiller as the next wave came in. Nothing.

The wave passed beneath the hull. She needed more purchase. As the boat levelled, she reached forwards over the cabin roof and grabbed a coiled mainsail sheet. No time, no knife to cut it free. She threw a few swift in-and-out loops about the tiller end and then drew the rope round a stern cleat. She put her feet to the cockpit wall. Using all her weight, she heaved on the rope.

Another wave swept in. Carrie felt herself lifted. Higher and higher. This could be the one that capsized her. She hauled, cried out with the strain as the boat began to fall off the wave peak, rolling, its mast approaching the horizontal. The rudder moved. The bow turned a little. She felt the current's titanic strength through the rope and rudder. She must be travelling at seven or eight knots just with the movement of the water. The wind caught the sails and abruptly, the sloop yawed into the tide. It swept down and across the wave like a vast surfboard, so fantastically fast for such a large boat that she actually barked a laugh as the pressure through her arms reduced. Riding the current, now, the next wave raised the stern rather than hitting her broadside on.

Carrie had control.

Jay

Jay watched the Chinook disappear forwards to land. He heard the ship's bigwigs rattling upstairs to greet them. He heard the arrivals descend the stairwell, straight on past the bridge deck and down. Heard the first mate cursing them because he'd laid on a welcome catering spread on the bridge. Jay watched through the radio room window as the VIPs walked out along the personnel footbridge towards the raised drill floor beneath the derrick. He watched them stop, have some sort of discussion. And he watched the *Bon Marie* taking an age of the world to veer away south. He answered their radio comms tonelessly. Over the walkie-talkie traffic, he heard the company men – these desolators – had arrived on the drill floor.

He watched and listened with his pulse beating so hard at his neck he put a finger on it and pressed down, as if he might calm himself that way. Then he ripped off the headset, stood, paced, his eyes unable to focus.

What was happening out there? Who was the Coast Guard operative who'd been lowered to the yacht? What were they doing at this minute? They'd be keeping whoever it was who'd been injured – and it could only be one of two people! – alive. That was their job: they were expert paramedics. But hang on, only one person had been mentioned! No one had said anyone was dead. What about the second? But Jay couldn't ask. There was just no reason at all for him to ask anyone anything of that nature. He had to fight the urge to smash the radio equipment to pieces.

He dropped into his seat. Opened the secret email. Wrote: *ARE YOU OK? What's going on? RESPOND!*

He sat, stared at the email inbox, the radio traffic a meaningless drone from the headphones on the table. He felt his hands turning to claws with the stress. The tension built until he actually shouted aloud.

'Y'all right, fella?' a bridge technician looked in through the radio room door.

Jay could not think of a single word to speak.

'It's no' so bad,' the older man told him. 'You'll be dangling your pecker down Free Man's Lane before you know it.'

Jay dug up a thin smile. 'Usual bullshit,' he said. 'Thanks, Micky.'

The man rolled his eyes in sympathy and disappeared.

He stared down at his little missile there on the table. The crew were good enough guys, most of them, however much they drove him nuts with their prejudices and material obsessions. And it wouldn't matter, it really wouldn't. Not to most of them. A hiccup, a reassignment, a few weeks off. Or just more work fixing stuff.

He placed his tiny missile – in reality, a USB stick – into the computer hub portal. An image appeared on his desktop. The icon was not that of a folder, but of a miniature nuclear explosion. His fingertips were sticky on the keyboard. He hovered the cursor over the little nuclear explosion, double-clicked, filled in the password box that appeared.

The whole screen swirled as if it were a detonation in reverse, millions of minute particles swirling slowly back towards the centre. After several slow seconds, it reached its apogee and a command box opened. Instead of the more usual 'Execute?', it read 'Execution?' with a Y and an N beneath.

There was a time Jay found such details amusing. Not any-more. Teen-hacker nonsense. Someone else. Someone he used to be. He hovered the cursor over the Y.

Don't...Do Not...Dot...Not...No...Do...No? Yes? No?

He stared at the mouse clicker.

Jim Ross

'Quite the show, don't you think,' Willetts shouted into Jim Ross' ear, 'tossing her out the helicopter like that?' Ross could barely make out the words over the roar of rig machinery and the Chinook's engines.

'Guess she didn't fancy the trip,' he offered up in reply.

Willetts laughed a collegiate laugh, clapped an arm over Jim's shoulders – avuncular, possessive? – and said, 'I do love a human drama.'

Ross glanced at him sidelong, not impressed, but Willetts was striding on ahead. Ross limped swiftly away from the Chi-nook. He hated helicopters. Ever since Venezuela.

They clambered down steel steps. The Inuvialuit crew-man, Joe Amaruq – Carrie's Russian spy! – took his arm as his walking cane slipped on the steel steps. He smiled a reluctant thanks as they entered the reception lounge, where they were greeted by a hail of gunfire.

At the far end, several off-duty crewmembers were play-ing some shoot 'em up on a huge screen. This end of the room, a welcoming party awaited. Leaning on his cane, feeling ridic-ulously bulbous in his survival suit, Ross made the introduc-tions.

The ship's master, Pavel Senko, gravely shook everyone's hands. His chubby cheeks and line-free face made the Russian look far too young for so senior a role.

'Gordon O'Sullivan,' Ross went on, 'our reserves engineer.'

'I know Gordon,' Willetts said, shaking hands with the dour, balding man. But Willetts spoke directly to Assistant Commissioner Grady. 'Gordon's our independent analyst. He'll be writing up the reserves statement, soon as the well test's complete.' He turned to Gordon. 'You'll need to hurry,' he said jauntily, though Ross could see the hard lines around Willetts' mouth, 'if we're to publish the statement today. Fortunes to make!'

Gordon looked dogged and Ross thought, Uh oh.

Lastly, Ross introduced the ship's Offshore Installation Manager, Mikhail Babushkin. 'The man in charge.'

Babushkin's hangdog face crumpled into a modest grin. 'If you follow me,' he said, 'we have coffee and refreshments on the bridge.'

'I'm heading straight for the drill shack with Gordon,' said Willetts. 'See our results.'

'I'll join you,' Grady said. And then everyone had to go.

A crewman helped them out of their survival suits and into cold-weather gear and hard hats. As he was signing them in on the computerised muster list, Babushkin said quietly to Ross, 'We must talk.'

Ross was not at all happy to hear it.

—

The group emerged onto the raised personnel bridge that led from the bridge to the derrick. Ross followed behind. Up here, sixty feet above the ocean, there was no protection from the gale. Ross's walking stick clanked the railings as he tried to keep his balance. Ahead, the derrick towered over them. Against the gloomy cloudscape, its brilliant lighting and enormous, tapering height made it a fantastic, almost religious edifice.

Hydraulic lines bulged from it like muscular arms. Ross smelled burnt metal and, more subtly, saltwater ozone.

His paranoia returned so fiercely he almost gagged. He stared out at the black, surging sea. Grady had explained why Carrie had so dramatically left them: some yacht in distress. Of course, she'd told him enough tales about her old job, but it was something else to see her in action. Positively erotic. Yep, he was partial to strong women. Like weak men are. He thought back to his ex-wife – strong or just psychotic? His father had liked to tell him, and indeed anyone: *You get what's coming to you.* And here he was. In truth, he felt more like a worried uncle at the moment. Still, he had more immediate concerns to deal with than Carrie black-belt-in-something-or-other Essler. He trailed after Willetts. Follow my leader. Tried not to think rust, leaks and liability. He should write a song.

The VIP cavalcade stopped at the far end of the bridge, clustering outside the closed steel hatchway to the drill floor. Three oil-grimed roughnecks leaned against the big shutter through which the pipe hoist's rails disappeared. Silent, insolent, they watched this spectacle of the money come aboard.

'Gentlemen,' Willetts called out, clearly gearing up for a sermon. 'All about us may be viewed the magnificent machine we lease from our Azerbaijani colleagues.' With a brazenly knowing smile to the Russian Yevchenko. 'And out there on the cruel sea, the *Bon Marie* travels between here and Tuktoyaktuk.' Ross followed Willetts' gaze towards the big supply vessel. The *Bon Marie*'s prow and superstructure formed a single red cheese wedge. It was in the process of turning away south, waves exploding against its hull.

'Our equipment,' Willetts continued, 'is either hauled fifteen hundred miles from Anchorage or flown in by heavy transport.' He pointed once more towards the ocean. 'Our ice-class tug, the *Raven*, on permanent standby.' It rose and plunged in the waves, supremely capable of dealing with anything the world threw at it. 'Crew helicopters fly from Tuk and Inuvik, crew jets to and from Yellowknife.'

Ross swallowed against the bile at the back of his throat.

'In summary,' Willetts said, 'I'm as near to stone broke as a stick horse.'

People laughed dutifully, only Grady remaining impassive. Ross crinkled his eyes at Willetts' Southern hometown schtick. He was a performer, sure enough.

'But am I concerned?' Willetts went on. 'I am not. We have arrived just in time to see the final well test completed, and...'

'In fact,' Gordon broke in, 'we're done.'

Willetts, for once, was stumped for words. Finally, he said, 'And?'

Gordon looked stolid. 'I'm still analysing the flow data.'

Ross felt suddenly seasick. If something had gone wrong with the well test...

But then Gordon relented, his face broadening into a narrow smile, about the most he looked capable of. 'I don't necessarily envisage a problem.'

Holy shit. Ross thought his boss might collapse. He wondered if he might himself. So. They'd get out the far side of this, after all.

Willetts very quickly mastered himself, grinned at his audience. 'I'll not rile the wagon master. Let us wait and see what his report tells us.'

A young journalist spoke up. 'Broadcasting a reserve statement from a ship is kind of unusual. Aren't they normally published in reports for regulators and shareholders?'

Willetts chuckled. 'Carpe diem, son. By the end of the day, we'll be richer than Rockefeller. I'll need a facelift for my *Time* magazine cover photograph.'

More obedient laughs. Babushkin gestured. 'You want, we all go inside?'

'It's cold as a banker's heart out here,' Willetts said. 'Lead on.'

As everyone shuffled past, Ross saw that the helicopter pilot had joined them. Don Escamilla, Carrie's ex, and the reason for her punishment posting to the Arctic, gazed about like a tourist.

'So,' Ross said, 'you dump Carrie in the drink. What's that, payback?'

Don stared at Ross a moment, but then he smiled good-naturedly. 'Some eco-crazy in trouble on a yacht out there.'

'The blogger. I've heard about him. You don't seem over bothered.'

'Anyone jumps out choppers for a living don't need her hand held.'

Ross conceded the point. 'She's on her way here?'

'She can sail off the edge of the world, all I care.' And Don went in after the main group.

Ross followed them onto the drill floor. Machinery thundered so loudly he put his hands to his ears. The others filed towards the drill shack, the protected space off to one side where the driller controlled operations. Directly over his head, the huge travelling block dangled on steel cables from the derrick's crown. From it, hung the sixty-tonne top drive. The sheer scale of all that weight poised over his head, like fate's pendulum, intimidated him.

At the centre of the drill floor stood the bright-red 'well test' or 'Christmas' tree, its body and arms bulbous with valves and spools, handwheels to open and close them. Pipes attached to different sections. Ross thought of some extra-terrestrial plugged in to a medical experiment. The tree split the various fluids and gases coming up the well into their component parts, sending them off to different areas of the ship to be processed, or burned off at the end of the flare boom, high above the ship. It was so small yet so critical a fulcrum, right here at the very heart of this vast behemoth.

Ross strode over to Willetts, explained what Don had just said about Carrie and the eco-activist blogger.

Willetts said, 'Oh that guy. We got him covered.' His cold eyes crinkled in triumph, then he turned and went inside the drill floor control shack.

Ross needed to get away from them all so he headed back out onto the raised personnel bridge. In a high window, he saw a face, framed by headphones, staring down at him with strangely wild eyes.

What had Willetts meant when he said he had the eco-blogger on the boat 'covered'?

Carrie

Carrie's heartrate slowed with the boat now under her control. But her skull felt as if it were encased in a lid of ice. Huddling in the cockpit, she pulled her balaclava over her head and, after that, the survival suit's hood.

Time to take stock of her situation. She ran through what she knew. Don had said she was some fifteen miles south-south-east of the drillship, which was course two-nine-five from her position. The GPS screen in front of her remained blank. She couldn't see a compass. Of limited use anyway, magnetic north being off somewhere in the Arctic Ocean en route to Siberia, more west than it was north from her position. All right, think. The coming storm was out of the south-west, Don had confidently told her. That meant the wind over her right shoulder was from that direction, which, in turn, meant the current was heading east-north-east. So the rig ought to be over her port quarter.

She squinted through the sea spray. The ocean hardly invited confidence, even to Carrie, schooled by her father on the North Sea. And that bore little relation to what she was dealing with now. Above, the granite-grey cloud cover seemed to hang almost touchably close. Visibility remained surprisingly good, however, right the way to the horizon. And on that horizon she saw now a yellow and orange flicker, exactly where she'd estimated it to be. Flames from the drillship's flare boom, though she couldn't make out the vessel itself. She remembered such sights with her father: night coming down, frozen stiff in the inadequate clothing he always provided his children. Flare flickers in the dark. Hell glints. Dragon breath.

In an ideal world, she'd beat up towards the drillship. Even in such heavy sea, she'd have been confident in a boat of this size and quality. But she'd need to get the electrics running once more for the automated sail-trimming equipment, for the radio, even – just in case – for the engine. Could she do it before the storm arrived? Technically, she didn't need to; the rig's support boat would be steaming her way. They'd find her, easily enough. So she'd play it safe, heave-to, let the yacht drift against the current, though it wouldn't be easy with the wind gusting, the heavy swell and the sailing system down. But first she had to see to the injured man below. She'd lost the securing nut for the tiller, but she had to take the risk. She used the mainsail sheet she'd looped around the tiller earlier to lash it tight, knowing the boat would yaw horribly in the waves, but without options.

The man remained unconscious, though his lips moved slightly as if he were whispering. Late fifties. Clean shaven. The heavily suntanned skin of a sailor. An eagle nose. Stiff, grey-streaked, auburn hair poked from his waterproof balaclava. He might have frozen to death by now without it, the heat escaping from his head. His face had blackened spots across it. She touched one and it smudged. Soot?

She noticed only now a faint smell of burning in the air, acrid, chemical. The man's hands were uncovered, raw, spotted with the same dark soot, his clothing also. The hands showed signs of blackening at the fingertips. Frostbite?

The boat surged as a bigger wave lifted its stern and ran beneath the hull. She had to get him secured quickly. Even if, with his broken neck, it risked killing him. He'd die anyway, if they capsized. She scanned the cabin.

Just behind the stairs, a door which ought to lead to the rear sleeping cabin showed the red square with white cross she was looking for. When she opened it, the entire space had been turned into a supply store. Just a few boxes remained. Guess he'd been out here a while. Close by the door, she found a first-aid cabinet and, stowed alongside, a two-piece emergency rescue stretcher. Whoever this man was, he'd planned well – even if he was a suicidal fool still to be out here, this late in the year.

She pulled the stretcher out. Rummaged among the first aid drawers. She took out a neck-brace, felt along his neck once more. The sixth cervical vertebrae had likely sheared. It could be resting against the spinal column, chipped or otherwise ready to kill him in a whole variety of ways. Could she risk straightening his neck? Paramedic's call.

Kneeling at his crown, her middle fingertips monitoring the vertebrae's movement, slowly she drew his head and neck straight. He groaned. She strapped the brace swiftly into position. Now to his spine. She slid her hands beneath him, trying to feel through the suit for anything misaligned. It was impossible to say. His body was completely limp. He might well be paralysed.

She drew his wedged foot free of the companion ladder. She pulled a thin cushion from the opulent seating that ran right round the cabin. Placed it gently beneath his head. Then she steeled herself, stood, stooped, put her hands under his armpits and drew him ever so slowly straight, his head sliding over the smooth, teakwood floor on the cushion. Her own breath came faster than the man's. She heard water slopping in the bilges. Something else she needed to investigate immediately.

The man now lay flat on the floor, muttering soft, incoherent words. She drew the stretcher alongside his body. She kneeled and drew him laboriously onto his side, making sure to keep his head on its cushion. Holding his shoulder, she pulled up a knee. Now he lay in an approximation of the recovery position. She tipped the stretcher so its raised edge was flat to the floor, pulled it tight against his body and levered him back. His torso rolled in, but not his legs.

The stern reared up. She had time to glance towards the hatchway just as water crashed in through the opening. Rogue wave? It broke over her, snatching her breath away, stinging her face like acid. She slid sideways, scrabbling for the stretcher as it skated across the floor. She'd not yet strapped him in. Then a blow to the right side of her head knocked her flat. Lights fired in her eyes. She felt herself drifting away.

'No!' she cried. Blinked, shook her head, though the pain was almost unbearable. She saw the cabin roof above, felt the boat lift, up and then level, before the stern plunged back down as the great wave passed under and round the hull.

'Get...up!' She rolled to one side, pushed herself to her knees. Retched three times, stopping herself vomiting through will alone. Knew herself concussed. She'd hit her head against the table edge. Something stung her eyes. She put her hand up and drew it back to see blood, already crystalizing on her fingers. The wind, even with the scraps of storm sail, heeled them a degree or two further over. It howled through the rigging. She needed right now to heave the boat to and ride this out.

The stretcher had come up against the table base. The man's legs had twisted round, still not in the basket. He made louder sounds now, half-words she could not make out. She cursed at the agony in her skull as she tried to lift his legs inside. Yet she slipped immediately sideways. The floor glistened.

Eyeing the open hatchway fearfully, she tugged at his legs. They were heavy, hip joints loose, no muscle tension. At last, they flopped in. He was speaking words now. He seemed to be saying something about someone named Eddy? Freddy? Teddy? Crudely, she rolled his suit hood up and over his balaclava-ed head, pressed cushions either side. She folded two aluminium blankets she'd taken from the first-aid drawers around him, careful to wrap his exposed hands as tightly as possible. Then she strapped him in with the basket secures.

She rested against the companionway ladder, seeing bright flashes of light, fighting nausea. She was panting: from the exertion, from the cold, from the fear that she'd kill him even while trying to save him, from fear itself.

'The ship!' he said now. His eyes glared up at her, so desperate, so horrified, she felt a surge of terror in her sternum, strong as heartburn.

'What?' she said.

'The ship!'

'This boat?'

'The drillship.'

She leaned in close by his face. 'The *Belyy Medved*?'

'He mustn't...'

'What? Who mustn't?'

'Tell him no!' Then his voice caught in his throat and he began to gag. Carrie dragged the stretcher onto its side to put him back in an approximation of the recovery position. He coughed once and his breathing eased. But his eyes had closed again.

Her helmet had jammed itself into the corner where a long bench that half encircled the cabin table met the floor. She snatched it, pulled it over her head, wincing with pain. Staggered up on deck.

'Donny, over. Escamilla? Essler for Escamilla, over.'

Nothing. She repeated the call, knowing how limited the lid-walkie's range was.

She heard a crackle. '...sler...prob...late...' and then the crackling voice stopped.

'Don, we've a possible threat to the drillship. Can you read, over?'

A short crackle burst, then silence.

She spoke into the receiver, over and over again. No response. She dragged the helmet off, slid down into the cabin, hurled it across the room. It bounced into the darkness of the forward hallway. She put her hands over her face, tried to calm her breathing, her head pounding, nausea threatening to overwhelm her. Tried to think. What had the man meant? A deeper panic caught hold, some inarticulate sense of shame, of culpability. Had she missed someone? It was part of her job to vet all crew travelling out to the rigs. In the new security climate. After the Persian Gulf events, after the eco-activists and Greenland. The Alberta Sands fiasco. Who had the injured man been talking about?

She kneeled over him, but he was out again. With a single bungee she secured the stretcher to the table leg. Best she could do. Then she had an idea. She rummaged in the cabin cupboards and drawers, came up with a black, rectangular box, hurried back on deck. She wrenched it open, drew out the flare gun inside. She popped the barrel, thrust a flare in, aimed it straight up. Fired. Then she repeated the action. She was about to use the final flare, but hesitated, put the gun back and resealed the box.

Nothing else to do. She went back inside for the helmet. Perhaps Don would have seen the flare. Perhaps someone would. Perhaps they'd radio the support boat as it was on its way. They'd get on the helmet mic waveband and be in touch.

Ross

On the personnel bridge, Ross rested his arms on the rail. For a moment, he allowed himself to enjoy the freezing air on his face. Two or three more days. Then he'd breathe easy.

He glared up at the derrick, as if at an enemy. Two maintenance men were suspended on ropes above the massive travelling block and top drive, carrying out some sort of maintenance.

'So, we talk,' someone said behind him. Babushkin.

Ross said, imitating Willetts' voice, 'Black gold beyond the dreams of Mammon.'

'You are bitter man,' Babushkin said.

Ross continued to watch the two men working up in the derrick. He said, 'What's left to talk about? Dammit, Mikhail, it's your ship.'

'But your responsibility.' Babushkin's lugubrious slab of a face turned sardonic. He placed one finger vertically before his nose, then pointed it at Ross and made to fire it like a pistol.

'Oh, drop *yourself* down the well, why don't you?' Ross told him.

'The heavy mud is going in. We are safe.'

'Not yet.'

'The well is good.'

'But?'

'But?'

'*But* everything. I wouldn't wipe my ass with the paperwork for any of it, Mikhail.'

'You are not usual in your bad language, Jim. The stress gives you pain. But the machinery did not fail. Gordon and the other teams saw nothing wrong.'

'It's not you with your name on everything. Sure, Willetts is the money. But it's my licence, my company hired your piece-of-shit drillship. They're my safety cert...' He stopped hard, before he lost control. Sighed. But that had been the deal – the deal, after all. 'Don't you worry about it all, Mikhail?'

'It is me who is out here on the water.' He waved his arm around to take in the ship, everything. 'I worry. And your Willetts: now he is a man who worries.'

'PentOil, Willetts, he took out a convertible loan to get us through this. Big enough to crush him. Me too, of course. But I'm just collateral damage. It comes due Monday nine a.m.'

Babushkin laughed his basso laugh. 'And today is Friday. They will take his company. Bankrupt him.'

'And do worse to me. Unless Gordon's a good wee laddie, and gets that statement out before close of day. Then everyone goes rah rah rah.' Ross shook his arms like a cheerleader with pompoms.

Babushkin knitted his fingers together, stretched them until they cracked. 'We have some readings at the seabed, the well-head,' he said, speaking so slowly each word hung in the icy wind. 'There are – anomalies.'

'Don't do this, Mikhail.'

'Readings, they are not...consistent. I think you would want to know this.'

'It's Lokgas's equipment,' Ross said lamely. Lokgas was the company that owned the rig.

'But your lease. For the record,' he went on, speaking more formally, 'your inbox now contains the details. So you know.'

Ross stared through the stinging wind after the support boat. It was going after Carrie. Carrie, who leaped out of helicopters, saved people.

Babushkin said, 'Why did you take this job, Jim?'

Ross shook his head slowly.

At last, he said, 'I'm the patsy.'

'I do not know this word.'

Ross didn't know how to explain. But, anyway, that wasn't good enough. He wasn't a patsy. Not really. He'd walked into this, eyes open. If you choose to be the fall guy, are you one? Or are you just plain-and-simple guilty?

A little orange arc of light burned for a few moments near

the southern horizon. Initially, Ross watched it, aimlessly, thinking of how close they were to getting out of here. He saw another light follow the first. It transcribed the same tiny arc, hardly to be made out, except as it was set against the glowering black clouds behind.

'You see that?' he asked Babushkin. The only thing in that direction was sea and weather and...Carrie.

Then all the lights went out.

—

Babushkin swore in Russian. From his elevated position on the personnel bridge, Ross could see the entire ship had gone dark. It was scarcely conceivable. The ship's features cut sharp black lines against the churning, shifting grey-scape of the sea and sky.

'This *glupyy* tin can,' Babushkin said. 'Better we sell for scrap.'

Now Ross noticed that faint, constant judder had also stopped. And, just as he understood the reason, Babushkin shouted, 'No!' The dynamic positioning system – the four huge thrusters that kept the ship in place above the well – had stopped. Stopped, when they must never stop.

Babushkin spun away and ran for the bridge. Ross limped after him. The wind came heavier by the minute, and he had to cling to the railing. The dark and silent ship had become an eerie place of shadows. The sea pounded at the hull, immediate, bullying, threatening. Men called out, swore. Two raced past him in the opposite direction. He could not think, could only follow Babushkin.

He passed through the doorway. Darkness encircled him. He edged forwards, tapping his stick like a blind man. He found the stairs, followed the sound of loud discussion above. But then a terrible shame stopped him. He wanted to creep away, to stoop, hug his knees, hide. There was fate in this, inevitability. He who believed in no such nonsense. Still, it gripped him until panic, like nausea, seemed to press up into the back of his throat.

But he forced himself on, arrived on the bridge deck. The crew were not more than vague silhouettes against the outer windows. Hand torches flickered back and forth. No screens were lit anywhere. Conversations overlapped in a jumble of voices. Frightened faces appeared in the torchlight. Senko, the ship's master, stood as if frozen in the midst of it all. Babushkin had his head down, one forefinger running across text in a handbook as a crewman held a torch for him.

'The engines?' Ross said.

'We have no power anywhere,' Babushkin replied, still scanning the text in front of him.

'The standby generators...'

'Redundancy systems, all have failed.'

'That's not possible,' Ross broke in. It was beyond probability that all three engines – triple redundancy – should fail together. He tried to control his breathing.

'Everything is down.' Babushkin eyed Senko, but still the ship's master just stood there, lost as Ross felt. Babushkin said, 'Where's the chief engineer?'

'Here,' said an able-looking Filipino of many years experience.

'Check every circuit breaker,' Babushkin told him.

'On it already,' the engineer said. 'It don't make sense.'

'Do your job.'

Ross stared out the window at the darkened ship. He shook

with dread, had to grasp the window frame. Felt the cold there trying to reach through from the outside, to snuff out...He expelled air forcefully from his lungs. He had to get his shit together. What was happening on the drill floor? How embarrassing must it be for Willetts right now? How damaging for their future licences with the Canadian authorities? It already constituted a major incident requiring significant formal investigation.

The derrick lights flickered back on. They were shockingly brilliant against the thick, black clouds. A few deck lights began to come on as well. Ross saw the two men who'd been working up in the derrick on ropes. They were frantically rappelling down towards the deck. He wasn't surprised. It must have been terrifying up there when the lights went out.

Then he noticed sparks crackling in the derrick's crown.

'Mikhail!' he said, grasping Babushkin's arm, swinging him to see.

At that moment, the travelling block and top drive, that great pendulum that swung above the drill floor, began to fall. Ross heard, even through the thick glass, a furious whirr of heavy steel cables. Then the dozens of tonnes of their combined weight disappeared into the sealed space below. Even the bridge deck shuddered with the deep, bass crash of their impact. The derrick lights went out again. A long, rumbling growl followed, loud as an avalanche, seemed never to end.

As plumes of dust poured up from the drill floor amid the derrick's girders and out across the decks, the bridge crew fell silent. Babushkin snatched up the public address mic, pressed the button, spoke. But there was no sound, no operating light. He pulled his walkie from his belt. Swore as he flicked between channels. Numerous confused voices overrode each other. Ross heard, 'Got to get to the safety...'

'Drill floor!' Babushkin shouted into the radio. 'Drill floor, come back.' But no one answered.

Ross said, the words seeming to come from some great distance, 'The well's not yet sealed.' And in the full implication of that statement, he awoke once more. If the drill floor machinery had been destroyed then all the gases, the crude oil, the well-test materials, all of them under vast pressure, would be free to explode up out of the well in a blowout.

'I'm going down there,' he said. Snatched up a walkie. Heard the engine control room reporting all systems still dead.

'We're going to fall off position, tear the riser off the wellhead,' someone said, voice shrill. And if that happened, oil would flow directly out into the ocean from the seabed.

Babushkin handed Ross a torch. 'Tell me what you find.'

Ross limped towards the door. Joe Amaruq, the Inuvialuit crewman, stood there.

'I'll come with you,' he said as calmly as if they were heading out for a drink.

Carrie

Inside the cabin, still clutching the helicopter helmet with its silent radio, Carrie felt the boat lift on another wave, higher than any before. Her head rang with concussion, her stomach heaved. She held on to the table leg, the injured man's words – *Tell him no!* – playing in a loop.

Tell who no to what?

She had too much to attend to. She'd have to trust the tiller arm keeping the boat steady for a while longer.

She lay down on the cabin floor at the vessel's midpoint

and listened. She could hear the water in the bilges sloshing around, as yet unfrozen. It didn't sound too bad down there. Evidently, they weren't sinking. She'd have to find the pump soon, though – hopefully a hand pump in this nightmarishly automated boat.

She stood at the navigation table. The nautical chart clipped to the surface showed the eastern Beaufort Sea and surrounds. She had to throw herself onto the bench seat as the stern shot up. The seas were growing out there. She put her finger to the chart: she had to be about here, a hundred miles or so north-north-east of Tuk, on a broad reach heading east-north-east, wind from the south-west. Banks Island loomed somewhere to the east, a two-hundred-fifty-mile-long lee shore. All right, so she had to heave-to, wait for the drillship's support vessel to arrive.

'Always check what weather's coming up behind,' her dad used to say. She hurried on deck.

The wind forced her to lean and squint. The sea had grown more skittish and choppy. The wind lashed the wavetops into a curious haze, fragmented somehow as it frosted into ice. The sky seemed blacker, lower. In the south-west, the storm's fog-like shroud raced towards her, its leading edge so clearly de-fined, as often they were at sea. It would arrive in a few min-utes, much sooner than Don's estimate.

The tiller arm had inched partially loose without the se-curing nut. She punched it hard, twice, her concussed head throbbing with each blow. It slid back into position. She flopped onto the pilot seat, dry-retched. The sloop pitched dramatical-ly between waves. A blue-canvas dodger was wrapped around the front of the cockpit. The vessel's name had been written along the fabric's side. She could see 'The.' She stood, leaned out, read *The Carrick*. Of course. There had to be a connection between this boat and the image chiselled into the Tuk barroom table. She still hadn't been forward, below deck, to see what or who was up front.

Her watch was hidden inside her suit, but she guessed it must be late afternoon. The Arctic sun, which hardly rose into the sky, this time of year, would be descending still lower, bloody orange, to bounce along the horizon behind the storm clouds. Soon it would be as near-as-dammit night. No light, no navigation instruments.

Off the starboard bow an iceberg rolled a quarter mile away. Just perfect. Icebergs in the dark. And growlers: those invisible chunks of broken floeberg bobbing a few inches above the water line, often bigger than a car, more than capable of ripping a hole in the hull or shearing off the keel.

A massive wave rolled in, many feet higher than the transom. It lifted her as if she were on a fairground ride. She flicked every switch she could see. Nothing. There were hardly any ropes visible on deck, everything sleek, hidden away, automatic and requiring electricity. How was she supposed to trim the sails? She'd never been aboard anything this automated.

She unstrapped the tiller, leaned hard on it. The prow turned. A wave caught the boat broadside and it rolled alarmingly, Carrie clinging to the loose tiller. The boat levelled and she saw the jib begin to back. She might do it after all, ride this shitty weather out. The mainsail shivered, reefed too small really.

She stared out in the direction of the drillship, seeking the support boat.

When last Carrie had looked, just the flare boom had glimmered on the horizon. Now she saw a towering pillar of fire, like an erupting volcano. Binoculars were strapped beside the console array. She snatched them up, gazed through the eyepieces. Saw a gigantic column of black smoke and yellow flame, tapering to red. Above, lead grey and cobalt blue thunderheads of smoke churned out and up to merge with the clouds.

She stared through the lenses, unable to think.

In the foreground, a brilliant red support ship was turning, the *Bon Marie*, turning away from her, turning back towards the burning drillship.

She heard the hiss, barely had time to turn, before a great rolling wave broke directly over her. It crushed her into the cockpit console, choked her as it came on and on. Her ribs lanced with pain. The boat pitched until she felt it might capsize. Then the wave flowed under the hull and was gone. She lay on the cockpit floor, gulping air, too stunned to think, her ribs agony, head pounding. The tiller swung wildly.

All Carrie could see in her mind's eye was that pyre of smoke and flames.

Then the storm hit.

Ross

Ross and Joe Amaruq felt their way down the black stairwell, along the hall and out onto the personnel bridge. The freezing wind came harder, directly from prow to stern. Dust filled the air. Both began to cough.

Ross could hear a fierce, constant rumble, so deep his abdomen trembled. It grew rapidly louder as they hurried along the high walkway. A few lights flickered on and off through the machinery caches and deck below. Some fifteen metres from the drill-floor, a group of men, one holding a lamp, stood in silence beneath the yellow pipe hoist. They wore hard hats, filthy cold-weather gear, smudged faces. Ross wondered what kept them from heading inside.

Close up, the deep rumble became a roar almost beyond bearing, like some titanic waterfall. And it came from inside the drill-floor walls, two stories of thick steel plate that rose before him, with its closed access hatch and huge hoist gate. Debris was falling. Materials from inside the well – mud, the gluey spacer material, sea water – jetted upwards under enormous pressure to explode against the derrick's girders, careening in all directions. A chunk of hardened mud as big as his thigh struck the walkway just in front of him.

A blowout, he realised. The drill floor machinery had, indeed, been destroyed.

He and Amaruq ducked beneath the hoist's protective canopy.

'We got to get in!' Ross shouted into Amaruq's ear.

Amaruq nodded. 'Wait here,' he said. He gestured to two of the crewmen huddling under the canopy with them. They disappeared down a steep stairwell.

Shortly, they returned, carrying a steel sheet. This they held above their heads. Ross stood in the middle of them, hating his walking cane and ruined knee. They inched towards the drill-floor hatch.

Abruptly, the debris falling around them and clattering off their makeshift umbrella diminished. The sound of the well blowout changed. Now came a hissing, a sound beyond anything Ross could have believed possible, like static played through an unbearably loud speaker system. It beat so hard at the ears the men holding the steel sheet stumbled, trying to keep it over their heads and at the same time cover their ears.

Ross crouched down behind the hoist's front end. He pressed his hands to his ears, genuinely fearing his head might explode. If he was twenty feet from the drill-floor door and the far side of a steel wall, what was it like in there?

It came to him, then, what this new sound meant. He gaped at the other men, screamed, 'Run!' but his voice was lost. Only Amaruq squatted down beside him under the hoist.

'Gas!' Ross shouted in his ear.

But it was too late.

A titanic explosion. The entire drill-floor housing pulsed. Then an immense ball of brilliant yellow flame boiled out of its roof and up, enveloping the derrick. A second later, the explosion burst the drill-floor walls.

Spinning shards of steel, yards wide, flashed past the hoist in a hurricane of superheated air. They smashed through everything in their path. One of the men, standing in the open close to Ross, just disappeared. Horizontal jets of fire burst out, all of it happening inches to either side of he and Amaruq, protected by the hoist. But then even the hoist's front section came loose. It caught them up, threw them along with it until Ross slammed into something solid.

The horizontal flames withdrew as quickly as they'd come. Ross found he was lying on his back, staring up through twisted metal. The derrick had become a great, flaming tower. Fire rose in churning waves, white hot in the centre and brilliant yellow. It travelled past the crown itself, two hundred feet overhead, where gigantic, quivering tongues turned to thick, black smoke.

Ross whispered, 'The men. Oh God, the men inside.'

Ross felt something soft on his forehead. Amaruq was kneeling over him, silhouetted by the inferno. His face looked strange, half-melted. It took Ross a moment to realise that he had a long cut on his scalp, from which blood was dripping down across his cheek and congealing.

'We got to get to the bridge,' said Amaruq.

'Was this me?' Ross whispered.

'You gotta shut it.' Amaruq put a hand each side of Ross's head, gripped him so hard it hurt. Blood dripped from the man's cheek, the drops like glowing rubies in the firelight. 'The well! We can still seal the well! The blowout preventer!'

And at that, Ross's consciousness returned.

Amaruq lifted the bent girder that lay across Ross as if it were balsa wood. Dragged him to his feet. Ross groaned, pain lancing through his knee. But, scanning himself in the violent, flickering light, he saw no visible tears to his cold-weather gear. The heat, even this far away, scalded his face.

'The other men?' he said.

Amaruq didn't answer, just stared at Ross until he lowered his eyes.

Ross staggered forwards, Amaruq propping him up. His walking cane was gone. Men ran past. One stood in their way, just gaping up at the fire. Ross caught hold of him, shook him.

'Go to your safety point,' he said.

The man did not move as they pushed past him, his eyes returning to the spellbinding dance of the wild flames.

At the bridge door, Ross hesitated, not wanting to face the many people there. They might believe it was his responsibility, his culpability. There was still no electricity, no control screens. A few lanterns had been rigged. Senko spoke into a walkie, instructing fire brigade teams to muster at their stations. Babushkin was issuing orders to a crewman. He noticed Ross and Amaruq.

'Help these men,' he told a young woman.

She approached Ross with wipes, looked confused, as if unsure where to begin. He touched his face. His fingers came away bloody. He swayed, thought he might fall over. She spoke softly, telling him he was all right, he was fine, her face belying the words.

Outside, another huge explosion rocked the ship. A pillar of fire rose beside one of the forward derrick stanchions.

Ross pushed the young woman's hand away from his face. 'Mikhail!'

Ross, Senko and Babushkin stared at each other – three men with control of a hundred-thousand-tonne drillship, ablaze, without power, drifting inexorably off an open well on the sea floor in the Arctic Ocean.

As one, they turned to look in the same direction. A red and a green button, two hydraulics gauges and several indicator lights, all beneath a plastic protective cover on the control desk. 'Emergency Disconnect System,' a sign beside it read.

Ross stepped closer to Babushkin and Senko. He spoke quietly, so only they could hear. 'We must! We won't be able to control a spill. Not this late in the year. We all know this.' He wanted to say, 'We've always known this.' But, even now, he didn't want to confess that much, even to himself.

Babushkin and Senko nodded. The bridge had fallen silent. Everyone now watching. Babushkin flipped open the cover, depressed the green button. Paused.

'Do it,' Ross said.

He pressed the red button, held it down for several seconds, released it. Ross imagined the hydraulic fluid pressures racing down to the sea floor, the massive shear rams in the subsea blowout preventer that rested above the wellhead biting together to seal off the well.

No one spoke. No one moved.

'And?' someone said, their voice cracking.

Babushkin only pointed. No indicator lights winked. The gauges showed zero pressure. 'The button push is hydraulic,' he said. 'It could be only the indicators, the electrical, do not work. We have no computer to tell us.'

It was possible. Surely it was. Surely they might have closed the well. But Ross knew the truth. An awful passion seized him, so strong he clenched both hands into fists, rocked like a madman caged in an asylum. The ocean, this beautiful, barren place beyond the edges of the world, made a grave for the crew. Because of him. Every falsified safety certificate he'd put his signature to. Every shortcut.

He shook his head, pain spearing across his face and scalp. The pain provided a form of clarity. He limped to stand beside Babushkin at the control desk. Something: something had to be possible.

'The tug,' he said. 'It can take us in tow. Hold us over the wellhead while we make a plan.'

'The disconnect can have worked,' Senko said.

'We must assume it didn't.'

Babushkin looked at the young radio op. 'Jay,' he said. 'Can we contact the *Raven*?'

Jay was rubbing his forearms with his hands, as if trying to rid them of insects. But he spoke clearly enough now, though his face was lined with tears. 'I'll try walkie channels,' he said. 'And we've the prow signal lamp. The tug will be maydaying on our behalf already, sir.'

Ross walked to starboard, looked out. The tug was positioning itself at the *Belyy Medved*'s prow.

'They know what to do,' Babushkin said.

Ross saw they'd got a bandage on Amaruq's head and cleaned the blood off his face. Ross's mind kept replaying the VIPs walking ahead of him into the drill shack. Ross turning away...a gif on endless repeat: the men heading into the drill shack; the crew on the main drill floor, filthy with grease and oil; men with children. Willetts had two. They were only in their teens, weren't they? Crooked Willetts whose fault this was. Willetts' fault. Not his.

'Jim!' Babushkin called. 'If the well disconnect worked, the fire will die.'

'Yes,' Ross said automatically. Then, 'Yes.' Understanding. The well pressure would be cut off and nothing would be left to burn. 'How long will it take?'

'A minute?'

They watched out the aft window. But the inferno boiled up through the derrick tower.

And it did not diminish.

Carrie

The hull shot up then dived down into the ocean's turmoil. The rigging squealed. The wind tore at Carrie's head, howled gigantically in the darkness, suffocating her if she turned to face it. Rogue waves would appear from odd directions, lay the boat almost on its side, water crashing over her, filling the cockpit until she was submerged to her chest. Then, as quickly, it would sieve away, jellying into slush, as the yacht flung itself upright. All of this in almost pitch darkness. Only a vague, ambient light outlined the whitecaps breaking all around her, jagged white lines that appeared behind, ahead and, terrifyingly, above.

At least the sleet had stopped. She breathed through her nose to minimise the fogging in her visor. The tiller jammed into the crook of her arm, feet wedged wherever she could, she kept the wind over her right shoulder. From the south-west, as Donny had told her. With zero visibility, it was all she had to rely on.

After the storm hit, she'd made the decision to run for shelter. The nautical chart had shown her a spit jutting from the south-west corner of Banks Island's Cape Kellett. She'd felt confident the current, at least, would indicate the approaching shore. But the fury of the storm now made her less certain.

Still, she was in control with a clear plan of action. The thing was, she would've expected to have arrived at the coast long before this. Perhaps the wind veered further into the west and she'd missed Banks Island entirely.

Carrie's injured ribs, the nausea and headache of her concussion had, at least, all but disappeared. Her stomach groaned with hunger; thirst troubled her more. Her mouth had become so parched, the back of her throat so dry, she could no longer swallow. She'd remembered the innovation in her suit, the thermal inflation device. It had puffed the suit still more bulbously, a tiny battery light flashing on her forearm. She might well be dead already without its additional insulation. Yet, still, she was cold. And nothing drained energy faster.

She sang to herself silently, given her racked throat. 'That syphilitic, hypocritic, fornicating, royal-mating, dirty lecher, asshole stretcher, bleeding fucker, weenie sucker, navigating, masturbating, Christopher Columbo.' One of her salty father's 'specials' he'd so delighted in teaching his children, to her mother's outrage. Carrie had taken them with her like shields when she enrolled in the Navy at eighteen. Now, however, they did her little good. Even amid the storm's black nightmare, her mind kept replaying those huge flames rising from the drill-ship. Had she failed in her duty? Had she expended so much, fighting the reality of being stationed in Tuk, it had blinded her into missing someone? *Who* had she been meant to stop?

She could now see beyond the prow for the first time. Faint light.

Abruptly, the sloop rose as if it weighed nothing. High, higher than anything before. She felt herself racing along in the current, faster and faster. This was the one, the one that finished it. She slumped, exhausted, over the tiller arm. A swift plummet and then she'd be beneath the water.

But, instead, there came a different sound. An irregular but louder booming. The sloop held high and level. And she grasped what it meant. A lee shore – hours later than she'd estimated. To starboard, breakers crashed on an invisible coast. A hundred yards to port, the same: she was caught between the two.

The boat slid round until it was side-on in the channelled current. She could see nothing ahead. Ever faster, the sloop ploughed on. Carrie hauled on the tiller. Then it came loose, at last, from the unsecured rudder stock. She slammed forwards, screamed. And then there was a massive, grinding crash. Carrie shot out of the cockpit. She had a second of breathless suspension, before the lifeline she'd secured earlier bit into her waist. Her head was driven into her knees. The visor crumpled, came partly loose. Water – freezing, shocking – washed over her face. She was in the ocean.

Ross

Ross listened as Senko attempted to direct fire crews via the walkie, but it was evident that most fire systems were not operating properly, and even when they were, it was impossible to either make headway or control the secondary fires that had started up around the ship, let alone the blowout itself.

He caught sight of himself in a window. One long wound ran from the top of his cheekbone into his hairline. Other lacerations littered his face, so many he was barely recognisable. The young woman had applied antiseptic gel and the little binding plasters that acted like stitches to the larger wounds. The top of his right cheek had swollen up, the bruising topped with a ragged lesion.

He glared in hatred at himself. Hobbled back to the bridge, his knee threatening to collapse with every step.

Through a walkie, he heard the voice of the young radio op, Jay. 'We're getting ropes from the tug. I'd say ten minutes.'

Babushkin turned to Ross. 'If we stay over the wellhead under tow from the tug...'

'...the fire won't stop. The ship will be destroyed.'

'So,' Senko said, 'we let the ship fall off, free ourselves from wellhead. We save the ship and lives.'

'But we cause an environmental catastrophe.'

Senko slapped his hands together in frustration. His earlier stasis had been replaced by a kind of shrill dynamism. 'We save ship. Stop fire. After, we take her over the relief well. We make to stop the spill.' Ross hadn't thought of the relief well that exploration regs insisted be drilled several hundred metres away in case of just such a disaster. But it wasn't going to help this time.

'For God's sake, look!' Ross pointed out the rear window. The storm wind fanned the flames everywhere across the vessel in brilliant, terrible whorls and flurries. 'The ship's already lost.'

Everyone fell silent.

Senko said quietly. 'We order evacuation.'

Babushkin stared out at the inferno raging up through the derrick, the increasing numbers of fires starting all across the decks. Walkies squawked, but otherwise the entire bridge fell silent. 'Abandon the vessel,' he said finally.

Senko began issuing orders.

Ross was trying to think it through. 'We can trigger the blowout preventer manually on the sea floor, using the submersible.'

'Not possible,' Senko said. 'The sub's control shack, it is too close by the derrick. And the derrick is on fire.'

Ross glared round at the faces. 'The submersible, can we get it aboard the support boat?'

Joe Amaruq said, 'It weighs the same as a bulldozer.'

Babushkin said, 'The sea it is too heavy. And no one can go up in crane to lift it on the support boat. It cannot be done.'

Ross gazed out the window. Amaruq came to stand beside him. Down by the bottom of the derrick tower, on the main deck below the drill floor – up from which the inferno blazed – a shipping container sat beside the submersible itself. For some reason, lights shone there, where it was dark across the rest of the deck.

'Maybe,' Amaruq said.

A wild hope filled Ross.

—

Ross and Amaruq emerged onto the main deck. Ahead, the blowout silhouetted everything else by its brilliance. Huge embers cascaded like streamers into the wider darkness. The wind almost knocked Ross to the deck. He planted the metal pole the young woman had found for him, clung to the railing. Sleet thrashed at his wounded face. Amaruq caught hold of his arm. Together they made their way aft, towards the flaming derrick.

They had to skirt smaller fires which had broken out on the deck. Two men appeared in front of them. They supported a third, limp, his face black with burns.

'Get to lifeboat. Idiot!' one of the men shouted at Ross; then they moved on forwards.

'Actually,' Amaruq said, 'this might be a shithole idea.'

They bypassed a knuckle-boom crane's foot. All about it, flames crept up through chinks in the deck like hellish fingers. The crane arm had not been secured properly. The wind and the motions of the ship had it swinging back and forth above them in a dangerously wide arc, its vast beams moaning and creaking with the see-saw. They scurried beneath it in half-crouches.

The submersible's control shack was a repurposed twenty-foot shipping container bolted to the deck. A couple of arc lamps were working. Ross saw electronic lights blipping through the shack's open door. A young man peered out, his boyish face earnest, frightened.

Ross introduced himself.

'The company man? I'm Krajichek. We got to get the sub in the water, try to seal the wellhead on the sea floor.'

'Good man,' Ross said. 'Good man.'

Krajichek beckoned them in, closed the door. 'I got my backup battery working,' he said. 'But the controls keep...I can't get through to the bridge. What the hell happened?' He glared at Ross.

Ross couldn't meet his eyes.

'Ship was a disaster waiting to happen,' Krajichek went on. 'All the crew been talking...'

'What do we do?' said Amaruq.

'Use the hoist. But I need more hands. Scoresby...my boss. I don't know where Scoresby is.' Panic made him look more a boy than a man.

Back outside, the ice-sleet raged along the deck. Ross had to turn his face away. The whole ship seemed to squeal with stress. High above them, the loose crane arm beat against its securing station, lending a terrible rhythm to the chaos.

The remotely operated sub itself was a twelve-foot-long, fat cylinder of bright yellow panels, infolded prehensile limbs and directional lights, boxed by an exoskeleton of steel tubes. The hoist arm resembled a gallows. Where the noose might have been, a block and chain connected to the top of the sub.

Krajichek stood by the hoist control. Green lights flickered on the console. An amber beacon revolved on the hoist. Ross and Amaruq unclipped the rope clamps. Krajichek pointed upwards, then twirled his finger to indicate he was starting. The submersible shifted on the deck, as if shaking itself awake. It lifted off – one foot, two feet. Ross and Amaruq hauled at the ropes to keep its nose pointed out over the side. It rose above the rail, stopped and swung; its many tonnes uneasy in the air. The wind gusted harder and Ross almost lost his feet. The sleet attacked his face so he had to keep his eyes almost closed. His cold-weather gloves slipped on the rope. He clung on as the hoist extended its arm, carrying the sub out over the side.

It was almost clear of the deck when the lighting died. The hoist stopped. Now only the fires illuminated everything. The sub swung out and back. Ross dropped to the deck just as its rear corner fizzed past, an inch above his head. He rolled to his back, the rope slack in his hand. Saw the massive machine twisting above him. He scrambled to his knees, hauled and hauled against the rope on its pulley.

Gradually it centred and stopped moving. Ross snapped the rope clamp shut to hold it taut. Unclenched his knotted hands. Krajichek was busy behind the control console. Ross caught Amaruq's eye. He gave him a wry smile back.

The hoist's amber light blinked on again, though the two deck lamps did not. Krajichek was spinning his finger in circles. Get on with it! Ross unlocked the rope. The hoist began to inch the sub out over the water once more until it hung six feet clear of the ship.

'Do it, do it,' Ross shouted.

The hoist paid out its line and the submersible dropped into the firelit chaos of foam-spray and turbulent black water. Suddenly a brilliant light illuminated them. Some hundreds of yards away, Ross saw the support ship, the *Bon Marie*, its cheese-wedge prow carving the waves. It was shining an arc lamp in their direction, trying to help.

Gazing down over the rail, Ross watched the sub touch the surface. It tipped, drawn off centre by the fierce pull of the current ripping along the drillship's hull. By the time it disappeared below the surface it was almost on its side. Ross could see its lights glowing dimly beneath the waves.

The control cables came up through a groove in the gunwale. When he released the rope, it whistled through the pulley and into the water.

'Now what?' he yelled.

'She has to get deeper than the ship's hull,' Krajichek replied. 'I'm going to the shack. When I signal, you press this button, okay? It'll disconnect her from the drillship and we'll remote control her down to the wellhead.' He headed inside.

Amaruq came to stand beside Ross. He pointed upwards. The crane arm was nearer the deck, nearer them. The fire by the crane's base burned ever stronger.

'It's coming down,' Amaruq said.

'We have to finish this.'

Amaruq stared up at the crane, while Ross watched the shack door. Shortly, the young man looked out and gave a thumbs up. Ross pressed a control panel button, saw the sub's hoist arm spring up. He hurried over to the shack. Amaruq remained where he was, staring up at the crane arm. Krajichek was seated in front of twin joysticks and a number of monitor screens.

'How long?' Ross said.

'Let me work, would you?'

The riser – a pipe linking the ship to the sea-floor wellhead – came visible on the monitors, somehow menacing amid the green-black gloom of the ocean. Still, Ross felt the awful clenching in his lower abdomen ease off a little. Krajichek hunched over his joysticks as the submersible plummeted into the deep.

A claxon sounded outside. It hooted six times, audible even through the clamour of the blowout and the storm. Then the ship-master's voice, crackling and broken. 'This is Senko. Abandon ship. Abandon ship. This is not a drill. Abandon ship. You all know your muster point. Bring survival suit and life jacket. But nothing else. Abandon ship. Abandon ship...'

Krajichek was breathing so hard Ross thought he might hyperventilate.

'What do I do?' he said.

Ross said slowly, 'Whatever feels right, son. I won't pressure you. But if we don't get that wellhead sealed, there's going to be an almighty oil spill. And there won't be much we can do about it this late in the year.' He put his hand on the kid's shoulder. 'But the master gave an order, clear as day.'

'We gonna die?'

'Could be.'

Krajichek dropped his chin to his chest. Then he took one big breath, caught hold of the joysticks again. Ross squeezed his shoulder harder.

The sub's depth meter showed a thousand feet. Ross thought, I'm playing with this kid's life – what, to appease my guilt?

He squatted behind Krajichek's chair, clinging to its back. If he could not save the drill floor crew, if he could not save the drillship, then he had to – he just had to – get the well sealed.

The whole shack quivered. Was it the storm? His mind went to Carrie. He thought of the appalling, violent ocean. She was out in that, on a small boat, alone. And the support ship had returned to the drillship. Was she already dead? But he couldn't believe it. Not Carrie.

'Nearly there,' Krajichek said.

Abruptly, they reached the bottom of the riser. The flexible connector that joined the riser to the wellhead's stack of seafloor components became visible.

'Christ,' Krajichek said. He must have tilted the sub to make the riser appear vertical through the CCTV cameras. Now they could see it was angled way off centre. The ship must have dropped a long way off its position already. The flex connector was designed precisely to allow for a large degree of give. But they could see the strain being exerted on it. The water around it shivered with stress.

'It'll pull the whole wellhead stack off.'

'Hurry,' Ross told him.

The sub dropped down beside the tower of components inside their steel tubing frame. It slowed to a standstill.

'You know what to do?' Ross said.

Krajichek didn't deign to answer. The sub circled the well-head stack's bulbous protrusions. The little submarine's arms became visible in the monitor now, Krajichek busy at his controls. The monitor view went suddenly awry.

'What?' Ross said.

'Just a current.' Gradually the view centred again, and the sub continued its tortuously slow journey.

The wellhead's blowout preventer's manual controls came into view, with its array of handles designed for the sub's hands to grapple.

Ross said, 'Good work.'

Something impacted the outer wall of the sub's control shack. Again and then again. They sounded like rifle shots.

'Lord almighty, what is that?' Krajichek's voice was a squeak.

'Just rivets blown out of their housing by the heat. Keep going.'

Ross hurried to the door, opened it a fraction, looked out. Amaruq crouched beside the hoist's base, both hands over his head. When he saw Ross, he pointed. It was way too loud even for shouting. Ross saw the fire at the crane's base had spread across the deck. In some places, the steel itself glowed. Amaruq was making signs with his fingers to indicate running.

Ross shouted, 'Two minutes.' Raised two fingers.

Amaruq shook his head, but resignedly. Stayed where he was when Ross signed he should go.

A rivet cannoned off the shack wall beside Ross. He ducked back inside.

Krajichek was reading from a thick technical file. In the monitor, a submersible arm was extended towards the control panel. Krajichek manipulated the joystick. The arm snapped shut its gripping hand and missed the handle. He tried again, failed.

'I'm just the junior,' Krajichek said.

'You're doing great.'

The monitor's view skewed once more. When it came back into focus, the control panel had disappeared. Krajichek was cursing softly to himself now, over and over. He played the joystick and the view turned sideways until the panel came into view once more. He closed in. The gripping hand extended. Slowly. Slowly. Ross held his breath. It started to close round the handle.

'Yes,' Ross whispered.

Behind them the door flew open. Amaruq burst in. He snatched hold of both of them by the collars of their jackets. Yanked them back so hard, Krajichek's chair flipped over.

'We're there,' Ross shouted. 'We're there.'

But the big man hauled them both to the door, fought them when Ross attempted to grab the door jamb. Outside, a monumental grinding noise drowned out even the blowout's howl. Ross had time to look up as he was dragged along, stumbling. He saw the giant crane arm collapsing right on top of them. It smashed into the deck beside them, its impact sending the three of them skidding across the deck. Ross collided with something, which spun him in a full circle. Then he lay still, winded, utterly stunned by the closeness and scale of the accident.

When he could look once more, the submersible control shack was completely crushed. He'd failed. The ship would burn, the wellhead would collapse without being sealed, and, even if they survived, they'd have no way to stop the oil spill that would follow.

Carrie

She was in the ocean. Yet, instantly, she hit bottom. Agony about her waist, blind, unable to breathe with the cold, yet her head still above water. Her backside rested on something solid. The sea poured over her. It dragged her this way and that, as if she were a fallen waterskier zigzagging on the surface, still towed behind a powerboat. She rolled over onto her hands and knees, fought the current, which ploughed into her chest and sprayed up across her face.

The *Carrick*'s hull loomed over her. It listed, twitching against whatever it had struck beneath the water. If it came free it would crush her in a second. She cast a quick look over her shoulder but could only make out the fast-running tide vanishing into grey gloom. Were they not ashore? Not on a beach?

The full terror of being overboard, in the ocean, alone in the Arctic dark, seized her. Crying out at the pain in her waist and ribs, she clawed her way madly towards the boat. Her feet scrabbled on what felt like shingle.

She reached the stern but could not fight her way through the violence of the freezing surf. She lost her footing again and tumbled back the way she'd come. The lifeline drew her abruptly to a halt, choking in the seawater. She rolled onto her back and sat up on the underwater bank.

She could just sit there with the tide rushing round her. Go to sleep. Wait for the *Carrick* to come loose and crush her. The cold felt less severe in the water.

In fact, it was the cold itself whispering in her ear.

'No chance, buster,' she croaked.

Now, the tide felt less intense and the light was marginally brighter. She pushed through the water, more careful now with her feet. She approached the stern. The waters swirled beside the vessel, which made screeching, grinding noises as it shifted against the underground barrier.

She ranged sideways a few steps until her lifeline came up taut. At its very limit, she edged out into the tide. The waters immediately tried to take her feet from under her. But she was ready this time, planted them widely apart. The muscles in her thighs quivered so hard she knew they'd give out at any moment.

And then there was no more bottom. Her feet slipped down a steep slope and she was plunged in up to the inflatable part of her upper suit. Frantically, she thrashed her arms, trying to twist round, and then her feet hit the shallows again and found purchase. She swivelled over, gasping. Pushed again through the water, at the lifeline's end, until she was abaft the stern.

The tide came markedly less strong. She strode forwards, made the bottom of the ladder. The boat had been bodily hurled by the tide onto this submerged bank. She dragged herself onto the ladder, pulled herself up, her arms shaking with exhaustion. She crawled onto the transom. Mechanically, she drew herself towards the cockpit, rolled down into it. She worked at the cabin hatch, fingers numb in her gloves. Lifted it, slid on her bottom on to the companionway ladder's top step, untied her lifeline, drew the hatch closed. Sat slumped, gasping.

When she looked up, the stretcher remained jammed against the table where she'd secured it. It had tilted almost on to one side, however. Everything was covered in a diamantine patina of ice. It glimmered faintly, bleak, like some long-forgotten ice tomb just unearthed. She slid down the steps and pulled the stretcher flat. Astonishingly, the man still breathed, if fitfully.

On a wall by the navigation desk, the second hand on an antique brass clock moved around the face. She heard it as well now, ticking in the comparative quiet; a quiet – after all those hours of relentless pounding noise – that was somehow all the more terrifying.

She unzipped a glove, pressed fingers to the man's throat, watched the second-hand ticking. Her own blood pulsed so hard it all but drowned everything else out, even the random gun-cracks from the flapping sails outside. She had to focus, feel the pulse. Watch the second hand ticking, ticking. Just calm down for a moment, just stop for just a moment, just for a moment…a moment…

Ross

Someone was shaking Ross. 'We got to go,' Amaruq said. 'Right now.'

Ross opened his eyes. Jets of fire shot horizontally across the deck in different directions. He lay close by the moonpool. In a sudden frenzy, he dragged himself up, clinging to the rail. Directly overhead, the blowout's inferno raged. The drill floor's underbelly – heavily rusted thick steel plate – had begun to sag. Sections glowed a violent red with the heat. The ocean sucked and heaved in the huge rectangular pool. It hurled towering jets of water to explode into steam against the superheated drill floor base. Ross had to duck away as it fell hissing around him.

The riser was still intact. It dropped into the water, and on down to the seabed. As it slid to its new home, it slanted diagonally, edge grinding against the moonpool's lip. The steel cylinder shook with the force of the blowout it contained inside itself. Ross heard the grinding of metal stressed beyond its limit.

'We must get away from here,' Amaruq shouted in his ear. As they headed towards the ship's starboard side, Ross took the walkie from his belt.

'Babushkin,' he shouted. Held it close by his ear.

'Who is this?' a voice said.

'Ross. Get me Babushkin.'

'Babushkin gone.'

A great sea surge flew up over the moonpool rail, cascaded down over him. The freezing water snatched his voice away. He was dimly aware of his hair solidifying into ice, even here amid the fires. Somewhere, he'd lost his hard hat. When he could speak again, he said, 'Gone? Who is this?'

'Is Senko. I am sorry. He was try to save crew from the accommodation decks. Now he say nothing in his radio. There is fire there.'

Ross tried to think. His mind was so slow. 'The tug has us under tow?'

'I think so.'

'You *think* so? The riser's being dragged off the wellhead. We failed with the sub. The tug needs to bring us up into the wind, keep us directly over the wellhead. It'll tear off otherwise!'

'If we break from the well, then the blowout stops.'

'But the spill, man!'

'Mr Ross. Is about people now. Get to lifeboat.' Then Ross heard him growling orders in Russian.

'He's right,' Amaruq said. He'd been leaning in close to listen. 'It's about saving lives.'

Ross gripped the moonpool rail, bent so his forehead rested against it. The ship groaned and squealed, the blowout roared, the storm tore at him. He breathed in huge gulps.

And he was back in the helicopter in Venezuela, after the rebel missile hit. Dense, black smoke filled the cabin. He was thrown forwards and sideways and back in his shoulder harness. The wounded chopper was spinning, the thwock of the rotors changing abruptly to a terrible clatter. One smashed in through the cabin roof. The smoke blew clear, even as the blade sheared half the head off the woman beside him. His Caracas agent, forty-five years old with four children. As her blood sprayed across him, he praised God it wasn't him. That it was her instead. The copter twisted down towards the jungle...and Ross was drunk, clipping the door on the way out of the Tuktoyaktuk bar, collapsing into the snow outside. He was apologising to Carrie, again, for making another pass at her. And always weakness ate the heart out of him.

'Get on, you prick.' Amaruq wrenched him violently back. Ross opened his eyes to find he was leaning far out over the moonpool.

Ross allowed himself to be dragged across the deck. Krajichek had hold of his other arm. The huge crane's ruin resembled some vast mechanical dinosaur's bones, the wreck of a giant child's toy. Embers flashed by like fireflies in a hurricane. He wanted to grab one from the air. It was intolerable that he should catch so fleeting a glimpse of them and then they should be gone.

'Stern lifeboats,' Krajichek shouted, and tugged him aft.

His knee gave with each step, a blinding pain he welcomed for its clarity. 'We go forward,' Ross shouted. 'The tug.'

Amaruq shook his head. 'It's over.'

'No.' Ross pulled away from him. He hobbled round the moonpool. The blowout bellowed. Molten metal dripped from the drill-floor's belly. Ross could feel his skin beginning to scald. Only the sea-spray made it possible to continue.

The main deck on the far side of the ship was less debris-filled. But when he emerged from beneath the derrick, the blowout's heat hit him so ferociously, he had to duck back beneath the overhang. Twenty yards on another fire burned, gusting madly in random directions, right across the otherwise open space. But Ross had to try. 'To the tug,' were the only words now that his mind could manage. He prepared to dash out between the jetting flames.

Before he'd taken two steps, Amaruq caught his arm. 'All right. But not this way.' And he led Ross and Krajichek towards a hatch.

They descended into absolute darkness. The heat, at least, was less. And, once the hatch had been closed, the comparative quiet came as a shock. They entered a cavernous space. Lights flickered on suddenly. With the lights came the emergency evacuation claxon that Ross had heard earlier. It shrieked, on and on, as they hurried across the bay. Then, abruptly, the lights went out again and the claxon stopped.

With only the firelight to see by, Amaruq led them to the far side. Passing through a hatch, they climbed a steep staircase, emerged cautiously through another hatch onto the deck. The bridge superstructure loomed above. The blowout lit everything with a flickering crimson glow. Beyond the rail, oil and other debris burned on the ocean's surface. Ross saw the support vessel, the *Bon Marie*, two hundred yards off the port side. Two of the *Belyy Medved*'s lifeboats pitched wildly beside it. People were trying to leap across, while the support boat's crew clung to the mooring ropes. A man went into the water in his lifejacket. Ross turned away, unable to watch. He limped around the bridge superstructure with Amaruq and Krajichek towards the prow.

Amaruq swore. 'Lifeboats,' he said.

Each of the muster points, either side of the bridge superstructure, usually had a lifeboat suspended beside the railing. Now, no personnel could be seen – and no boats.

In fact, just one man remained. Ross saw him, standing right at the V-shaped prow, regarding the freezing gale, the tug's lights visible ahead. It was the young radio operator.

'Jay,' Ross shouted, remembering his name. He shouted again, so hard his throat ached. The man turned. Ross held up his walkie. Jay nodded, showed four fingers. Ross switched to channel four.

'The tug has the ship under tow?'

'Yes.'

'She needs to draw her into the storm. Come forward, what...?' He turned to Krajichek. 'What do you think? How far off the wellhead have we come?'

Krajichek had to blink, try to find focus. He mumbled, and Ross saw he was beyond reason. So Ross tried desperately to do the sums. Forty feet down to the waves from the underside of the drill floor. The riser at an angle of maybe ten degrees. Add eleven hundred feet. God, he should have stayed by the moonpool! Used the walkie.

'What are you talking about?' Jay said on the walkie.

'We have to keep the riser over the wellhead, stop it coming away. Or the oil will...'

'The oil will spill into the ocean, unchecked. And there'll be no way to stop it before the winter ice arrives.' Jay's voice,

77

even with the fierce wind and the almost continual minor explosions about the ship, bore the strangest tone.

'And no known way to fight an oil spill under ice,' Ross said.

'I never really understood,' said Jay.

'What are you saying?'

'How beautiful the industry can be.'

And, somehow, Ross knew exactly what he meant. 'Yes,' he said.

'Even here, now. Look.' And he threw a hand out to indicate everything.

'I know, Jay.' He kept his voice calm, in spite of the panic the young man's weird fatalism invoked. 'But I have to talk with the tug. Can you help me?'

'And how terrible everything will be now.' Jay nodded, acknowledging the truth of his own words. Then he removed his lifejacket, clambered up onto the rail.

'Jay!' Ross shouted, but the young man fell away out of sight.

Ross stared at the empty prow. He felt the vertigo in his stomach as if he too were falling. He remembered once telling Carrie how much he'd come to love the Arctic. 'More than I believed. More than I should.'

'Hey.' Amaruq gripped his shoulder. He swung him around. The massive, towering flames of the well blowout sputtered. Though many fires burned all over the stricken drillship, the huge central inferno diminished, until the tilted, broken skeleton of the derrick became visible.

And Ross understood. Eleven hundred feet down, deep in the ocean's darkness, the riser had torn from the wellhead. Oil now flowed free into the Beaufort Sea.

—

Amaruq was shouting at Ross and Krajichek, then speaking on the walkie. Mutely, Ross followed them inside the bridge superstructure. He and Krajichek waited in silence while Amaruq disappeared into the darkness.

'Did you see?' Krajichek said. 'Why did Jay do that?'

But Ross had no answer.

At last, Amaruq returned with survival suits and lifejackets. Dressed, back outside, Amaruq drew them forwards. Ross limped as best he could through the deadly fireworks raining down from the burning helideck that jutted out from the top of the bridge overhead. Ice particles thrashed Ross's wounded face. The fires, the storm, the blink of lights from the two other vessels out there, the ozone stink of ocean here to windward of all that was behind: they came ever more distantly to Ross.

Krajichek was speaking. The young American seemed to have emerged from his stupor. 'Man,' he said, 'you got to be joking.'

Ross forced himself to listen.

'Burn here.' Amaruq had his face close to theirs. 'Or freeze, but with a chance to live. I choose freeze.'

'Yeah, cos you're a fucking Eskimo,' Krajichek shouted. 'I'm from San Diego.'

'What's this?' Ross said vaguely.

'We jump. Look.'

Ross saw something bouncing madly in the foam, twenty yards off the starboard bow. From this distance, it looked no more than a rubber ring with webbing in the central hole. A rope ran from it to the tug, *Raven*. A man clung to it with one arm, beckoned with the other as he rose and fell in the steep, breaking waves.

'Jump and live,' Amaruq said.

A steel girder, warped and glowing with heat, collapsed to the deck nearby. Overhead, the helideck sagged off the horizontal when its supporting strut gave way. The tail end of the Chinook appeared, hull awash with white-hot fire. So slowly, it felt as if the earth itself had paused to watch, the aircraft slid over the edge. It fell, tail first, impacted the drillship's starboard gunwale close beside the three cowering men. A rotor slammed into the deck beside Ross. For a moment, the Chinook rested there, perfectly balanced. The wind whipped the flames about it, like a dragon's fiery wings. Impossibly huge and close, it towered over them. Then it plummeted away into the sea.

'Oh, man, did that even happen?' Krajichek said.

'Jump!' Amaruq shouted. He dragged them further forwards. He grasped Krajichek's survival suit, hauled him up onto the rail.

Krajichek shook his hands off. 'I will goddamn do this myself.'

He disappeared into the water, swiftly came up. Flailing, he twisted round, disoriented.

Amaruq and Ross frantically pointed towards the life raft, but Krajichek could not get his bearings. Still twisting, left and right, the tide swept him away along the drillship's side. The life raft's cable paid out. It bounced and swung back after Krajichek, drew in close by the ship's hull. Amaruq ran back along the deck, trying to keep them in view. Ross didn't move. He was staring up as the whole gigantic helideck structure, six storeys tall on its struts, began to collapse.

Now it was Ross who chased after the big Inuvialuit, grabbed his arm. 'We got to go.'

They pulled themselves up. Amaruq leaped into the water.

Ross stared down at the appalling spectacle of the colossal waves smashing into the *Belyy Medved*'s prow.

He jumped.

Jay

A wave lifted Jay. He slid down its front edge and under the surface. Salt stung his eyes shut. Had he just hit the water or been here an age? He wanted to die – that was right, wasn't it?

Instead, he bobbed once more to the surface, the air trapped in his cold-weather suit keeping him afloat. He couldn't feel his face. He forced open his eyes.

Of course, he'd had his doubts. Of course! But he'd assumed the ship's systems would reboot automatically. Wasn't that a fair assumption?

He had to do what he'd done. Yes, it had to be what it was. Simple. Effective. And, it sure turned out effective. No one could deny that. But it hadn't been anything approaching the plan. Not this. He didn't want to be responsible for anyone's death. He wasn't a monster. It shouldn't have become...

But what price the Arctic's destruction? What price the future dead, those countless millions? His mind flicker-imaged TV clips: New York and Mumbai submerged, Australian heat storms, Bangladeshi refugees attacked by vigilante gangs in their own capital city, Chinese floods, drought babies like dust-caked stick toys. And the unnumbered animal dead? The sixth great extinction. Academic papers. Horror graphs. How many human lives was it worth? You had to act! And there would be no one could say now that he hadn't acted. "Better to die on your feet than live on your knees," right?

He'd leaped from the ship to die. His death was surely its own justice. You shouldn't survive. Not as the acting party of such as had happened. So he was a pragmatist? A dying pragmatist, but that was the price. The sacrifice.

But what if the wellhead was compromised? And you, Jay, the polar-bear hugger, caused an unchecked spill in the Arctic winter? Justify that! Ah, he'd put a bullet through a polar bear's forehead any day of the week for the greater good. '*Belyy Medved*' was 'polar bear' in Russian. The corporates sure understood contempt. They were the despoilers, the world-burners.

So the payback was in kind.

And it seemed to Jay that he was no longer freezing in the Beaufort Sea, amid the burning wreckage. Instead, he was aboard a yacht, squatting at the prow in the cold Arctic sunshine.

'Keep a lookout ahead,' a man told him from the helm. It was the man to whom he had been directing his thoughts. His inquisitor. The man it hurt so much to think about... Jay lifted his hands before his face. They were the hands of a child.

It was Jay's job to watch for growlers and small bergs as they entered Lancaster Sound. Low, white Bylot Island lay off their port bow. His inquisitor told him the Dorset Island ice cap might show as a peculiar brilliance to the north, on these late summer days when the sun was shining. A pod of beluga whales accompanied them, white and sleek in the clear black water. He hoped to see narwhals. A flock of black-and-white little auks zigzagged amid the rigging, humming with life. He watched them flit away across the waves, unbearably poignant, like living sea foam, like a dream. Like a whirling, racing, dissipating dream...

And now, he dragged his frozen eyelids apart one last time. Above his head, through the polar storm, he saw a dragon perched on the drillship's gunwale; a dragon with wings of brilliant fire, bright against the black sky. It loomed there a moment, and then fell down upon him.

'Anything ahead?' his inquisitor asked.

But Jay saw nothing.

THE CARRICK

Ross

Ross lay in a narrow bunk, the ceiling eighteen inches above his head.

'Anyone?' His voice was little more than a whisper.

'You alive then.' It was Joe Amaruq, sounding remarkably normal.

'Krajichek?'

'Asleep,' said Amaruq.

'You saved me. Saved us both...'

Amaruq butted in. 'What I been thinking: that lady jumped out the chopper? She got me so angry. Back in Tuk. She was asking me questions like I'm some sort of...'

'It was – is – her job.'

'She thought I was a terrorist, chrissake. I come from Sachs Harbour, not Beirut. She's the one is foreign.'

'Scottish.'

'Wherever. You all are the outsiders here. Not me.' Amaruq's voice held such resentment that Ross kept silent. 'What was she doing, anyways?'

Ross stammered about the small boat in trouble but what was rattling around inside his head was Willetts saying, 'That guy, we got him covered', about the yacht's master.

When Amaruq didn't answer, Ross turned his head to see him sprawled on a bunk just across the way, fast asleep. They lay in a tiny cabin, three tiers of bunks either side of a space two feet wide.

Ross just couldn't put his memories in order. Shock, he supposed. To close his eyes was to be back in the water again. The vicious pull around the drillship's hull. Drowning, his lungs filled with brine. But Amaruq caught hold of him, as he'd done so many times that night. Then Ross somehow clutching

87

the life-raft's safety line. Choking, blinded. A flurry of indistinct activity. Voices audible through the gale. A hard surface beneath him. Pain like burning needles as something or someone beat at his frozen limbs. And, at last, he lay flat, a person telling him to sleep.

He was aboard the tug boat, *Raven*. The realisation made him relax – safe, safe at last. And once more he drifted.

His father was speaking. 'Work, James, it's the ground on which all else is built. Love, family, life. A day like today? It's only made possible through work. There's nothing else otherwise.' Dreary and repetitive. Jim glanced up to see his mother shut her eyes, inhale deeply, her lips thin and pale.

They were standing in a long room in some mid-west museum, the only people there. Another of his father's carefully planned road-trip stopovers. Display cases stretched along either wall, occasional high windows casting light-beams down through dust-filled air. Little geological exhibits either twinkled or remained resolutely dull beside their descriptions. Jim wanted to dash up and down, stare in at everything, read the names and remember. Because he genuinely did find it all fascinating, he really did!

Instead, each new shard proved the basis for another lecture. His father taught petroleum geology at Columbia. He and his mother bore the full burden of that vaunted career wherever they went.

'Ah, you'll both love this,' father intoned. 'Gadolinite. Bet you didn't know it's among the first rare earth minerals named...' Jim watched his mother's knuckles whiten. He thought of the pressure within a petroleum dome as it pushed up against some resistant salty stratigraphic layer. Mum had been almost silent the entire trip. Ten-year old Jim wondered if she were having one of her 'woman moments', as dad described them.

His father glared at the label beside another exhibit. 'Bastnäsite?' he said, incredulous. 'Not a chance is that bastnäsite.'

Jim glanced at his mother, whose lips thinned yet more.

'Too deep a red, too cloudy.' Then his father was striding towards the little museum's reception, his waving finger at the ready.

Abruptly, Jim's mother took his hand. 'Come along now,' she whispered. She pushed through a fire exit door. And they were out in brilliant sunshine. His mother dragged him out onto the tarmac surrounding the single-storey building on the edge of some small town Jim couldn't remembered the name of. They walked quickly round towards the building's rear until his mother, breathing ever more heavily, stopped and leaned one arm against a red oak trunk where the tarmac petered out into scrub. She rested her forehead against her forearm and Jim might have heard a single, dry sob.

She stood straight once more.

'What're we doing?' Jim asked, but she just led him away along a tamped earth path through low trees. The sound of traffic grew louder until they emerged onto a highway verge.

Some time later, Father pulled up alongside. By then, Jim was quietly weeping while his mother hummed a monotonous jingle over and over. Jim let his hand fall from hers as his father got out. He didn't say a word, though. Just came round the car and opened the front and rear doors. Some silent exchange went on between his parents, but eventually his mother slid into the passenger seat and so Jim clambered into the back.

It was his mother's only moment of resistance.

Now, on the bunk aboard the *Raven*, Jim's thoughts turned

from that memory to another. He and Willetts leaving the chopper. Draping an arm about Jim's shoulders like he owned him. Would Jim ever escape domineering men?

He thought of Carrie living up here in a world of men, taking it in her stride. At least she'd managed to avoid this mess, and he felt a surge of relief at that. Though hadn't he seen a flare? A distress flare? No. She'd have sailed back to Tuk, a sea sprite at the helm of that stricken yacht, storm or no storm. Be overseeing the Coast Guard response even now.

He couldn't just lie here on a bunk. Would not. He was responsible – for it all, and not only in terms of his authority but also culpability. At the very least, he could do something about the former.

As Amaruq began to snore, Ross pulled himself to his feet. He clung to a bunk ladder as the cabin plunged and rolled. He wore borrowed clothing: a thick fleece and deck pants, thermal socks. Someone had thoughtfully left a pair of boots and a knitted, heavy wool hat at the end of his bed. For a time, he could only place his head against the cold steel of an upper bunk handle. The kindness of people when he hadn't deserved to be saved. For a time, he sobbed, but as quiet as he could, not to wake Amaruq or the young Krajichek.

Eventually, he put on the gifts, the boots a size too big. The wounds on his face had begun to sting, but he bore the pain as his due. He hobbled out the cabin, and up the almost vertical stairwell outside, clinging to the rails as the boat pitched. His ruined knee gave way every time he put his foot down, the pain making him gasp.

On the bridge, the *Raven*'s master, Peary, sat in the captain's chair. His ruddy, deeply lined face showed the strain of the past hours: mouth narrow, heavy bags beneath deeply-set eyes, his thinning grey hair standing on end. He had a pair of headphones in his hand, one earpiece to his ear.

'Captain Peary,' Ross said.

Peary waved one finger to silence him, pointed at a sailor and then at Ross. The sailor nodded.

'Over here, sir,' he said.

He directed Ross to a chair at the back. Shortly, a tin mug of black coffee was given to him. Ross had to clutch the mug in both hands, he shook so badly. He glanced through the glass behind him, felt coffee scald his fingers.

A few hundred yards astern, waves exploded against the *Belyy Medved*'s prow, bursting in huge fountains of spray that swept away along her deck. The spray became eerie, speckling light particles as it streamed past the many fires still burning on the gigantic ship. While the inferno from the well itself was no more, flames still curled about the derrick, which had visibly sagged towards the bridge. Ross could hardly see anything of the bridge superstructure itself, however. The foredeck was a wreck of bent, mangled and partly melted steel girders. Fire still burned where once the helideck had been.

'Will her fuel tanks go up is the question.' Peary stood beside him, staring back at the *Belyy Medved*.

Ross squeezed his forehead with his thumb and forefinger. 'Or leak into the ocean,' he said.

'I hardly think a ship spill's your foremost concern.'

'She's got ten thousand barrels of crude in her hold. From the well test.'

'Sweet Christ. I'm going to pay out her line to a quarter mile.'

'Can you keep a hold of her?'

'We're steering head on into this blow with lines on a drill-ship that displaces a hundred thousand tonnes. We're slipping astern all the time.'

'Then what did we hire you for?'

'You can go take a shit in your own mouth, my friend. You hired one solitary tug and the Arctic winter's come. Your outfit was always a shambles. I told my paymasters we should deep-six you a dozen times. Well.' He blew a loud breath through his nostrils. 'So, we cling on, ride out the storm. If the fires don't part the cables. Or a lee shore don't come up on us.'

'What about help?'

'Are we sitting pretty in the Gulf of Mexico? Ports and rigs and safety boats every which way? No. Coast Guard's got an icebreaker, but she's still caught up trying to enter the Barrow Strait. Thick ice there already. Days away. There's a rig supply vessel from Mackenzie Bay coming, but she's still a hundred miles off, and not a whole lot of reason to come now 'cept for fire duty. They can't launch choppers out of Inuvik till the storm's done. What use they are even when they get here, I don't know. No other souls will we drag from the water.'

'What news from the *Bon Marie*?' Ross asked quietly.

Peary looked down at Ross like he was an insect. 'Only now you ask that question. They got all the lifeboats. Skipper'll win a medal for it. Deserve one too. Senko's alive. He's calling the muster.' Peary called to the mate manning the radio. 'Get this individual on the line to the *Bon Marie*.' He stared back out at the *Belyy Medved*, spoke less harshly. 'An early winter's coming. Bad like before all this climate shit dug in. Lots of ice. Meaning, you will be most righteously fucked. And the whole world watching. Remember, was Bob Peary told you first.'

Then he turned away at a sudden blast of frigid air. Cursed the sailor entering in minute detail, who just smiled.

Ross gulped his coffee down, limped over to the radio, barely keeping upright with the tug's violent motion.

'Can you get me Senko, the *Belyy Medved*'s master?'

He had to wait several minutes. Eventually he heard, 'This is Senko.' The man sounded so low and weary that Ross could hardly bring himself to ask the question.

'Did you do the muster?'

'You have Joseph Amaruq and Andrew Krajichek, no?'

'Only them.'

'Then twenty-eight souls are lost. Four more likely die before evac comes.'

Sleet and sea spray hissed against the *Raven*'s bridge windows. It was impossible to see ahead. 'Could there be anyone left aboard?' Ross asked.

'I not think so.'

Closing his eyes, Ross said, 'Babushkin?'

'No.'

'Did anyone at all make it off the drill floor?'

'Only the helicopter pilot, the young journalist and your man the boss.'

'Wait. My...You mean Willetts?' Ross began to ask how but then realised details were irrelevant. 'Can I speak to him?'

'He is one of those maybe dies. A bad injury. Coma.'

'How could this happen, Pavel?' It sounded like an accusation, when what Ross really wanted to say was, 'What have I done?'

Senko just said, 'Twenty-eight souls.'

R.C.M.P. Evidence File

Belyy Medved – Suspect "A", Tablet mobile computing device
[evidence code: A12] – Journal Fragment, dated 23 June [no year]

Helideck Reception, screening area – evening.

So here I am, working our rusting rig, cos the ice has generally retreated so far north we can drill more safely now ("more" safely!) and I'm watching a Russian movie about an icebreaker trapped in the Antarctic ice! Corporations don't do irony.

During the pandemic, the talk was about the fossil fuel business getting wiped out. Remember "negative oil price"? Producers pay you just to take it away – they'd run out of storage space. There was "hope" (toe-curling word) for a new age of eco-socialism. Gaia breathes again, forgives us our sins. Then Ukraine, Gaza, Russian gas pipelines to Europe shutting up shop. Bang!

Anyway, us tree huggers didn't reckon on "resource localisation." Thought the "local" was *our* pitch, didn't we? Down with globalisation! Get the *V for Vendetta* masks on, chuck a brick at Davos. No one's throwing bricks now: kettling, drone cameras, riot-cop psychos down every side street, outnumbering the protesters. It was populists who stole the "local" from us. Post-pandemic blame games. Brexit. The Orange Fascist and the new world dis-order. Everything that followed after.

The oil-men got the message, though. "Drill baby, drill!" And sure, they'll source our fuel locally for us! Why not? Lower supply costs, reduce risk and fuck those Russky invader scumbags (he writes on a drillship that's Russian in all but flag and Azeri beard of a company registration). They'll "boost local skills, develop communities"... those local-lovin', good-ole-boy multinationals. So Canada ripped up its offshore Arctic drilling moratorium in 2026 and way hay hay, come on in: government subsidies on offer, state-sponsored pipelines a promise. Do it through a local shell company's all we ask. Jim Ross and "Pentada"! One last fossil fuel fart before the Fall. Russians are doing it up north, anyway, Greenland's getting drilled, so why not the rest of us?

I should've brought popcorn.

Ross

Ross sat quietly at the back of the *Raven's* bridge as the drill-ship burned in the Arctic night. Ross the puppet, the passive. And when he'd tried to act, tried to save the ship, he'd failed. Too late, too little. Definitely too little. He'd known the ship's condition, known the risks, allowed himself to be used, signed the paperwork, finessed the bullshit. Ross the patsy, as he'd described himself to Babushkin. Dead Babushkin.

Willetts still lived, though Senko had said he'd likely die soon. And if he died, Ross really was screwed. Willetts. If Ross was anyone's patsy, he was Willetts'.

He remembered the first time he'd met the man. Some big-ticket Italian restaurant on Mott Street, New York City, three years ago. Willetts was lounging in a booth when Ross arrived. He offered Ross a limp, languid hand but didn't rise.

'I'm guessing people in our business shake your hand,' Willetts said, 'but only in sympathy.'

Ross slid in opposite, on his guard.

'They look you too deep in the eye, don't they?' Willetts went on. 'Seeking the scars inside. They're wondering how you'd deal with the pressures of work if they take the risk of hiring you.' Willetts stared so hard Ross felt like something in a petri dish. 'A risk too far, they decide, given all you've been through.'

'I'm resilient.' Ross wasn't going to offer up his despair so easily. He didn't know this man, had never heard of him when Willetts' office had first called. Yet here he was. Where else was there to be? Frankly, he was happy with a free lunch, even in the knowledge there was no such thing.

Still. Willetts did seem exactly to comprehend Ross's predicament.

'In your own way, Mr Ross, you're quite the legend,' Willetts said, once the pasta primo had arrived. 'But mostly, you're a pariah. Americans won't tolerate a sanctions buster. Even, dread word: a *traitor*.'

Ross watched the linguine on his fork unravel back onto the plate. Willetts sucked appreciatively on a vongole.

'What exactly *were* you doing in Venezuela, Mr Ross? The Orinoco basin. At the height of the insurrection.'

'We'd company assets stranded even before full sanctions came into effect. As I guess you know.'

'Indeed. I followed the court case. You were still in a wheelchair.'

Ross didn't answer.

'Some said you only escaped prison because of it.'

Again, Ross said nothing. He'd learned from his mother that silence was, at times, his only defence.

'Some said you'd been walking fine for a year until the day you showed up at court.'

Ross sipped the excellent Vernaccia Willetts had chosen. Their table seemed afloat in a sea of the soft light and hushed dialogue of expensive dining. But for a moment, Ross was back in that Virginia courthouse, hearing the federal charges being read out against him and the company he worked for. His mind had been filled with documentaries he'd seen about supermax prisons, multiple life sentences. Once again, he'd been the fall guy. Passive. The law, not him, deciding his future. The wheel-chair had been, indeed, his lawyer's idea, if a pretty damn good one nonetheless.

'What is it you *desire*, Mr Ross?' Willetts asked.

'To work.' But what he wanted to say was: to be part of the world again.

'You have no living blood relations.' Ross stared across at this sharp operator whose underling had done his homework for him. 'But for an ex-wife in the Philippines.'

'Don't remind me.'

'When they shot you down in that helicopter,' Willetts said, his voice an ever-deeper Southern drawl, as though he were beginning to weave some grand narrative, 'were you thinking it was all over? Did the rebel missile seem to you like some God-sprung lightning bolt of *destiny*? All alone as you are.' Willetts held the crystal wine glass before his lips, a mordant twist to one side of his mouth. 'Or were you merely thinking how *screwed* you'd be once you returned to US soil?'

'I was too busy dying to think anything,' Ross said.

'But *die* you did not. And now, here you are in hope I might offer – what –redemption?' Willetts drank, but his eyes never left Ross. Then he set his glass down as if in resolution. 'Jim, let me level with you. I hear you're a man who wouldn't bite a bis-cuit. But I also hear you got horse sense and plenty of notches on your gun. I have a project and I need someone who's going to say yes when I tell them what needs doing. Someone I can bet my farm on. Should the need arise.'

Willetts' Southern schtick was growing stronger and stron-ger. Ross said, 'You sure you're not really from New Jersey?'

Willetts smiled his big-tooth smile. 'I am just a digger in the dust.'

Ross eyed the perfectly manicured nails about the wine glass stem.

'You think it possible we might come to an understanding, Jim?'

Still, Ross said nothing, that lone defence of his. Willetts laughed, a low explosion of sound, a laugh so carefully crafted that Ross could not fault it.

'Lord Heavens, Jim, I see I'm painting myself the dark practitioner. I'm not suggesting anything that smacks of malfeasance. I just want a right-hand man I can trust, trust inside out –' Willetts smiled the perfectly affable smile '– and upside down.'

The helicopter spinning down into the Venezuelan jungle; the pickup truck ride through the forest, an agony so great he shrank still from its memory; the court case; his medical bills sucking every last cent out of him. He didn't pretend he wasn't guilty – at least not to himself. And what had been his sin? Allowing a boss to browbeat him into going somewhere he shouldn't have gone. His sin had been weakness.

Now, Ross clung to the arms of his chair on the *Raven's* bridge.

The same sin, played out again and again, like some eternal Buddhist cycle. He'd been around enough to know that they surely wouldn't all be going to jail, even after this catastrophe. They didn't after Venezuela. They didn't after Deepwater Horizon. They wouldn't now.

Twenty-eight. Lokgas's owner dead. Grady the Coast Guard assistant commissioner and the person with oversight of their drilling licence, dead. The members of the PentOil board: all gone. Even Babushkin. And eleven hundred feet down, the well lay open on the sea floor.

Ross had known. Oh, he'd known everything.

'Hey,' the tug's master, Peary, called. He was holding a telephone receiver in his hand. 'You the big cheese now. Coast Guard Command want a word.'

Carrie

First, she heard a sound. A whisper in the silence, then it was gone. The silence was a puzzle. Why silence? But, equally, why should it not be so? She couldn't remember. The whisper again, so faint, muffled. What was it?

'Water.'

Water? Oh, but she needed water, her mouth so parched her tongue could barely move. She forced open her eyes, felt the lashes separate painfully. Blinked. An image came into her mind of an offshore supply ship turning in the high seas of an Arctic storm – turning away from her. Leaving her alone. She moaned, the sound like that of a little girl.

'Water.'

Her head lay on her arm. One leg was bent under her, agonised and numb at the same time. She forced herself to move her limbs, her shoulders, to roll away from the hard, narrow bar on which she rested.

'Water.'

She was cold...Arctic cold. She drew her frosted eyes open, blinked, saw a man's gaunt, bearded face close to her own.

'Water,' he whispered.

She pushed herself to her knees. In fact, it wasn't quite silent, after all. The soft hiss of a breeze stirred the rigging outside, a light flap of sail.

She tried to speak, to say, 'Water, where?' But her parched mouth could not form an articulate sound. He understood, directed his eyes behind him. She clambered to her feet, clung to the table as her numb leg came alive in an explosion of pins and needles.

In the hallway, an open door on the left revealed the galley. Moisture had frozen into the corners, glistening rime frost trails down the cabinets and walls. Her breath billowed like thick fog. She stooped beside a low fridge, plucked open the door to see resealable bottles of water, at least ten of them. The bottles were frozen solid. Without power, the fridge was as dead as the boat itself. If the power had been on, the fridge would have kept the water warm enough not to freeze.

She eyed the galley stove. Twisted and pressed the hob lighter. It clicked without reaction. She tried again. Nothing. Cursing herself for an idiot, she searched around until she found the gas control valve. Cursing herself for an idiot, she searched around until she found the gas control valve. It was closed. She opened it. But, of course, no electricity for the spark. A handheld lighter hung from a hook. She tore it away, ice splintering. Clicked a couple of times and the hob caught.

She set all four to burn, the flames an almost invisible blue. Lit and opened the oven as well. Everything on full. As much for the relief of discovering something on the boat still worked as for the warmth.

A half-filled kettle was frozen solid too. She set it on the hob. It didn't take long to thaw, so the atmosphere couldn't be too cold. She was no expert, but she remembered tales of Arctic explorers burning ice for hours before it turned to liquid. She poured water from the kettle directly into her mouth. It was so cold it made her teeth ache. She gagged, drank again and again. Could have drunk an ocean dry. But she took the kettle back to the main cabin.

His eyes were closed. She used her finger to wipe water

around his lips. He gasped, licked, his eyes half-opening. She poured the tiniest amount into his mouth. He croaked. The galley fires hissed.

'More.'

She let him have another few sips.

'Enough,' she said. 'More in a while.'

'No.' A defeated whisper.

She put the kettle back on the hob, then rummaged in the first aid box. A white metal case read 'IV Saline Solution' and the word 'Ice' with a line through it. She unfastened the tags and inside, found five unfrozen bags of saline solution along with drips and feeds. She took one out, drew down the blanket she'd covered him with earlier. The fingertips on his gloveless hands were blackened. First sign of frostbite, even below the soot-like dirt she'd noticed earlier. He might well lose the ends of his fingers.

'Can you hear me?' she said. He didn't respond. She took his fingers and squeezed them. 'Can you feel that?'

He didn't react at all. Not good. She worked the saline drip into the back of his wrist, used surgical tape to suspend the saline bag from the table. She wrapped it in an aluminium blanket. Would it freeze? She'd keep an eye on it. The man stank. He must have defecated in his suit. She'd had to pee herself during the storm. Something else to deal with.

The cabin was noticeably warmer with the oven and hob gas burning nearby. She fed him more of the now-warm water, but didn't try to speak to him. He took it quietly, passively accepting everything. She felt increasingly certain he'd been paralysed.

The scale of her predicament fell down upon her. The drillship explosion, the support boat turning away. Had anyone seen the flares? She was panting, hands jumping from place to place. Panicking. So, stop. Get outside, get the lie of the land, go from there.

'Back before you know it,' she told the man. He didn't react.

She came on deck, stepped up on the cockpit bench, better to see. The *Carrick* was listing to about twenty degrees. It had grounded almost broadside on to a low shingle bank that lay partly above the water now. Smooth, granite pebbles stretched away for ten yards, then dipped below the surface, the whole shaped like a teardrop, the wider end of which they'd crashed into. She remembered struggling across it the night before, when it'd been beneath the surf. Looking over the side, she saw through clear, green-dark water a steep slope disappearing into darkness. She had to get an anchor into the shingle while she had the chance at low tide; heft it out there herself.

Twenty yards away, a head appeared. A whiskered snout twitched faintly. Huge, black eyes gazed at her. The seal drifted sideways seemingly without effort, its head completely balanced.

'I'm sorting it, so buzz off,' she told it.

The head vanished beneath the surface. Her voice had sounded strangely hollow, as if it had carried only a few yards before bouncing back off an invisible wall. She pulled off her suit hood. The air pinched her ears. Yet still, the day was comparatively mild. She guessed it to be around minus four or five. Warm for October, she knew.

The shoreline, two hundred yards away, formed a broad, pebbled crescent a half mile wide. Dotted along the shingle, a few beached floebergs lay in various states of decay. Beyond the shore, a low flat country of snow, ice and lifeless earth stretched away as far as she could see.

Back the way the *Carrick* had come in, several low islets and pebble banks resembled the one on which she'd crashed. They formed what might be considered a kind of funnel. She guessed the boat had been channelled between them by the storm current as it ran along beside the mainland shore. She'd struck the underwater barrier at such speed she felt certain there'd be no re-floating the *Carrick*, not without a larger vessel with a crane or tug. And a tug might well rip the bottom out, even as it pulled them free. The bottom might be holed already. She needed to investigate.

She stepped down from the cockpit bench and sat. Her ribs hurt when she breathed. One or more was either broken or badly bruised. Her concussion headache still pressed at her temples, though that might also be a product of hunger or thirst. She watched the horizon-bobbing Arctic sun, which lit the broken, stratus clouds with a colour she thought most closely resembled apricot.

She'd moaned more than once to Ross about how this whole foul dump at the top of the world was black, white and grey and nothing more. The terrifying bloom of the drillship firestorm came into her mind, seen through the binoculars, played out once more. An act of terror? Accident? How many were dead? Had the Chinook survived? Ross? Grady? Oh God, had Donny made it?

It was too much to think about.

All she knew was here, this place, her own situation.

And so she pulled herself back from the brink.

Perhaps she'd been saved by her decision to take control of this vessel. A boat named and emblazoned with the same emblem as that scratched into a tabletop in the crew bar beside the base in Tuk. The same Carrick knot as from her childhood.

It felt almost mystical. Like destiny, though she didn't believe in any of that bunk. Out here, though? Did the world work differently?

Maybe the concussion really was getting to her.

Which all took her back to the man below. Time to assess his injuries. Meanwhile, she was probably just over the horizon from some Inuit settlement or scientific base, radar station or something. She'd been headed for the south-west coast of Banks Island, and the hamlet of Sachs Harbour was near that. A Coast Guard vessel would likely appear in the offing an hour or two from now. Small world nowadays, even in this backend of nowhere.

She dropped into the cabin. His eyes had closed again, breathing shallow yet even. The saline drip should be starting to help his body sustain itself. She'd look him over. But hang on: she'd not yet investigated the rest of the boat! As she moved into the hallway, she realised how terrible an omission of her duties, both as an investigator and paramedic, that had been. What if someone had died while she'd slept? It was negligence, no other word for it, concussion or no concussion.

She opened the door opposite the galley. Low light from the doghouse windows in the ceiling revealed four bunks. Two of the berths showed signs of habitation. Ruffled blankets. Paraphernalia of personal effects. A tablet in a bulkhead web. The other two had clothes scattered across them, though the blankets were undisturbed. At least two people had been aboard.

She moved on to the door at the end of the corridor. Turned the handle.

First, an overpowering reek of burning – acrid, like plastics and other man-made materials. It was dark. This space was forward of the doghouse, so no ceiling cabin windows. If there were portholes, they'd been blacked out. Her pupils widened and she began to see.

A table shelf ran round the far end of the cabin, into the narrowing prow. It was stacked with electronic equipment. Screens and keyboards, switches, dials. All of it dark, lifeless. Much of the array had deformed with heat. In front of it, a swivel chair had been secured to the floor. The ceiling was blackened, charred. She coughed, retched now with the smell, retreated and shut the door.

Back in the main cabin, she sat in the navigator's seat. An internal thermometer on the wall read plus-one degree Celsius. Melting frost glistened across surfaces. The sea chart was still clipped to the table top. She brushed her hand across, wiping the slush away. She'd run on through last night for hours longer than she should have in order to reach the southwestern tip of Banks Island. So where was she? She must have missed Banks entirely, the current taking her further south into the Amundsen Gulf. She must be on the mainland somewhere, or even Victoria Island. In any case, she was a long long way from the base in Tuk.

She needed the electrics working again, or at least a clear sky and a sextant.

Given the amount of communications equipment in the forward cabin, this was certainly the infamous eco-blogger's yacht. Okay, what about that second crew member, as suggested by the used bunks? The dinghy hoist had been deployed, so he or she had disembarked because of the fire. This would be the skipper at her feet. He'd ordered the other person into the dinghy for safety, while he'd tried to put the fire out. He did well to succeed, given all the woodwork in here. The boat could have gone up like a bonfire. That stood up to reason.

How long before she'd arrived had it happened? Long enough so that she and the chopper crew hadn't spotted the dinghy.

Or the dinghy had left for some other reason. It was one hell of a coincidence that a fire had broken out in the pimped-up comms cabin up front, the same day as whatever had befallen the drillship. Now that was a query to put to the injured man – if he came round.

So the fire had shorted the boat's electrics. Could they be repaired? That was the single most important issue to address in the short term. She noted the open cockpit hatch and the sound of the galley burners working on full. How much gas was left?

She had to get a grip or she'd kill them both.

R.C.M.P. Evidence File

Belyy Medved – Suspect "A", Tablet mobile computing device [evidence code: A12] – Journal Fragment – Dated 19 July [no year]

Stern canteen – breakfast.

I'm poking at a piece of Russian blood sausage that's leaked into my beans. What was I thinking?

Two Louisiana drill crew at the next table talk supercharging a vintage Chevy. News the other day reckoned our best-case scenario now – 4 degrees of warming by 2100 – means $600 trillion of damages, twice the world's entire current wealth or something. Still, the earth can 'suck my swinging dick', to quote the redneck petrol-heads. Last time the Earth was 4 degrees warmer, the sea rose 260 feet. That'd make barrelling along beside the bayou kind of redundant, wouldn't it?

My bunk-mate, Alexi, offered me a slice of 'salo' earlier. Sliced pig lard, if you can believe that. Eating meat's the most stupid part of my cover. What was I thinking? I mean, come on.

I've got heartburn all the time now.

Ross

Ross held the satellite phone to his ear.

'PentOil, good morning,' a female voice said. It was eight a.m., Texas time. He remembered the receptionist's name just as she began to speak.

'Mary Jane,' he said, 'This is Jim Ross. Who's in the office?'

'Only me. I came in early...' He heard the catch in her voice if she were fighting tears. 'I been watching the news all weekend. I tried to call Mr Willetts...'

'Mary Jane...'

'The phone just rings and rings. I don't know what to tell folks.'

'Who's been calling?'

She went through a list. Everyone from the Canadian Prime Minister's Office to the US Minerals Agency, CNN, Fox, Willetts' wife, everyone's wife. 'What's happening up there?' she said when she'd finished. 'How bad is it?'

'Mary Jane, I need to talk to the PentOil company lawyer.'

He wrote down the number she gave him, shut off the satellite phone. Through the *Raven*'s bridge windows, he watched the Coast Guard icebreaker that had recently arrived, and the support boat that had come in from Mackenzie Bay, fire-hosing the *Belyy Medved*'s still-smouldering hulk. A huge jet of water burst from the tug's foredeck as well. A half-mile away he could see the low cliffs of Cape Kellett on Banks Island's south-west corner. Clouds hung thick and dark overhead. The sea showed a low swell, the water black as night. A pod of seals bobbed nearby, watching the spectacle. Their heads moved comically from one ship to the next to each other. He didn't want to know what they might be thinking.

He got through to Jameson Adams, PentOil's legal counsel.

'Mr Ross,' Adams said, 'there's very little I can say to you at this time.'

'You've spoken with the Canadian authorities? With Crown-Indigenous Relations and Northern Affairs?'

'I cover PentOil operations stateside, Jim. May I remind you that your company, Pentada, owns the licence, leased the drillship from Lokgas, which is not based in the USA but a foreign nation, Azerbaijan, I believe. Technically – and the law is all about the technical, Mr Ross – PentOil has nothing to do with the Pentada beyond as a financial sponsor. Operational responsibility lies with you. Get yourself some independent legal advice. That's all I have to say.'

'You're telling me not to speak to you? But I'm about the only one left alive.'

'Quite.'

—

Ross was talking with his company accountant when Peary caught his attention.

'Inbound,' he said.

A small fishing boat with an upright wheelhouse drew alongside. Two crewmembers helped a woman cross to the *Raven*'s deck, a man with a thick briefcase following behind. Both wore what looked like brand-new parkas, the hoods pulled up against the cold. The woman spoke to the crew then stared up at the bridge. Ross saw spectacles with heavy black frames, wrinkled skin, a soft expression. She looked to be pushing seventy, if vigorous in the way she'd hopped between boats. Still, the thin line of her mouth was so sternly set, Ross just knew she must be looking for him.

'Permission to come aboard,' the woman said in all seriousness to Peary, when they arrived on the bridge. She had a homely voice, like a grandmother. When she pulled her parka hood down, she wore a scarf over her hair. She drew it off. Her hair was grey and bouffant, like the late British Queen.

'It's him you're wanting,' Peary said, pointing.

'You're Mr Ross, Pentada's CEO? I'm Margaret Hathaway, Crown-Indigenous Relations and Northern Affairs.' She introduced the man with her as Mr Oates. 'May I say how very sorry we all are for the loss of life this incident has caused.'

'Perhaps you'd care to use my chart room?' said Peary, grace itself.

Ross closed the door on the private torture chamber Peary'd offered up. Hathaway and the man, Oates, pulled off their parkas and hung them on hooks behind the door. Both wore suits, crumpled as if they'd been in them too long. Hathaway sported a pale-green trouser suit with a cream-coloured shirt. It made her look considerably younger. She held her hand out, inviting Ross to sit. He remained on his feet.

Hathaway said, 'How are you bearing up, Mr Ross?' Her pale blue eyes were faintly rheumy in the hard, fluorescent light. Yet they gazed unblinkingly at him, taking in the lacerations crisscrossing his face. Ross's mouth formed words he could not speak. After a few moments, he held his hands up helplessly, felt tears at the corners of his eyes.

She nodded with sympathy as Oates passed her a document folder. She drew papers out. 'Assistant Commissioner Grady was aboard the drillship,' she said, staring down at the paperwork.

'I'm sorry.'

'Plus several other members of our Coast Guard.'

Ross said nothing.

She looked up. 'And if I may just hear it from you: the well remains open and uncontrolled?'

Ross put his hands on top of his head. 'Far as we know.'

Oates made a sound like the cluck of a chicken. He was maybe thirty-five, squat, bullish, his hairline low across his crinkled forehead. He had a pad open, head down, making notes.

Ross said to Hathaway, 'You're in overall control of the, ah, the situation?'

'The government has a cascaded system to deal with these kinds of emergencies. Coast Guard's DG Operations Nares has charge of emergency actions. There's a government minister.' She paused fractionally. 'The simple answer would be yes.'

'When will the crew be allowed home?'

'We'll have them on their way once they've all been interviewed and cleared,' she said quietly. 'It's for the Coast Guard to decide.'

'And how long's that going to take?' Ross surprised himself with his anger. 'It's been thirty-six hours since the *Bon Marie* docked at Tuk.'

Oates said, 'We're short on interviewers, since your company killed most of the operatives we had nearby.'

Hathaway, her smile unchanging, said, 'I imagine it'll be later today.'

Ross sat down opposite Hathaway. His body seemed to melt into the chair's contours. Just to sleep....

Hathaway said, 'If you feel able, Mr Ross, do tell us your version of what happened out there.'

'I wish I...The ship went dark. I mean it all went dark. I've never seen...Then the travelling block collapsed on the drill floor. There was a blowout. I tried to get the submersible down to...I tried. I really...'

He stopped, choked with tears. He didn't know how to go on. However many times he'd rehearsed his story in the hours since they'd brought the *Belyy Medved* into the bay, it never came out the same way twice. And he just kept going back to the young radio op, Jay, pulling off his life jacket, leaping to his death. He couldn't shift the image.

'The ship's master,' Oates said. 'Senko. He also "doesn't know" what happened.'

Ross said, 'I've never heard of a technical fault on such a scale.'

Hathaway gave him a shrewd look. 'So it was a "technical fault"? A fault on the ship owned by the Russian company Lokgas.'

'Azerbaijani. I'm not trying to pass the buck, just to be correct.'

'And PentOil's entire senior management died on the drill floor.'

'Bar Willetts himself.'

'Who remains in a coma,' she said, 'with serious head, shoulder and pelvis injuries.'

'The *Belyy Medved*'s owner died as well,' Ross said.

'Which leaves you, Mr Ross.' Again that sympathetic smile. 'The man holding the exploration licences.'

Ross could hear the whine of electrical systems, the distant rumble of idling engines.

Oates said, 'You didn't trigger the emergency disconnect system.'

Ross remembered Babushkin – dead Babushkin – pressing that hopeless button. 'We tried.'

'And it failed,' the man said. 'Senko said the same. How's that even possible?'

Hathaway spoke before he could find an answer. 'Perhaps a more pertinent question for now, Mr Ross: can you tell me your plans for sealing the well.'

'I'm sourcing a submersible team. We'll get them aboard this tug and back out there. Manually seal the well.'

'Assuming that tearing the riser off didn't fatally damage the wellhead,' said Oates. 'Which it likely did.'

'At least we can see what's happening.'

'Otherwise?'

'We put a drill unit over the relief well to intersect with the original well; seal it off from the bottom that way.'

'I believe,' Hathaway said, 'the relief well's six hundred yards south-east of the main wellhead?'

'As per regulations.' Ross felt like telling them, I did my homework too. But he knew that wasn't good enough. Not any more.

Oates said, 'And this miraculous "drill unit" will come from?'

'I'm working on it.'

Oates made exasperated sounds. Hathaway held up her hand, and he fell silent. She said, 'I wonder if you've seen the latest weather report?'

Ross nodded. 'A cold spell's coming.'

Oates said, 'My boss's wider point: you were out there too late. The ice is coming in, worst for years. Coming now! Could be nine months before we can even access the wellhead again. We don't have weeks for you to source sub teams or track some fictional replacement drill unit. We don't even have days.' His anger pressed down on Ross's exhaustion, until he felt claustrophobic. He had no strength to defend himself.

'You know, Mr Ross, you really ought not to have still been there,' Hathaway said. 'Pentada had overrun its licence period.'

What could he tell her? Willetts made me do it? It was all Willetts' fault? He wanted to say it'd been her government that had granted the licences in the first place. That it was her government that ought to have known the potential issues. That Canada knew to turn a blind eye when required. Same as everywhere.

'You've seen the news?' Oates said.

'The story's out.'

'"Story's out?" This is *the* global lead item, I mean everywhere. Once the oil-soaked seabirds start flopping around on Instagram, the blinded seals, we'll be...'

A crewman came in with mugs of coffee. The three of them sat for a time, sipping their coffee in silence. 'We'll be... ' Oates was as aware as anyone of their entwined guilt.

At last, Hathaway pushed her cup away. 'Now, Mr Ross, I want to turn to disaster finance.'

'I was just speaking to the company accountant...' He stopped, aware that the critical moment had arrived.

'Yes...' Hathaway prompted.

Ross turned a spoon in his cup, watched his coffee swirl like a little whirlpool. 'There might not be anything in the, ah, the accident provision fund.'

'To be clear,' Hathaway said softly. 'Nothing in the cash account your company must evidence to secure your licence? But your company had produced the evidence of a sufficient cash account, initially, to secure the licence. Now there's nothing in it?'

'That's the suggestion, yes,' Ross said.

'Let's be clearer still, shall we?' said Oates. 'Whose money is it that isn't there?'

'The accident provision fund was offered by PentOil. So Alexander Willetts.' Ross squirmed.

'But it isn't in the fund now, is it?' said Oates.

Ross knew where it was. He'd arranged the money transfer himself back to the US, right after he'd produced the bank statement to secure the licence. Hathaway and her feral sidekick were moving in for the kill. They knew it. He knew it. They were going to make him the scapegoat. The patsy. Oh yes, yet again.

'Forgive my pedantry,' Hathaway said. 'Pentada acts as PentOil's representatives: we understand that. But Pentada is a distinct company under law, here in Canada. Your company. Pentada holds the exploration licence. Hires all equipment, all vessels. Ergo, the project is under *your* operational and legal control.' She never stopped looking at him, never dropped her sympathetic expression.

'I'm a shell company for PentOil.' He could hear the whine in his voice, hated it. 'It's Willetts who has control...'

'Let us not travel in circles, Mr Ross, at so difficult a time' Hathaway said gently. 'To be more pedantic: this exploratory drilling operation has been using an ex-Russian drillship long past its decommission date, owned by Lokgas, an ex-Russian company trading out of Baku, Azerbaijan, flying a Chinese flag, funded by money from a small US exploration company, PentOil, through the shell Canadian company, Pentada, that you own in its entirety. Is that about the long and the short of things?'

'All of which you were happy to licence! So add Canada to that list.' But Ross looked down as he said it, saw his fingers clutching the table edge, his broken nails, the bruising and minor cuts right across the skin there. Damaged goods.

'And the rescue salvage company,' Oates said slowly, enunciating every excruciating word. 'You know, the outfit you're obliged by law to hold under contract while drilling.' Ross felt their gaze on him like jackhammers. 'The salvage company's up and running?'

'They're sourcing transport.'

'And are they aware you're without funds to pay them?'

Ross hurried on. 'First task is to get the fires out aboard the *Belyy Medved*. Drop her anchors.'

'She's leaking fuel?'

'We've not seen any.'

'Going to sink?'

'Nothing suggests it.'

Hathaway said, 'We need to see your well control and spill response plans.'

'I'm sourcing them. Our Cloud system's offline.'

Hathaway's smile didn't waver. 'We will be taking control of your computers and files, Mr Ross.' Her eyes, as they had throughout, remained locked on him. She said, 'What is your estimate of the well's pressure?'

'Around six-fifty bars. Sustained.'

'So you could have thousands of barrels a day leaking out,' said Oates. 'Tens of thousands.'

'And there're ten thousand barrels of crude aboard the *Belyy Medved*,' Ross went on, 'from the well test.'

'Christ Almighty, and you tell us that now? There are still fires on board...'

'We've seen no sign of oil in the water.' A knot in his stomach made him lean forwards until his chest almost rested against the table edge. 'I, we did all we could.' He looked at Hathaway, entreating her to understand.

In the windowless little room, no one spoke for a time.

At last, Hathaway said, 'Every one of us has failed in our proper diligence. But you, Mr Ross.' She pointed at him. Her fingernails were perfectly filed, narrow, sharp. 'You are going to prison.'

Carrie

Carrie heard the sound again. Couldn't place it. Not the wind: that low-pitched moan amid the shrouds and stays. Not the slap of waves against the hull. Not the creak of the boat shifting slightly on the shingle bank. Nor the snuffles and groans of the man asleep. Again, it came: soft, a scratching, as if of something heavy yet gentle.

She gazed round the cabin. Melting rime frost trailed down the walls. The kerosene lantern above her head made the droplets glitter like jewels. In the hallway, a faint pale fire flickered through the kitchen door onto the wall opposite: a single gas burner to ward off the cold.

She watched the man, noting the irregular rise and fall of his chest, his face pallid, grey, his cheeks beginning to sink as he came ever closer to his end. She'd rigged him a low bed in the cabin. With his broken neck, it was too risky to drag him through to the bunks. As yet, she'd not managed a conversation. When she did speak to him, he just gazed at her in mute bewilderment. She'd got his name out of him, at least: Bastien d'Urville. Yep, the eco-blogger guy.

The sound had stopped. She gazed once more at the charts. She was starting to suspect she'd ended up on Banks Island, after all. Could the wind have backed into the south during the storm, even south-south-east? In the storm-dark, it was possible she'd not have noticed. The current could have swung north as it neared the Banks Island shallows, drawing her along. That contrariness she'd noticed could have had something to do with the general direction of the eastern Beaufort's current being southerly.

So, Banks Island's west coast. But where? The coastline looked to be just one long, low mish-mash of tiny islets and waterways, much like what she saw outside. She couldn't match her visible surroundings to the chart. But that didn't signify anything. A hamlet called Sachs Harbour lay on Banks' south coast. About a hundred people. The only settlement. She might be ten miles away round the Cape Kellett headland. But the amount of time she'd spent sailing in the storm suggested further north. So she could equally be two hundred and fifty miles from the nearest human. Heavy cloud meant she'd seen no sun nor stars for a reading.

The sound came again. Scratch, scuffle, scratch. Something bumping against the hull. Some random tree root, long adrift, hundreds of miles north of the treeline. Scratch, scuffle, scratch. Louder now. She ought to go on deck and check it out. But even the effort of getting out of her seat seemed too much. God, only a couple of days and already she was becoming lethargic. Or her body was healing itself, carefully expending its resources where they were most needed while depriving the rest of energy. The good part was it meant she didn't spend her time obsessing about the *Belyy Medved*. But it lurked there in the back of her mind, waiting until she was strong enough to deal with it.

Outside, the external temperature gauge she'd rigged had read minus five degrees Celsius, last time she looked. Weirdly warm, far as she knew. Hadn't there been some talk of a cold winter coming?

She'd turned out all the yacht's stores. They had four weeks of food. Five on shorter rations. Gas for heat and cooking could likely be eked out a bit longer. Water wasn't a problem yet. And there was ice all about, right? She'd have to look into salinity and sea ice. But things could be worse. A rescue team would come looking for them. Once things calmed down with the drillship. Wait for the sky to clear, get a reading, fix the electricity, maybe, get on the radio. It'd be all right.

The scratching started again, stopped. She shrugged, returned to the map.

Then came a huge thud. The entire boat shifted sideways. A long, loud scrape down the hull, followed by a splash, and the boat righted. Then another sound she could make no sense of, like rasping wind through a hollow.

Now she was on her feet all right. Up the steps, clawing at the hatch-bolts. Automatically, the sailor in her checked conditions. Still that south-westerly. A gentle sea swell. Twilight, even at midday.

Then a thunderous splashing in the water to seaward. A deep-throated grunt. Scratching again against the hull – far louder out here. She took a step that way, but a thickly furred paw the size of her head appeared over the side, black claws two inches long. She skittered backwards, fell on her backside on the cockpit floor. Watched the paw catch hold. An oddly breathy growl. Another paw, a black nose, bared canines.

For a second, she just sat there, awe-struck, as the boat rocked under the polar bear's weight. Then she grabbed the boat hook behind her head. It wouldn't move. She whirled round on her knees, tugged at the securing straps behind its barbed points and further along its shaft. The bear growled, an odd, rumbling, rasping sound, so thick and low Carrie's abdomen quivered. She tore the boat hook free.

The bear had its forelimbs aboard, like a swimmer with their arms resting on the side of a swimming pool. Its head swung left and right with effort, biting and snapping at the deck. So huge was it that Carrie stood, unable to move. It slapped one paw further forwards. Its sodden, yellow-white fur clung so tightly to its forelimb that it resembled a heavily muscled human arm.

She jabbed the boat hook, caught the bear along the side of its nose, opening the skin in a long slice. It snapped, thrashed ever harder as it tried to lift itself aboard. The boat shuddered beneath Carrie's feet. She smelled brine, sour meat. Its eyes were black, unreflecting, like empty sockets. She drove the boat hook again and again at its head, its shoulders. It tried to catch the hook in its mouth each time, but now she pressed it into the neck, thrust forwards. The bear lashed a paw at her. It whipped past, one claw tearing a long slice through the chest of her survival suit, and knocked the boat hook from her hand. It bounced away over the side. She collapsed forwards to her knees, right in front of its face. Even as its nose wrinkled in a snarl, head cocking slightly to bite at her, it lost its grip and slid backwards to disappear from sight.

Carrie pulled herself to her feet, searching for another weapon. But the bear didn't reappear. Instead, she heard its breath coming in throaty rasps. She scrambled up on the cabin's roof and dared a look over the side. The bear still clawed at the hull, but it didn't seem able to lift its paws high enough now. Instead, it turned to swim alongside the boat.

'Oh, do me a favour,' she said, remembering the shingle

bank on the far side. It could easily climb aboard that way. Helplessly, she watched as it swam along to the prow. She could only lock herself in the cabin and hope it wouldn't beat its way through the thin door. Where had she put the flare gun?

However, instead of rounding the hull, the bear headed straight on to shore. She could see now, it was exhausted, paws flailing, its head almost sinking beneath the surface with each stroke. She wasn't sure it would even make it.

Carrie also was gasping. She wrapped her arms around herself, felt how cold her unprotected hands were. Realised she was mumbling aloud, incoherent. Her whole body quivered. Shock, she realised, though the diagnosis didn't change anything.

'Maybe you'll see polar bears,' some work buddy had said after Grady gave her the posting. Hah bloody hah. The bear crawled through the thin shore ice and collapsed onto its stomach, half in, half out of the water. Its flanks heaved as it drew in gasps of air she could hear even two hundred yards away.

'Me or you, big man,' she told it, voice cracking.

She dropped back down into the cockpit, took a look overboard. The boat hook was twenty yards off already. She went back inside. Secured every bolt on the hatch door. Felt her pulse beating in her wrist, her body soaked with sweat. She wrapped her arms around herself and rocked.

—

After a while, she noticed the man, Bastien d'Urville, watching her. He looked about as awake as she'd ever seen him.

'Polar bear?' d'Urville said in a voice whisper-soft but recognisably human.

She wanted to scream, 'It had fangs the size of carving

knives. My face was inches from its horrible great snappers.' Instead, she shrugged, said, 'I made it clear we weren't included in its diet plan.'

'You fought off a polar bear. With what?'

'Harsh language.' She got up, working to stay steady on her feet. She stood over him. 'Back in the land of the quick, are you?'

He coughed twice. His eyes tightened into a grimace. His head and face muscles still functioned, even if his body did not. He said, 'It would have swum in from the sea. Probably a juvenile male. But to fight off a bear! You are a latter-day Nansen.'

'I don't even know what you're on about.' She went into the galley, rooted in a cupboard, found what she was looking for, brought it back into the cabin and sat down. She fought to open the frozen bottle top. It cracked at last and she rubbed her hand vigorously around the lip to warm it before taking a swig. The Scotch sang hosannas down her throat.

'So, Lazarus, what happened here?'

D'Urville looked confused.

'You in a sloop shouldn't be here,' she went on, 'winter on its way. Electrics fried. More than one berth occupied, but no one else about. What happened?'

His eyes narrowed. Pain? Grief? 'Some whisky,' was all he said.

'Blood full of morphine, nil by mouth last couple of days and paralysed from the neck down.' Ticking them off on her fingers. 'Sure, why not? I'll scoop your eyeball out with a spoon, while I'm at it.'

Her entire body still trembled. She fell back onto the cabin bench, could hardly lift the bottle to her mouth. Her desperation to know what happened, to the *Carrick*, to the *Belyy Medved,* made her want to grab him, shake the story from his blue lips. But first things first. She drew the flare gun case from a cupboard, opened it and slotted the final flare into the breech.

'Someone is coming?' Strain showed on d'Urville's face as he tried and failed to move. 'We will be saved?'

'Sure, troops on their way.' She tried to look encouraging. 'But I need this for the bear.'

'Why not the rifle?' he said.

'What?' Incredulity lent her strength. 'Where?'

Feebly, he gave directions. Then he seemed completely spent. She found the key. Found the boat's safe, wide and deep behind a burned, plyboard front piece in the radio room. Inside, the thick steel casing had protected everything from the fire. She saw passports and maritime ID documents. A thick dossier file of some kind, along with a few USB sticks. And a Tikka T3x Arctic rifle. Everyone who lived north of the 60th parallel was packing and a crack shot, far as she'd seen these past months. The Inuvialuit Arctic ranger who guarded the airport had exactly this weapon, precisely as protection against polar bears. This one looked second hand or otherwise well used, its stock scratched and notched but serviceable. She could see no additional boxes of ammunition. But when she cracked the magazine, several rounds were lodged inside.

Carrie gripped the rifle. A rage was in her, and it felt too good to resist. She'd had no reason to carry a weapon since her days in the Royal Navy. She strode unspeaking through the cabin. Climbed the steps, almost tore out the hinges as she wrenched the doors open. She stood atop the cockpit, glared through the twilight towards the shore.

She saw the bear immediately. It was on its feet, though patently in an advanced state of malnutrition. It had the bent appearance of a third-world street dog on its last legs. Okay, a dog impossibly substantial, heavy-pawed and shaggy. Its filthy yellow fur hung wetly from its visible rib cage. But it seemed to have no stomach at all. The ribs curved steeply up towards the spine. It rocked bizarrely, rolling its head from side to side like she could imagine an elephant might. Carrie followed its gaze.

Further along the beach, three seals had dragged themselves from the water. One rolled on its back as if scratching an itch. They must be recent arrivals; she could see their sides rising and falling as they drew in great lungfuls of air, obviously tired themselves.

She went down on her knees. Drew off her gloves. The metal part of the stock was so cold her fingertip instantly stuck. She drew it sharply off and felt a piece of skin peel away. Clutching her over-mitten where it hung by a connector from her suit, she rubbed at the stock, the trigger guard and trigger. Then, gingerly, she let the tip of another finger lightly draw across the metal. Breathed. She found her teeth were bared as she stared along the rifle sights.

The bear was making small movements with a front paw. Its rear flanks quivered. Gusts of steam blew like small eruptions from its nostrils. She took a moment to gauge distance and fiddle with the rear sight. The bear set off towards the seals. She took aim at where she thought its heart must be, slowed her own breathing, rested her finger lightly on the rifle trigger, lifted the safety with her thumb.

Gradually depressing the trigger, she followed the bear as it charged the seals. It was emaciated, it couldn't truly charge, though. Rather it shuffled, its rear legs barely able to keep it erect, let alone drive itself forwards. The seals slithered for the water, though they were in no real danger.

A bullet would be a kindness.

But then she sighed, muttered, 'Oh, go on then.'

Her aim swung left. She held her breath altogether. Sighted. The rifle bucked, slammed into her shoulder, hard enough for her injured ribs to squeal in protest. But she did not flinch. The muzzle returned to its first position and, beyond its steaming length, perhaps three hundred yards away, she saw the explosion of blood, saw the body flip over backwards. The rifle's roar fell directly away to silence across the flat terrain.

Everything seemed to stop. The bear slowly swung its head Carrie's way. Did she read some quizzical expression there? Then it loped towards the dead, bloody seal rolling back and forth against the pebbles in the feeble tide. The other two seals were gone.

Carrie watched the bear rip and chew, its muzzle flecked with pink foam and tangles of gore and blubber. She and the bear: two equally sorry specimens here at the ragged end of nowhere.

'Guess it's you and me,' she told it, but it paid her no attention now.

She glanced down at the rifle on her knee. Cracked it open. Four rounds left.

R.C.M.P. Evidence File

Belyy Medved – Suspect "A", Tablet mobile computing device [evidence code: A12] – Journal Fragment – Dated 21 Aug [no year]

My bunk – evening.

Curtain drawn. Ignoring Alexi and Kusma in the upper bunks. Alexi's soon going on shift, Kusma's just off. He works the engine room. It takes him half an hour just to stop shouting. I have to unclench my fists to type.

Sent a coded trans packet today. An email chain: Jim Ross and the OIM agonizing even as they cover up the fact the blowout preventer hasn't been serviced in three years.

I'm re-reading an article on the Earth Liberation Front to cheer me up. Back in the 90s, they torched a few research labs, logging company HQs, car parks full of SUVs. In 20yrs they never hurt a human being – so the story goes. Didn't stop the FBI making them the No.1 US domestic terrorist group. Some of them regretted what they'd done. Well, you would, once you're locked up in a supermax with bin Laden's best buddy in the next cell. The "violence hadn't helped", they said, even set back the cause. But they agreed on one thing: every peaceful protest they'd been on came to nothing.

You despair. Watching the 500-year-old redwood chainsawed into toilet paper. Then you rage. And rage gets you hopped up for anything. You blow shit up. Open some eyes. Most people would stick their head under a jackboot before they'd change. Sure, drive a hybrid, pour almond milk in your porridge. Say a prayer to the Church of Science: it'll come up with something.

Won't be so simple when there's malaria in London and Chicago, heatwaves killing 200,000 white folk every year. Might see a few offshore-asset billionaires strung up after all. Either that, or the mansion walls double in height and Judge Dredd's patrolling the streets.

'You like fuck Taylor Swift?' Alexi wants to know.

Didn't she hang off a wrecking ball? Or was that someone else? 'She's my girlfriend,' I tell him.

Ross

Hathaway and the four accident investigators had already gone ahead. Reluctantly, Ross made his way up the heat-buckled staircase. He bent his head as he passed through a hatch, miraculously still in its original shape, and emerged onto the *Belyy Medved's* drill-floor.

Hathaway and a male investigator – a serious, young French-Canadian in white coveralls – stood off to one side talking quietly. Ross gazed about in dread. A newly-rigged arc lamp threw harsh light from above. The floor formed a wasteland of collapsed girders and cables. Items of machinery had melted into gargoyles. Almost nothing remained of the drill-house. The blowout's firestorm had obliterated it. There were no signs of human remains.

Hathaway came to stand beside him. She handed over a tissue. He wiped his eyes, blew his nose.

'We failed them,' he said. He had to cough to clear a blockage in his throat. He meant to say, 'I failed them.' But, even here, even now, he did not have the courage to say it.

'Yes,' was all Hathaway said. She turned back to speak with the investigator.

She had told Ross he was going to prison. How could he cope with another court case? This time, with all the faces of the dead arrayed before him. All the men and women – thirty of them now – whose lives he'd held so glibly in his hands as he signed each document. But it had been, after all, Willetts who'd put him in this situation. Willetts in his coma, dodging the responsibility. Ross had not yet made it back to Tuktoyaktuk, to his office. Hathaway'd told him they would be taking control of his files. But not that they already had them. He had to get back, to go through them. But so far she hadn't let him out of her sight. Once the police had them, they would tease out every last detail of his culpability. Guarantee he carried the whole can. Hathaway would see to that, he felt certain, if only to deflect attention from her own department.

He picked his way among the ruins, stooped through a deformed hatch to emerge at the top of another steep staircase. Only the top few steps remained. The rest fell like mangled steel tentacles, broken, melted, towards the main deck below. Ross ignored the wreckage's shudder as he sat on the top step. He stretched his bad leg out straight, massaged the quadriceps. He stared down at the collapsed crane below, and the submersible shack it had crushed as it fell. How near they'd been! But none of that counted now.

He felt a hand on his shoulder. It was Hathaway. 'You might want to come see this.'

Carrie

Carrie's watch alarm chimed. Five minutes to midday. She'd been dozing at her seat in the main cabin as she waited. D'Urville also slept. He'd hardly been conscious since the bear attack and, when he was, he didn't speak. She could easily drift away again herself; her sleep had been erratic, dreams disturbing. But, duty. She sealed her survival suit, felt along the bear claw's rent she'd darned. It would do. Then she took up the sextant from the table, and went on deck. Clambered, half-blind with tiredness, onto the cabin roof. Turned the sextant in her mittened hands as she looked around.

The sky had cleared at last. The sun bumped the southern horizon, an oily yellow, like an egg yolk. She could stare directly at it. Otherwise, the sky ranged from pale azure to a somehow comforting indigo in the north. The barren flatlands to the east stretched away, blank and drear.

Her watch chimed midday. She took her sextant reading,

far as she could recall the process anyway. As she lowered the device, she saw a speck in the sky. Her breath caught. But it wasn't a Navy recon drone, a CG chopper, SAR team come swooping in to save them. A raven, it flapped inland, disappearing as it landed. Four days already. Where was everyone? She supposed it was a big Arctic.

A low, grinding rumble sounded from seaward. She stepped across, looked over the side. Larger waves than before now buffeted the boat. She saw a jagged black line running for several feet along the hull below the waterline. She'd found other cracks, when she'd squeezed below the cabin deck to look, on either side of the keel, where it had been nearly sheared away when they ran aground. But the water inside the hull had frozen to form a kind of plug. Still, she didn't know the full extent of the hull's damage. And she'd no idea what would happen if the tide rose and they did re-float. Probably sink to the bottom. Ice stretched out from the shore now. Soon it would reach them and they'd be frozen in. Either that or the ice would destroy the boat. Basically, there were no good options.

She watched the polar bear on shore. It was eating again. Another seal. Although starved, it almost danced round the carcass, slapping at it, playful as it tore at the flesh held beneath its paw.

She felt oddly protective, watching blubber morsels fly out in bloody arcs as it ate. She could see the long wound on its nose she'd inflicted, black now, and the puncture marks where she'd jabbed its shoulders and neck. Once it regained its strength, would the bear be back?

She might throw d'Urville to it, if he didn't start talking.

Back in the sleeping cabin, she pulled off the suit. Underneath, she still wore her vest and officer's shirt, crumpled and filthy as they now were. She'd had to abandon her underwear and trousers. Washing clothes was just too ridiculous a job; it took fifteen minutes to unfreeze a litre of water on the hob. She pulled on a fleece she'd found in a wardrobe. The temperature stayed above zero inside now, the single gas hob providing a surprising amount of warmth.

Reluctant to work out her exact geographical position on the map – to learn just how bad the news might be – she made her way forwards. The burnt-out radio room had become one great tangle of cables and scattered radio set parts. She lit a kerosene lantern and sat, plucked the yacht manual from the chaos with a sigh. They needed power, plus a means of communication. But the wiring diagrams made no more sense than before. AC/DC meant high-voltage rock-n-roll to Carrie, and not a lot else. Her Navy officer training courses had tech stuff, but she'd barely scraped through. She'd been all about the action. Even if she got some charge somehow into the engine's starter battery, the vibrations from the engine running might shatter the hull.

She threw the manual across the floor. It bumped up against the open safe. She stared at it for a while, then drew the fat document folder from the safe's interior. She carried it back to the main cabin. D'Urville stirred, a rumble deep in his throat like the beginning of a cry. She put her hand softly on his forehead. He murmured, then drifted deeper into sleep. She watched him for a while, hand still on his forehead. Eventually, she leaned in close.

'You're going speak to me, laughing boy,' she whispered in his ear, 'before you slip off into the beyond.'

She slid into the L-shaped bench seat round the chart table. Took a swig of sixteen-year-old Lagavulin. At least the booze was quality. Drew the safe's folder close. It was a fat, double-width, lever arch file, filled with papers. A large, handwritten title on the front read *PentOil Dossier*.

'Well, well, well,' she said, and began to flip through the file.

R.C.M.P. Evidence File

Belyy Medved – Suspect "A", Tablet mobile computing device
[evidence code: A12] – Journal Fragment, dated 2 July [no year]

I sent – of all things – a fax today. Babushkin to Lokgas HQ in Baku Azerbaijan. Where the Russian company moved to escape sanctions. The fax was trying to make a point by using the outdated comms tech. Some vital machine part's busted on engine three. After the fax went off, Babushkin laughed like a steam valve, said, 'They will come back, for sure, tell me you have two more engine, why you care? I'll tell them, "Suck my mother's dick."'

Sunshine, 18 degrees today, if you can believe that. Average supposed to be 5. Beluga whales, a whole pod, circling the ship when I took a lunch break. Later, sent off a coded transmission packet to the Carrick containing the OIM's fax and the engine room report.

I like Babushkin, he cares about his crew. But it doesn't change anything. The plan remains.

Carrie

Carrie lifted the bandage away. The pressure sore above d'Urville's pelvis had grown, despite the thorough cleaning she'd given it yesterday. The skin around the central wound was blackening already. Other areas of his back also showed signs of sponginess and darkening. He was moaning with distress.

'For heaven's sake,' she said, 'you're paralysed. As in, your nerves aren't functioning.'

'Mademoiselle,' he said, between gasps, 'your bedside manner...'

'So where is it hurting? And call me mademoiselle again, I'll punch you in the head.'

'I don't know.' He sounded close to panic.

Outside, the wind itself kept up a relentless wail. It sank down into the lowest registers, tugging at her guts, then rose in abrupt shrieks that startled her. It made the rigging creak and snap and whistle. There was a smell in the air, nothing to do with her patient. But, somehow, familiar. What was it?

She said, more quietly, 'I'll hit you up with some painkillers in a minute. But we're going to talk before you slip off to bye byes again.'

She cleaned the wound out with saline solution, applied antiseptic ointment and a new bandage. Then she drew an ampule of morphine sulphate from the medicine box, filled a hypodermic and shot him in the buttock. First time he'd needed it. Was that good or bad? What had changed? Something internal? Was he rotting from the inside out? She could see no additional bruising to indicate internal bleeding. It was all way beyond her paramedic's knowledge. Dump the injured at hospital and on to the next crisis: that had been her gig. Not this nursey stuff.

Soon, she had him back in his thermals, a fur-lined hat on his head. She slumped on to the bench opposite. Watched his eyelids flutter as the drug took hold. She could still smell that faint odour in the air, nothing she could connect to the yacht's interior. She shrugged it away, listened to the hull grinding against the shingle, waited to be dragged off and plunged to the bottom of the ocean.

Would the boat even last as long as their supplies? Four weeks, five? It should. But the ice was changing. And the bear was out there, hungry.

'Did you discover our location?' D'Urville's voice came more clearly than she'd yet heard it.

'Ah, Sister Morphine, she heals all.'

'You're not Canadian.'

'Nowhere's where we're at. You want to tell me what happened here?'

After a few moments, he said, 'There was a fire.'

'No shit.'

He closed his eyes. His eyeballs moved behind the lids. She put her hand on his cheek, concerned he'd fall too far into an opiate stupor. She hadn't had to dose anyone in a while.

'All right,' she said, in part to keep him awake, 'let's play a game: Guess The Cock-Up. I'll go first. The sleeping cabin suggests two people sharing. The dinghy hoist's got nothing hanging from it. So, the fire. Your what, first mate? he gets into the dinghy as a precaution while you're putting out the flames. Dinghy loses its line to the boat. You got no engine. Nothing. So off he or she bobs into the offing. Something like that?'

D'Urville's eyes flickered like he'd hardly heard. But when he glanced her way, his expression seemed calculating. 'Something like that,' he said. He stared up at the cabin ceiling now, speaking hesitantly, as if searching for every word. 'He went on deck to trim the sails for the storm. I was making the fire safe. We were rolling dramatically. He wore no life vest.'

'What sort of a first mate falls overboard?' But she saw the pain on his face and relented. Still, the question remained in her mind.

D'Urville said, quietly, 'I dropped the dinghy, but too late. I don't remember...'

'Then you fell down the hatchway,' Carrie said. 'Woke up with me saving your arse.'

'Frederic. He was twenty-three.'

She leaned forwards. 'And what about the drillship?' She watched a confused play of emotions pass across his face.

'Why?' he said. 'What has happened?'

'Bit of an, oooh, coincidence your boat going boom the same day...' But she stopped. She'd held back on telling him what she'd seen yet. Wanted *him to* tell *her* what he knew first.

'What has happened?'

He sounded so alarmed that she took two steps towards him, holding the whisky bottle as if she were about to beat him to death. 'What did you do, you fucking little weasel?'

His jaw moved as if he were grinding his teeth. Drops formed at each tear duct. He tried to turn his face from her, but could not even manage that.

Several minutes passed. Carrie twisted the whisky bottle in her fingers.

At last D'Urville asked, 'What happened to the *Belyy Medved*?'

Carrie's fists clenched. 'Why is it you think anything happened?'

His lips formed silent words.

'Here's what I know,' she said. 'You're Bastien d'Urville. French and Canadian dual passport holder. Though I'm not hearing much of a froggy accent.' She lifted his passports from the table, flipped them over to land on his stomach. He made no reaction. 'You're some sort of polar-bear hugger. Blogging to the world on the sins of Arctic drilling. Did a decent enough job the oil-biz boys complained to Ottawa. Even I got the memo.'

He didn't reply. What *was* that smell in the air? Some trick of her memory, perhaps. A partial hallucination, the kerosene lamp swinging about, making zigzag shadows round the cold cabin. She poked at a tendril of melting ice that snaked down from the cabin window above her head. Frost whited out the window itself on the outside. She wondered if she should tell him about the drillship explosion, after all. See his reaction. No, first she wanted to find out his version. He certainly knew something.

'I smell oil,' he said.

'That's it!' She eyed the kerosene lamp. No, not kerosene. The hob was gas, not oil. Engine oil? Fuel? Not quite. Like a gas station, but...'Oh, sweet Jesus.'

She ran up the companion ladder and drew back the latches. The wind snatched the door from her hand and slammed it into the wall. She heard the kerosene lamp shatter. The cabin went dark. She clung on to the jamb, hauled herself out into the cockpit. The stink came stronger on the wind, even cold as it was.

Crouching, clinging to a handrail, she gazed outwards. Away to the south, the horizon was the colour of burnt orange. Above, a half-moon bobbed in a clear sky of darkening blue. Ice had formed through the rigging. It crawled across the mast and yard like a pale virus. The ice atop the shingle bank looked solid now. The wind had veered into the north. It was plucking an eerie song from the rigging.

And the smell. She remembered running with her brothers, she the youngest, the only daughter, always struggling to keep up, running past the huge container cylinders, alongside pipelines by the Aberdeen port. You could always find a leak if you followed one far enough.

The smell: unrefined crude.

She stared more closely at the sea. The water heaved like dark mercury, gentle and sluggish. Moon-glimmers refracted into snaking curls of rainbow light where the long, winding slicks of oil crisscrossed the sea's surface.

Carrie understood the disaster that must be unfolding out there. For a moment she just stood there, absorbing the reality of it, until the cold became too punishing.

She raced back down the companion ladder and through to the kitchen. Doused the hob fire. Darkness engulfed her. She felt her way back into the main cabin, wrestled the outer door shut. She stood over d'Urville, though she could barely see him.

'Was this you?' She shouted the words close by his face. Took hold of his suit at the neck, made to drag him up before she recalled his injuries. She let go, groped among the drawers until she found a torch. Clicked it on, stood it upright on the table, swept the broken kerosene-lamp glass to the floor. The torch wobbled slightly as the wind shook the boat. D'Urville's eyes were open and she saw understanding there.

She said, 'I saw the drillship explode.'

He tried helplessly to move, the frown-lines on his forehead deepening to ravines. Tears poured down his face. Phlegm gurgled in his throat as he sobbed.

'My husband and my best friend were headed there!' she said. 'Tell me!'

R.C.M.P. Evidence File

Belyy Medved – Suspect "A", Tablet mobile computing device
[evidence code: A12] – Journal Fragment – Dated 7 Sep [no year]

Stern Common Room – evening.

Watched a colony of seals playing in the moonpool today. I wish the ship had a swimming pool. Showers just don't get me clean. I scrub and scrub. Need to sink down in the water.

Sitting in a corner, same as always. Today's topic of public debate: this Arctic shithole. Cold, dark, food's shit (Russians jeering about that), money's shit compared to the Gulf, takes half your downtime just getting here and away. I want to say, You're right, because a shithole's a place you take a dump. And that's what we're doing.

But I've always been bad at small talk.

Do they know what I am? Do they *see*, when they look at me? Do they *see* the truth of what I am?

Ross

'Jim, come and join us.'

Ross followed Hathaway's voice to the B*elyy Medved's* radio room. She and two investigators stood looking down at the main computer array.

Hathaway said, 'Over here.'

He stepped closer, peered down. Started to say, 'It's the radio control...' but then he saw what they meant. A USB hub rested beside the computers, plugged into the array. And poking out of the hub was a USB stick attached to a key fob.

'What do you make of that?' Hathaway said.

'It's a memory stick. I've half a dozen in the top drawer of my desk. So what?'

'But what's it doing there? In the ship's computer array?'

'You got me.'

'Take a closer look at the fob.'

It was more of a gentle suggestion than an order but Ross obediently examined it. The fob was a pyramid, maybe two inches along each side. The connecting ring at its peak formed an all-seeing eye. Each face of the pyramid had a different design, hand-drawn. He saw an interlinked knot shape, perhaps something nautical. Another side contained a capital A in a red circle; another, a tiny green fist in a green circle.

'Okay?' he said, not sure what he was looking at.

'Still nothing?' said Hathaway.

Her nails clicked on the desktop. But she smiled. 'Jim, the eyes must see. We have, here, an anarchist "A". We have an *Earth First!* design, the fist in the circle. And we have the conspiracy theorist's ur-symbol: a pyramid with an all-seeing eye. Freemasons, lizards, Zionists ruling the earth. Are you following me?'

Ross said, 'And this?' pointing at the sailor's design.

One of the investigators said, 'The knot's a Carrick bend.'

'There was something about that, wasn't there?' Hathaway said, looking up at the ceiling.

Ross knew. Straight away, he knew.

'That yacht,' the investigator said. 'The one the Coast Guard operative went down to. It was called the *Carrick*.'

'I know him,' said Ross.

'Who do you know, Jim?'

'The radio op whose desk this is. He was…distraught that day.'

'You mean,' an investigator said, deadpan, 'distraught while the drillship was exploding?'

'No, more than that...and then he jumped...'

'What do you mean jumped? Jumped where?'

'Overboard.'

'You jumped overboard.'

Ross saw Jay again, at the prow, the flames burning all about them in the dark of the storm. 'He looked at me...he took off his lifejacket before he jumped overboard. It was...' he didn't want to say the word, 'suicide.'

'What was his name?' Hathaway had hold of a sheaf of documents she'd pulled from her knapsack.

'Jay.'

'Yes.' Hathaway sounded elated. She was looking at a particular page. She showed it to Ross. 'That him?'

Ross stared at the photograph. Boyish but faintly haggard, skin tight over the bones of his face, hair unruly, as if he didn't get outside enough. Another dead young man. He nodded, turned away to gaze out the rear window at the wreck of the *Belyy Medved*, the low, grey cliffs beyond.

Hathaway was telling the investigators, 'We need to get this analysed fast. I want everything. Everything. He was comms. He may have gained access to all systems. Could be we got our man.'

Ross didn't listen to the rest. Jay was staring at him before he jumped to his death. What was in the young man's eyes?

'The stick could be anyone's,' Ross said. 'Ship's full of people with software engineering degrees.' His vision blurred with tears. 'We can't blame some poor kid just because he loses it at a bad moment.'

Hathaway came to stand beside him. 'Get some rest.' For once her face had relaxed from her set smile into something that looked genuinely happy. 'You don't look at all well.'

Carrie

Carrie ate a last mouthful of the canned cheese, tuna and kidney bean pasta. It was cold, though she'd lifted it from the hob two minutes ago. She took a saucepan of melting ice from the hob, replaced it with the food pan. A candle guttered in a saucer. She watched its soft yellow light reflecting in the water drops meandering down the walls from the rime frost on the ceiling.

The hiss of charring food startled her. Cursing, she scraped at the pasta and sauce in the pan, ladled it into a bowl. Replaced the melting water pan. Scooped water into a beaker.

In the main cabin, d'Urville muttered angrily to himself in his sleep.

She said, 'Reveille.' Put the food under his nose. His eyeballs rolled beneath the lids, face contorted in confusion. His lungs gurgled. He blinked, tried to clear his throat. Looked at her without recognition.

Then he croaked, 'Carrie.'

'Time to eat.'

'Not hungry.' The muscles in his neck convulsed. He coughed, spat black fluid into the wad of tissues Carrie held by his mouth. Blood from his lungs.

'Like I give a shit,' she told him. But she offered him some water first. His cheeks were concave, the shabby beard like scrub on wasteland. She fed him slowly, tiny mouthful by tiny mouthful. He chewed, his eyes closed, swallowed uncomfortably. Gagged several times. Each meal was harder, but she spooned it all into him somehow. The bowl empty, she heard water bubbling in the galley.

'Time for your bath, laughing boy,' she told him.

'Sounds diverting,' he said.

139

She fetched the water and sponge, poured some of the hot water into a bowl with salt. Set that aside. She had to work fast. It was desperately cold, even inside. Their breath lingered in frost-cloud billows, before condensing to ice on the walls and ceiling. With the rest of the water, she set to cleaning him. She stripped each part of his body in turn, wiped him down, towelled him dry. He wore thermals, two pairs of socks, thick loose trousers and a Shetland cardigan. Layers of blankets on the cushions below, opened sleeping bags and more blankets on top.

'I...am...a...very...patient...person...' she said aloud.

'I'm sorry,' he whispered.

His feet and toes were in surprisingly good shape. She'd worried about blood flow to his extremities. Still, the muscles of his legs were withering so rapidly it shocked her. They'd only been marooned for six days. She didn't know how much longer he'd last. And he hadn't told her yet about the *Belyy Medved*. In fact, today he was the clearest she'd yet seen him. She'd been playing nice since her anger after discovering the oil in the water outside. She found she'd been more afraid he'd up and die, leaving her alone out here. He'd been mostly rambling on about Arctic winds and different kinds of ice, polar exploration and stuff. If he went off-piste it was into quoting Shakespeare. But it was all driving her wild with anxiety and rage and fear. What had happened to the drillship? What was his involvement? Well, she'd pick her moment, and she'd get it out of him.

She removed the soiled diaper she'd constructed out of bedding sheet strips. His penis curled like a forgotten prawn in the grey fur of his pubic hair. When she rolled him on his side, the pressure sore on his lower back had worsened, the skin around the wound black, crinkled and wasted.

'That bad?' he said.

She'd drawn in her breath. She made a noncommittal sound. Pus had dried into yellow flakes. She cleaned it with her homemade saline solution and some antiseptic wipes. 'I'm going to have to cut some flesh away. If you're lucky, it might hold off the sepsis a few days.'

She took the medicine cabinet's scalpel into the galley, heated it over the gas flame until the blade edge gleamed like a line of white fire.

'This shouldn't hurt,' she told him.

'You'll be the first to know,' he said, gazing sidelong at the scalpel.

'You got a head full of morphine and you're paralysed from the neck down. I could saw your leg off you wouldn't notice.' She held it like a fine paintbrush, between thumb and forefinger.

'"Sweetest nut hath sourest rind."'

'Shut your mouth, will you?' But she admired his courage nonetheless.

She sliced away the blackened flesh in tiny sweeps, touching a wipe to them to lift them away, dropping each little morsel into the food bowl. They lay like blackened fingernails amid the scraps of pasta and cheese.

D'Urville began softly to sing. '*She swore that she'd be true to me, mark well what I do say. She swore that she'd be true to me, but she spent my pay-day fast and free. In three weeks' time I was badly bent, mark well what I do say. In three weeks' time I was badly bent, then off to sea I sadly went...*'

'...and fell down a ladder, like a useless lubber.'

'Carrie, I appreciate all you are doing for me. My stupidity has stranded us both, killed...'

She sensed her moment. 'Killed who?' When he said nothing, she set off on another tack – keep him talking about specific things, keep him present. 'Why *Carrick*?'

'Why...?'

'The sloop: why'd you call it *Carrick*? A name? The knot?'

He stared at the wall as she continued her surgery. 'My closest friend at school,' he said, 'Edouard, he was from a family of the aristocracy, with Africa connections of old. Environmentalists and activists. Very different people to my own family. I was fifteen, visiting with Edouard, aboard their yacht in Monaco.'

'Get you.'

'A deckhand was teaching us knots when Edouard's mother called us inside. We sat, watched the news. You've heard of the *Rainbow Warrior*?'

'Some video game character?' Carrie said, worrying at a dried ball of pus deep inside the wound.

'*Rainbow Warrior* was a Greenpeace ship. In 1985, they were to sail from New Zealand to protest a French nuclear test in the South Pacific. The French secret services blew the ship up, right in the harbour, killed one man. It was a cause célèbre, particularly when the police caught two of the French agents and convicted them.

'That day of the sinking, I sat with Edouard's family, swept up in their anger. We watched the television and I clutched the half-formed Carrick knot I'd been trying to master. That was the day everything changed.'

She sliced away the last of the black skin. Droplets of clean blood lined the wound.

'You feel this?' She poked the scalpel tip hard into the middle of the sore. New pus oozed out around it, making her sigh.

'Yes...no. I don't know,' he said.

'Same random pain?'

He grunted.

She applied antiseptic salve and a new bandage. She only had six more bandages. Eight morphine shots. Five days of antibiotic tablets. She flexed her fingers, cold and tight. As she dressed d'Urville, she said, 'There's a Carrick bend motif carved into a table in Tuk's bar. Some coincidence, eh? Bit like your fire the same day the drillship exploded.' She thought of Ross, sitting opposite her, the bottle between them, that dumb trilby of his.

D'Urville's lids pressed together, and his eyeballs moved from side to side as if he rocked himself in sorrow. But she'd had enough.

'Time's up, shitheel,' she said. 'I want answers.'

He shook his head. Weakly. Slowly. The movement made him groan in discomfort. 'I need more painkiller,' he whispered.

'Here's the deal,' she said, holding the hypodermic in front of his face. 'Tell me what happened or spend the last days of your fucked-up, tree-hugging life in agony.'

He looked at her in silence, his eyes full of tears. When he still didn't speak, she tossed the hypodermic onto the table in frustration. 'What, you think I don't mean it? I'm the person who reckons you killed my ex-husband and my best friend.'

Finally, he whispered, 'My son was on the *Belyy Medved*.'

R.C.M.P. Evidence File

Belyy Medved – Suspect "A", Tablet mobile computing device
[evidence code: A12] – Journal Fragment, dated 15 June [no year]

Radio Ops Room – pm

30 mins of my shift to go. Watching news in a corner of my screen. Massive tornadoes in the American Midwest. Dozens dead. Even this late in the autumn. A hurricane's brewing, north of Puerto Rico – could be one of the biggest ever. But we love it, don't we? Humans. Love destruction even more than money. Make it bigger...Make it worse...Bring on the apocalypse. We're all waiting for the Big One.

I'm also in process of running a diagnostics package on the faulty satellite comms. Faulty this – faulty everything, everywhere. This ship's already a corpse, it's only those in charge pretending it's not. Someone's got to show them how it is. Someone's got to show *the world* how it is!

Carrie

Carrie scowled down at d'Urville, but she spoke quietly. 'Say that again?'

'My son. He is...was...is...aboard the drillship.'

'How about that.'

D'Urville seemed not to hear her sarcasm. 'But he is a tough character. He's worked on rigs from West Africa to the Gulf of Mexico. He's not going to...' His voice died away.

'Blow himself up while he's blowing up a drillship?'

D'Urville grimaced. 'He was there for me. Just watching, keeping record. PentOil are corporate criminals. Read the files.'

'The little lamb doing a bit of corporate espionage for Daddy.'

'You must see what he found. They've been faking safety documents, altering machine parts' countries of origin. More. All of it filed through the Canadian service company, Pentada. Directed by Jim Ross. And they are all but bankrupt. They have no financial reserves against drilling in so treacherous a place.'

'There's been no ice here for years,' she replied, though she squirmed at repeating Willetts' words.

'You don't feel the cold? Climate change is a process. Two steps forward, one back. There will always be a cold year again, the ice returns. Then what? Would you trust Russian paperwork on the competencies of a drillship in such harsh conditions?'

'If anyone knows harsh conditions...'

'The *Belyy Medved* was to be decommissioned three years ago. Then suddenly the deal is signed with Pentada and it is here, all its paperwork miraculously in place.'

'There was an explosion. It wasn't ice, it was fire.' But d'Urville didn't answer. 'Let's keep it simple: you're saying your son had nothing to do with whatever happened?'

'No...no,' d'Urville said, and again softly, 'No.'

'"No" as in he did nothing? Or "no" you're not telling me he did nothing?'

D'Urville squeezed his eyes shut. His tanned skin had an ashen cast beneath the rough stubble. She slid onto the bench seat, tapped her nails on the PentOil dossier. In truth, she hadn't comprehended much of what she'd looked at so far. The files contained page after page of opaque technical documents: wellhead flowline schematics, blowout preventer maintenance reports, coil tubing unit specifications, borehole sites and operations regs, daily drilling reports – all in tiny print.

'Do you feel responsible for what happened?' d'Urville whispered.

'I'm asking the questions,' she told him, but the words rang hollow. She persevered anyway. 'What was your son doing on the *Belyy Medved*?'

'He was a communications officer.'

'And your comms equipment went boom the same day as the drillship. Your family's a coincidence magnet. So what, he'd talk to you over the radio, here, in your rich-boy's spy ship?'

'He sent me information via packet radio transmissions, ultra-high frequency, which is line of sight only. I had to stay close.'

'Which cost the mate's life and nearly your own.'

'Please, Ms Essler. Carrie.'

'When was he last in touch?'

D'Urville hesitated. 'The day before...'

'And what did he tell you?'

'That senior management were coming.'

'What else?'

'Nothing! I don't know.' Black spittle oozed from the sides of his mouth. Automatically, Carrie wiped him clean.

'What else did he tell you?'

But d'Urville only muttered in such a fit of anguish Carrie could not bring herself to continue.

She took up the morphine hypodermic she'd laid on the table earlier and gave him the injection. After a few moments, he became quiet. His eyes opened and he gazed at her as if he were a child.

'What are we doing here?' he said.

Waiting to die, she thought. The boat was safely locked in the ice for now, but if it came free, no way would it float for long. A starving bear out there on the prowl. Dwindling supplies. And when first she saw the oil spill, those rainbow curls on the black water, she'd realised rescue might not be coming for them after all. The world had bigger issues to deal with than seeing if Carrie Essler and some eco-nut had survived the storm.

'Waiting for the cavalry to arrive, Bastien,' she told him, easy in the lie. 'Be here soon.'

His eyes closed once more.

—

Carrie lit the hob, put ice in a pan to melt and went on deck. The cold stung her eyes, made her lungs burn. Thick cloud in every direction, low, black, almost motionless. Yet there was a faint breeze. The wind vane at the masthead showed it came out of the north. The sea surface looked almost flat. But now she saw it gently, subtly heave. The air smelled just faintly of tar.

The land was shrouded in gloom. The shore ice looked lumpy and irregular, grey in the wan light. It reached halfway to the shingle reef on which the *Carrick* lay. The water had frozen on the shingle itself. The open lead between it and the shore ice could not be more than seventy-five yards wide. She pulled the neck of her fleece up around her mouth and nose and perched on the cabin roof, helpless against the encroaching desolation.

She heard the polar bear before she saw it. On the beach, clear even in the dull light, it seemed to be dancing. It jumped forwards, pouncing at the shoreline, its paws smashing the ice. It jabbed its muzzle down, snapped and shook as if tearing flesh. Its face was oddly dim, unclear. Then it whirled this way and that, as if attempting to rid itself of something. It shook its massive, scrawny frame, before returning to its perplexing attack. Some weird bear behaviour? But now it looked up, directly at the boat, saw her. Its head froze, low. It began to sway slightly, as it had when preparing to charge the seals.

'Oh, you idiot,' Carrie said.

It paced out onto the shore ice, gathered speed. She took a step towards the hatch, eyes on the bear, but the ice gave way beneath it. It collapsed into the water, only its head still visible. Then its forepaws scrabbled the ice rim. Its back reappeared, and it obviously stood on the seabed. But the ice edge broke and its forepaws went under too. She heard that heavy, breathy growl. This time it almost turned into a yelp, though, as it tried to jump up, go left, go right. Then it heaved itself round and smashed through the ice, back towards the shore, fifty feet away. If she weren't of the opinion that alpha predators lived without fear, she could swear it was in a proper fluffy panic.

Back ashore, it began to jump and spin, a bit like a dog chasing its tail, as it attempted to bite at its flanks. It shook, then rolled on the ground, again and again. Its fur glinted, shimmered faintly. And Carrie understood the bear was drenched in oil.

And the oil was driving it mad.

To the accompaniment of its strangled yelp-growls, she looked more closely at the sea's surface near by the *Carrick*. She saw long, viscous curls of oil. The cold must be restricting its evaporation potential, which was why she could hardly smell it any longer.

A sudden gust of wind clattered the rigging, colder than anything she'd experienced in all her time in the Arctic. She turned her face away. Her eyeballs felt as if they'd shrunk inside their sockets. She could feel the hair in her nostrils, hard and brittle.

When the gust died down, she stared out again at the oil-sodden bear. It grew quiet, glared back at her across the few hundred yards of contaminated water and fractured shore-ice. Its head weaved from side to side, its flanks shivering. She wanted to shout to it. Tell it to run inland. To escape. She wanted to apologize.

Still, she knew the bear was going nowhere. It might be half-starved, half-crazed, but she and Bastien were the only deli in town.

Another, yet bigger gust of wind arrived, strong enough so she dropped back into the cockpit. This time it didn't die down, but grew and grew until she had to grip the wheel for balance.

She gazed north into the wind's terrible bite. She wondered what was coming.

NIGHT FALLS

Belyy Medved Disaster +3 Weeks

Carrie

A sound like a buzz. A bee buzz. A billion bees a-buzzing. She lay on a bunk inside a sleeping bag. Not asleep; not entirely awake. The buzz had drawn her from a dream. She'd been strapped like a husky to a Victorian arctic explorer's sled. Dragging it across broken floes, high on the polar cap. Watched from shadows by a bear. The dream in black and white, a 1940s movie. 'No way!' a part of her was saying. 'Absolutely no way.'

She twisted and stretched, rolled her shoulders a few times. Her body ached with inactivity. The ribs she'd injured still throbbed. Buzz, whirr, buzz. The bees were dying. Bastien had been lecturing her. Doom, doom. None of it was news to Carrie. Life formed an unbroken flow of human fuckwit-age.

Buzz, whirr, buzz – but growing rapidly louder now.

And then it clicked. She yelped, thrashed her way out of the sleeping bag. She wore men's thermals, loose and rolled at the waist. She hauled on her boots.

'Here! Here!' she shouted.

She stumbled into the main cabin. Bastien slept, breath erratic and gurgling. She tore at the hatch bolts, collapsed outside into the cockpit. The cold froze the air in her lungs. Ice coated everything. The throaty whine of a turboprop – single engine, light aircraft – was all about her.

She swivelled round, trying to see. Night, no moon, but clear blue-black skies. And then there it was. At maybe two hundred and fifty feet, coming from the south, the ambient light from the ice reflecting off its white fuselage.

'Here!' She leaped up and down, her breath frosting before her face. 'Here, you beauty!'

It was going to fly right over them. Couldn't miss. And then she realised what it was: its narrow hull and bulbous nose, the wide, swept-forward wings.

'No!' she cried. She tugged at the single drawer beside the wheel but it wouldn't open. Kicked repeatedly at the bolt until the ice shattered. The high-pitched engine whine from the drone – for that was what it was – surrounded her as she pulled out the flare gun. The drone roared overhead as she took aim and fired. The flare chased it in a long parabola. Burst in a shower of pink trails that robbed her of her night vision. When she could see again, the blur of its rear-mounted propeller was vanishing behind the dying flare-light as it headed north along the coastline.

It didn't turn back.

She flopped onto the cockpit bench, head down. But she was shaking so badly with the cold, she couldn't remain outside. She stumbled in through the open hatch. It was already freezing inside the cabin. She hurried through to the bunk-room, ignoring Bastien's enquiry. Retrieved her under-gloves, then huddled over the galley's hob fire, turning it up full.

'It saw us?' Bastien called, as best he could.

After a while, she returned to the bunk-room, pulled on a thick sweater and pants, then went to sit in the cabin. She couldn't look at him.

'A plane?' he said.

'HILEAD,' she told him. '"High Latitudes Environmental Assessment Drone." They're new; map environmental accidents.'

'But it didn't circle back,' he said.

'It's piloted by AI. Techs review the data.'

'It was mapping the oil spill.'

She looked at him, the straggle-bearded ascetic, his face gaunt as the corpse he'd soon enough be. That he'd survived these three weeks was miracle enough. 'Someone'll be keeping an eye out for us,' she told him.

She reached for the whisky bottle, almost empty. Last one. Took the slug anyway. Heard Donny's voice again: "Check in on the hour, every hour. So we know you're not dead."

Ross

'The strong Beaufort subsea tides will be dispersing the oil mostly south and west, also to the east and north, albeit more slowly. While oil slicks will appear on the sea surface, the entire water column will be polluted. The *Belyy Medved* disaster will have a very serious negative effect on fauna and flora throughout the Beaufort, likely for years to come. Beluga whales mate in the Beaufort. Bowhead whales, seals, walrus. Banks Island is an important nesting site for many species of birds. Smaller organisms that form part of the complex food chain will all be affected.'

Coast Guard Director General Operations George Nares glanced up from his briefing document. His heavyset face, all wrinkles and jowls, looked pinched, both from exhaustion and the report he was narrating. Ross sat beside him on the low stage lined with microphones. Alongside them sat Margaret Hathaway and Oates, as well as an Inuvialuit Regional Corporation representative and the mayor of Tuktoyaktuk. A line of journalists faced them. Those members of the local community who hadn't found a seat, stood along the walls. Behind Ross, an image of the Beaufort Sea was projected. A red mark showed the well site. Various coloured spill predictor lines spread out from it. The brilliant television lights had Ross squinting, as if he were under police interrogation.

As Nares began listing Coast Guard and other assets, Ross

put a finger between his shirt collar and neck before realising how guilty that must make him look. He wore a conservative suit and tie, but he'd put on a thick sweater as well, which he now regretted. Sweat boiled in his armpits. It must be shining on his forehead, accenting the ugly pink scars dotting his face. He wanted to slink back to his room, put his head under a pillow. To sleep, for once, without dreams of fear and fire.

'And lastly,' Nares said, 'a Hercules C-130 from the United States Air Reserve Command remains on standby to drop chemical dispersants wherever oil is discovered in open stretches of water.'

'Yeah, but what about us?' one of the locals called out from the back. There were rumblings of agreement round the room.

A journalist said, 'And have you discovered any "oil in open stretches of water"?'

'Our coordinated response has brought many federal partners together. As such, we're using everything from drones to satellite imagery. The Coast Guard's working with Pentada and oil spill response teams to locate such ah...'

'So, no,' the journalist said.

Someone shouted something. Another local called out, 'What about us?' A couple of others repeated the phrase.

'Our fishing! Our hunting!'

'You destroyed it.'

Now people were on their feet. Ross wondered whose idea it'd been to hold a public local event and let the press in.

'We've coastal response teams standing by,' Nares went on. 'Many of you here today signed up for those teams, and I want to thank you.'

'Cos we're the ones been screwed!' Ross saw it was Amaruq speaking. He sat near the front, looking strung out, his hair mussed, as if he hadn't slept in days. Join the gang, Ross thought.

'Right on that.'

'What about us?' A few people took it up, calling it out in unison.

Nares spoke over them. 'The Ministry for National Defence is putting in place significant military assets and personnel for use as required. However, it's predicted comparatively little oil will make it onshore.' His voice faded as he said that final word.

"Cept inside the dead fish!'

'What about us!'

A male journalist called out over the ever-louder chants, 'Has any oil been cleared up anywhere?'

'No.' Nares shouted the word and it stopped the crowd.

The silence seemed to pulse. Ross kept his head lowered.

'Oil weathering and dispersal under and through the ice,' Nares went on doggedly, 'mean it's unlikely we'll be able to burn off the oil. And dispersants work only with high levels of oil concentration that we're unlikely to find. Our ability to respond may prove limited.'

'Limited or impossible?'

'Previous research,' Nares said, 'suggests oil spill response is not possible in October between sixty-five and eighty-one percent of the time. This rises to around, ah, one hundred percent from November to May.'

'Basically, you can't do shit,' someone said. The room grew uneasy with the movement of bodies, whispers from all directions. Ross saw Amaruq deep in low conversation with an old lady sitting beside him.

A journalist at the front raised her hand. Wearily, Nares pointed at her.

'Do you have a more accurate estimate, yet,' she asked, 'on how much oil is actually coming out the well?'

Nares glanced at Ross. Ross, in turn, looked at the man sitting silently on the other side of him. Finally, Ross squirmed and stood.

'I'm Jim Ross, CEO of Pentada.' He coughed into his hand, unsure if his voice would hold. He heard muttering.

A male voice near the front muttered, 'Motherfucker.' Another shouted, 'What about us!'

'As yet,' Ross went on, 'we've not managed to return to the well-site. However, we estimate' – and he didn't want to say it, but had to – 'up to fifty thousand barrels a day.'

'Jesus, Mary and Joseph,' a voice said. Several local people stood, a couple raising their hands as if to ask a question. The chant took up again: 'What about us? What about us?' More people got to their feet.

The same journalist asked, 'We've heard all kinds of theories, but when are you going to close it off?'

'The ice-breaking tug, *Raven*, was on route to the well-site with a remotely operated submarine team, but the heavy sea ice...'

'Is it true,' a laconic voice asked, and Ross saw it was Joe Amaruq speaking, 'the *ice-breaking* tug's currently *trapped* in the ice?'

He wanted to say, come off it, Joe, what kind of hypocrite are you? Instead, he went on, 'The ice came early this year with the northern storm. Early and unusually thick.'

'Ice has come at its usual time,' said an old Inuvialuit man. 'Leastways, before you all bust the weather.'

'What about us!'

'So this just goes on till when?' a young woman called.

'Next summer? You had no plan against this?'

There were sounds of disbelief now. Someone shouted an obvious insult from the back of the room, although Ross couldn't make out the words.

Nares cut in. 'We've an ice-class drillship on route from Labrador. We're going to hook her up to the relief well already drilled. Cement the well hole at its bottom.'

'Drillships haven't worked out so good, have they?' someone said.

'When's it get here?' Amaruq speaking again, on his feet, voice strident.

'It's currently hindered by heavy ice at the north end of Baffin Bay,' said Nares.

Ross tried to speak over the rising incredulity and anger. 'We're still hopeful of getting the *Raven* over the well site. We'll attempt to activate the blowout preventer directly with the submersible. I've a slide I can...'

But no one was listening. Several local people crowded the front of the stage, throwing questions in such confusion Ross could make no sense of them. When had he last slept – nightmares or no? Two days ago? And, even then, only for a few hours. He noticed the news cameras panning round the room. He dropped his head, overcome with shame, exhaustion, grief.

An Inuvialuit man in a heavy, grey-knit sweater leaned across the table and grabbed hold of Ross's jacket lapels. 'You...' he began, but no words followed. Though not more than five foot six, he lifted Ross out of his seat, shook him. Ross hung limp, took it. Flash bulbs fired. It felt almost cathartic, the man's spittle flecking his face, hard knuckles against Ross's neck, the sea stink from the sweater.

Then Amaruq put himself between them. The guy released Ross, turned away, lifted his arms in a gesture of helplessness. Amaruq put a hand on his shoulder. The room calmed down. People – perhaps shocked by the violence – returned to their seats. Grady and Hathaway looked at Ross. He put both palms up to show he was all right.

A journalist stood. 'Richard Black, BBC,' he said. The room quietened down. 'The director of the United Nations environment program has expressed astonishment Pentada were granted a licence, given how small your company is and the scale of the disaster. Can you comment on this, Mr Ross?'

'We're a subsidiary of...'

'Yes, PentOil,' the journalist said, 'though Pentada's the sole licence holder here in Canada. And indeed, PentOil itself is currently under investigation in the US for operating without sufficient funds.' The journalist's eyes moved from Ross to the man sitting beside him.

Ross turned to look at Willetts as well. A head wound ran from behind the PentOil CEO's right ear, up and across his cranium to its crown. The hair had been sheared away, like a fire break in a forest. The wound still showed evidence of the pins that had held the skin in place, little criss crosses along the jagged, purple line of the injury itself. He'd chosen not to hide it. His hair had been brushed back, but it flew up in places, unruly. Despite his $10,000 suit, he looked like an inmate from *One Flew Over the Cuckoo's Nest*. Nonetheless, Willetts wore his habitual smile, the implacable calm in his eyes that showed he'd emerged from his coma unscathed. He'd propped his crutches beside him, visible to everyone. Ross had smiled grimly when he saw them there. The man did theatre.

'I do not believe it appropriate at this time,' Willetts said, his low, sibilant, Southern voice amplified by the microphones, 'to discuss details when the good people of the Canadian Coast Guard are still in the midst of their enquiries.'

'What about the good people of the Arctic?' someone called.

'And the good people of the US federal government too, I imagine,' the BBC correspondent said.

Willetts smiled widened. 'Oh, indeed.'

'And the current situation with the *Belyy Medved*?' This from a local reporter.

Ross made to stand. Willetts' suave deflections sickened him beyond reckoning. He just could not bear the guilt any longer. It was time he came clean.

But Hathaway spoke before he could. 'Salvage teams are continuing their survey. However, the *Belyy Medved* disaster is now formally a criminal investigation, and, as such, has been handed over to the Royal Canadian Mounted Police.'

Hands went up. 'Ade Greely, CBC News. Are you talking corporate negligence? Or do you mean the vessel was sabotaged?'

'Evidence suggests the latter.'

Ross stared at her, amazed. What *had* they found on that USB stick? He'd not seen Hathaway since their trip to the drill-ship, but when he'd emailed her assistant, Oates, to ask about it, he'd had no reply. The investigations team, which had swept into his room and confiscated every electrical device and all his hard-copy files, had been similarly unforthcoming. He'd had a few days to strip out what he could, but he knew there must still be mountains of incriminating evidence among them.

'By who?' the journalist asked.

'We're working on that.'

'Oh come on,' the BBC guy said. 'Are we talking Islamists, eco-terrorists?'

'There's no evidence of Islamist involvement.' Even the composed Hathaway was failing to suppress her satisfaction. 'Although we're not discounting anything at this time.'

Almost every journalist had their hand up now. The local community were all talking to each other. Oates was whispering in Hathaway's ear. Willetts didn't move his face, but out the corner of his eye he caught Ross's gaze. One eyelid twitched, just a tiny movement.

Abruptly the local people's hubbub fell away. The old Inuvialuit woman sitting beside Amaruq had gotten to her feet, about halfway back.

'Seems to me,' she said, her voice throaty and heavily accented, 'makes no difference who did it or how. Point is, it *did* happen. Point is, it *can* happen. Point is, it's *gonna happen again.*'

Nobody spoke.

Eventually Nares spoke into the silence. 'That concludes the briefing. Thank you all very much.'

Ross watched people shuffle out. The local Inuvialuit looked more despondent than angry now, as if at the hopelessness of dealing with these white defilers. Still, several were arguing with each other. He remembered the agonising that had gone on among the local population when the new port and growing the airport was being mooted. They'd fallen in line, though. How could they not? Money trumped environment every time. A couple of journalists clustered round the old woman, but she just waved her hand at them as she left. The TV camera lights went dark. Nares and the other senior Coast Guard and police officers had gathered at the far end of the platform, the Tuk mayor with them. Amaruq was still in his seat, his head lowered as if deep in thought.

'Eco-terrorists?' Ross heard the mayor say, his tone incredulous.

Hathaway edged along behind Ross to leave the raised platform. She put her hands on his shoulders, leaned close to his ear, Willetts watching.

'Hoo-ey,' she whispered, 'you should see the kid's diary on that memory stick. Working himself up to the dirty deed.' She squeezed his shoulders. 'Seems you're off the hook, after all.'

They all were.

R.C.M.P. Evidence File

Belyy Medved – Suspect "A", Tablet mobile computing device
[evidence code: A12] – Journal Fragment,
dated 14 Oct [no year]

Heard today we're going to overstay our exploration licence. Double-time pay's promised. And the suits are all flying in to see the well complete. Providence speaking. Gaia telling me, "You are Go for Launch".

The ship's command systems firewalls are like latches on a dollhouse. All its functions as ship and drill-rig controlled via a single network. They haven't bothered changing passwords since it was built. Same on every rig I've worked. The entire global drilling fleet's a security joke.

One little code-missile and 'KAPOW', 'VAROOM!' The media squealing 'This Could've Been Deepwater Horizon in the Arctic!' Dad releasing his documents.

You don't want me to do it, though, Dad. But the issue's bigger. What happens, even when it's done? What then, Dad? Story fades into the next diversion. Everyone's bored by climate events. How big's it got to get to change things? We'll never match the wave that kills New York in *The Day After Tomorrow*. And it's not like a quick ship systems failure's exactly THE END OF THE WORLD! It's Wake Up World! is all.

Let's call this a test run.

Carrie

Carrie slammed the hatch shut, drove the bolts home and stamped down the companionway ladder. She unzipped her face visor, pushed back the hood and yanked her balaclava from her head. She dropped a knife hilt onto the table. 'It just snapped,' she said, still gasping from the cold outside.

'You look like a badly crafted snowman,' said Bastien.

Frost had coated her completely white. She dragged off her survival suit in the hallway, made tea. Then she sat beside Bastien, offering him sips. The handsome older guy with the chiselled sailor's face was gone. His skin had become grey, his face cadaverous; only the eyes showed life, and they'd grown rheumy. At least the pain seemed to have disappeared. She wondered if that were a bad sign.

She'd slept twice since the drone had been and gone. No one had come. A chopper could make it from Tuk or Sachs Harbour. Maybe it was taking time to analyse the drone data.

'Know who I blame?' she said. 'Alexander Falcon Willetts the bloody Third.'

'You've been reading the PentOil dossier?'

She lifted the thick folder from where it languished on the bench-seat. Dropped it from a height on the table so it thudded. 'Got any Harry Potter instead?' she said.

Through the dark weeks of the storm, the dwindling supplies, Carrie'd lost much of her energy for conflict. But now, irritation making her voice harsh, she said, 'You know Willetts was on the chopper going out to the *Belyy Medved.*'

'Yes.'

'Your boy kept you in the loop, huh?'

Bastien went into one of his feeble coughing fits. She wiped mucus from his mouth. No chance of the damp rag's moisture freezing on his face now, he was burning up.

'Carrie,' he said at last. 'I must tell you something.'

'Your boy was doing more than just observing.'

Bastien was quiet for so long she thought he'd clammed up again. At last, he said, 'He studied computing at Concordia, here in Canada. His mother said I'd stolen him from her. She was right. I took him out on my boat, told him exaggerated tales of my environmental heroism. I encouraged him to take the marine radio courses, to work the rigs. To be inside the system. I succeeded absolutely in indoctrinating him.' He trailed off. Then started again. 'I love him as I love the natural world. The two...they became one.'

'That's what you wanted to tell me? Gaia and Jay united in Daddy's eco-fantasies?' Carrie said. 'Give me a break, Bastien.'

'Jay and I were worried PentOil would get away with it.'

'Get away with *what*?'

'We'd hoped for an accident. Everything was so run down and broken that it seemed inevitable. Nothing too significant, of course. Just enough to make the news. To spook the world. Then we could present the dossier.'

'Eco-warrior and his boy wanted oil in the water? You're shitting me.'

'It began to look like they'd be lucky: land their well, no accidents.'

'So you made a plan.' But she didn't want to hear what he

had to tell her. She didn't want to hate him. Not now, after all these weeks she'd kept him alive in the winter dark.

'Jay knew Willetts was coming. And he'd made a computer virus...'

'Oh, sweet Jesus.' She filled her cheeks with air, stared down at the dossier.

'He'd do it during the well test. The drillship would shut down. They'd be forced to trigger the emergency disconnect. The blowout preventer would seal off the well. The riser would separate from the wellhead, and the ship would reel it in. By then, the *Belyy Medved* would have rebooted its systems. Some well fluids would leak but nothing major and no one hurt. An emergency action to follow. Big costs. Millions of dollars. We could show PentOil didn't have the reserve funds to deal with even a small emergency, much less a big one. Show how drilling offshore in the Arctic Ocean was fundamentally unsafe. There's no proven way to deal with oil spills under ice. Bankrupt them. Cause so big a stink the other wildcatting companies would be forced off site as well.'

'While you pulled your whole Wikileaks act.'

'Like Deepwater Horizon in the Gulf of Mexico. But this time, a what-might-have-been.'

'Yeah but it could prove the opposite, equally; show how safety systems do work.'

'A blowout so far north in winter: there's no emergency plan for such a situation. Nothing that works in any of the science. But no one wants to hear about that. This would make sure everyone heard it whether they wanted to or not.'

'This is no "might-have-been" though, is it, Bastien?' She'd waited three weeks to hear the truth, and how squalid it was when it came.

Eventually he said, 'I emailed Jay the day…before the radio cabin fire. Rethought it. Realised the odds were too high, it could spiral out of control. Begged him not to do it.'

'You put him there. You who fired his radicalism.' She stood abruptly, began to climb the companion ladder, stopped. Came back and sat again. There was nowhere to go. 'It's on you, Bastien.' She turned the broken knife hilt in her hands. She had more rope to try and sever. Preparations to complete. But it was so cold.

'In fact,' she said, 'it's on me.'

'You couldn't have spotted Jay.'

'I was responsible for vetting the *Belyy Medved* crew.'

'We don't know what happened.'

'I was responsible.'

There was nothing else to say.

Ross

As the news conference ended, Ross remained in his seat. Jay Skelton: eco-terrorist? He didn't seem, well, substantial enough, somehow, to be a terrorist. And it felt corrupt that Ross's guilt should be so easily whitewashed by the young man's actions. A young man he'd watched commit suicide.

'Mr Ross?' The old woman who ran Tuk's bar stood in front of the stage. Her expression was so serious he couldn't see her eyes at all through the wrinkles on her face.

'Jeannie,' he said.

'What you thinking 'bout Carrie?'

'The Coast Guard found the yacht's dinghy floating on the water after the storm. She drowned.' But Ross was thinking about the work he'd been doing earlier that very morning with the HILEAD drone data analyst. They'd dredged through every scrap of information the drone had collected in its flights along the mainland and Banks Island coastlines. They were running through the northern section of Banks Island's west coast when Ross saw it.

'Scroll this back, would you?' he'd asked the young specialist.

'Ever got called obsessive before, sir?'

Ross made another handwritten annotation in the folder's six hundred pages of data printout. 'I'm responsible,' he said, pointed. 'Here. I don't get the heat analysis in this bay.'

They scrolled back and forth a few times, running through the heavily pixelated rolling image.

'It's a bay,' the analyst said. 'There's ice. It's cold, black. These're sandbanks or spits coming out the water. Sucks the life out of you just to look at it, same as everywhere else.'

Ross squinted, leaned close. 'Yes, but what about this? It's much warmer. Looks more uniform.'

'I don't know. Exposed igneous rock strata. Shallow melt-pond the last of the sun warmed up.'

'Something alive?'

'Whale carcass, maybe.'

'The lines look too straight.'

'It's the Banks Island Sheraton Plaza!'

'Could it be a boat?' Only in saying it did Ross realise what he'd been looking for all along.

'By Jove, it's the Titanic!'

'You got a real problem, you know that?'

'Not boat shaped, is it? More a square with a tail.'

'A boat's cabin?'

'It's an info blip.'

'You certain?'

The young man had shrugged. 'Don't look like a boat to me.'

Now, in the news conference room, Jeannie shrugged. 'She was about the toughest girl I ever saw. She seem like the sort just ups and dies to you?'

They gazed at each. He thought about the straight lines in that heat source.

'Maybe she lost her tracker,' Jeannie went on. 'Maybe the yacht radio was busted up.'

'So what, she's out there swimming with the narwhals somewhere, keeping quiet?'

'I just saying no one's talking 'bout her. And now it's eco-terrorists. And she went after that green fella's boat.'

'It's not some conspiracy.' But he had to close his eyes, overcome suddenly with the memory of his friend. When he opened them, Jeannie was heading out the door. Her words felt like a portent, even if he didn't believe in any of that crap. He pushed himself up, leaned against the table edge. He stared at the projected image of the Beaufort Sea, with its hydrocarbon plume flow estimates.

Willetts said, 'You miss her.'

Ross blinked, looked down at him, still in his chair. Willetts had been out of hospital for a week, though he'd only just arrived in Tuk. 'To face my many detractors,' as he'd put it, though he'd done no more today than position himself under the press microscope as injured victim. He'd certainly not been on crutches when he arrived the night before. Seemed like Willetts had the same lawyer as Ross did after Venezuela.

'It's the neurotic narcissist in you, Jim, wants to drag everything back to your own door. You got to let go at a time like this.'

'I'm just sorry she got roped into –' Ross began.

Willetts turned his hands palm upward, like he was offering some priestly benediction. They'd not had a private conversation before now. Willetts clearly hadn't found it necessary.

Willetts said, 'They'll bury whatever comes up your files, Jim. The eco-fanatic kid's plenty.'

'Hey Ross,' Nares called. 'Come join us, will you?'

Ross headed over to where Nares stood with Hathaway, the mayor and others.

'Jeez, I'm sorry about that guy shaking you up,' a local police officer said.

'Yes, perhaps a public briefing was ill-advised,' said Hathaway, though she looked pretty pleased.

Oates said, openly grinning, 'That's the kind of image goes viral.'

But Ross was hearing the echo of Jeannie: 'Lost her tracker…radio bust.' Something was in his mind. Something about the way things looked in the chopper that day. The image of Carrie before she jumped. All that equipment everyone was wearing. All the little blinking lights on everyone's chests. All except…

Jeannie: the bar-room sage.

Abruptly, he headed for the door, his cane click-clacking on the linoleum floor.

Amaruq was leaving also. Ross wanted to thank him for stopping the guy roughing him up earlier. But instead, he said, 'You're an oil worker too, Joe. Getting all riled up with the mob like that! Bit of a hypocrite?'

'Used to be,' Amaruq said. 'Not any more.'

Soon, Ross stood outside Carrie's room. Surely, they'd searched it, the Coast Guard, the RMCP. He tried the handle. It was locked.

'Here's what you'd do,' he said aloud. Leaning heavily on his walking stick he kicked out with his good leg. Nearly fell as his foot impacted but did not break the door. Pain shot through his bad knee.

Once he'd caught his breath, he saw the untreated pine doorframe around the lock mechanism had given. He kicked again. This time he did fall, but the frame splintered near the handle. He dragged himself to his feet, leaned his shoulder into the door, staggered in as it swung open. He limped over and collapsed on her bed.

It was unmade. Clothes scattered across it. He felt a sexual frisson. In her room at last! Shook the thought away, remembered the old Inuvialuit woman saying, 'Point is, it *did* happen. Point is, it *can* happen. Point is, it's *gonna happen again.*' He remembered Carrie in the bar, that last night: 'You're not the weasel you think you are, Jim.' She wasn't much of a judge of character.

He looked round the room and there it was, on the bedside table: the little square electronic box. Carrie's EPLT: her Emergency Personal Location Transmitter. Not attached to her suit. Still here in her room. Switched off. 'Her tracker...' Jeannie, the bar-room sage indeed.

He hurried out and away down the hall.

Carrie

She had to make the decision. The balance of probabilities had been reached, passed. She had to decide!

The ice on the *Carrick*'s rigging had frozen into crystalline forms like quartz nuggets. She chipped at them with an outsized jack knife, sturdier than the one she'd broken before. De-icing the main-sheet where it had been tied around a cleat took fifteen minutes. She shook the brittle rope free and, squeezing it to soften each section, coiled the entire length on the cockpit floor. She did the same with the spinnaker guys and jib sheet.

She'd found a few lengths of rope in the boat store, but she wanted all she could get. She tried to crank the manual arm that would lift the mainsail. Hopeless. The mechanism and the sail itself were frozen solid. She'd never get the sail-canvas free. Well, she'd found a spare sail among the stores. She might try the spinnaker later. But come on, honestly, it would be enough. If she just made the decision...

Exhausted, she flopped on to the cockpit bench and removed her visor, though the air was painful to breathe. She didn't want to frost her lungs, so she tucked her face deeper into her muffler, breathed through that. She'd enjoyed the labour after all those days holed up inside during the storm. Carrie had come out as soon as its thin, pale light of a new moon played across the cabin windows.

The bear had left. Or it had fallen asleep amid the low hummocks, fattened on seals, she hoped, not dreaming of humans. The shore ice had reached the shingle bar's ice-cover sometime during the northern storm. Ice now clamped the *Carrick* on all sides. To the west, the greyish sea ice disappeared into the distance, its surface jagged and uneven where the tides had shifted and raftered it into low ridges. It ground against the shore-ice, crunching, squealing, long laments, deep enough to make her gut tremble. 'A place of constant, angry dialogue,' as Bastien described it.

She went through the details yet again. She had perhaps ten days' hob gas and the same of kerosene for the lamps. Not more than a week's food. Perhaps ten to twelve if they reduced rations. He ate almost nothing already. Less would be to kill him even quicker than his injuries. So it would have to be enough.

Unless...

The alternative still appeared insane. But it represented action, at least. And it was Bastien's constant suggestion. For him, it could mean death just getting him up the cabin ladder. Death in transit, as it were.

A booming crash sounded behind her. She scrambled up. Saw a silhouette on the ocean, angular against the few stars visible to the west and north.

An iceberg, a hundred yards away. She guessed it to be more than thirty feet high, a sort of irregular hexagon, but with its sides nearest the water ground away by the waves, so it appeared top-heavy. It made slow but constant progress, driven by the tide, its leading edge splintering the thin sea ice. Drifting there – alone, weathered, glowing in multiple, ghostly whites, moaning internally as its uneven, internal structure shifted – it appeared unutterably forlorn.

She watched, hypnotised by its solitary passage. Myriad winding gutters etched the berg's sides: water run-off, as it had passed through an Arctic summer or two and survived. Some leftover chunk of pack ice, a multiyear floeberg, as she'd heard them called. It swung slowly round as it neared. Its far side was almost entirely hollowed out.

Then she realised: lazily, inexorably, it was heading directly towards the *Carrick*.

It must be following the same deep-water tidal path amid the underground banks that the *Carrick* had travelled before they crashed. God, it probably weighed, what, a thousand tonnes? More? Who knew. What to do? Get Bastien into the stretcher and over the far side onto the shingle ice? Fill a bag of provisions and throw it out? All impossible, in any case, the berg not forty yards away and closing.

Abruptly, it came up short. A terrible, fierce creaking emerged from its belly as it must have snagged on an underwater obstruction. The noise grew in intensity, so loud and singular amid the overall silence of the Arctic night that Carrie almost crouched down in terror and shielded her head, a child hiding from monsters. Instead, she climbed onto the cabin roof, clutched the mast, watched as the berg trembled and began to list.

Then the list became a plunge.

As it toppled, the berg came loose of its underwater obstruction and leapt forwards. Its upper side collapsed into the water, but a huge tail of jagged spikes and blades reared up behind as the vast mass rolled over towards the *Carrick*.

The moon disappeared behind a cloud. Carrie jumped down into the cockpit in the darkness and cowered. The whole boat, seemingly the whole shingle bank, shuddered as the huge berg hit.

Amid the maelstrom of noise, Carrie saw only dimly the ice-blades swing round directly above her head. They knocked the mast down. The steel backstays snapped, one whipping past her face. She was thrown up as the berg drove straight through the prow, lifting the stern. Then, equally suddenly, the monster came to rest, looming over her as she lay, prostrate on the steeply-sloping cockpit floor.

A whoosh of water inside the boat.

She ripped open the hatch and slid down the companion ladder. But she lost control and toppled forwards, only just catching her balance. The boat was canted way forwards and listing more steeply to starboard than before.

'Bastien,' she cried. He lay with his head and shoulders on the floor, his legs still half up on his bunk, his torso horribly twisted where he'd fallen.

'No,' she whispered, her hand at his hollow cheek. Thin, dark drool leaked out of his mouth. She could see his tongue, black and cracked.

She pressed her fingers inside his neck brace, felt for the artery. A faint pulse beat there. Carefully, she lifted his legs from the bunk to the floor so his torso was less twisted. He made a soft sound. Carrie rested her head on his side, her breath coming in gasps. She understood that she was close to hyperventilating.

But she heard the gush of water again. Lifted her head. The kerosene lamp still swung from the collision. Shadows danced through the cabin. She pulled herself to her feet, opened a drawer and snatched out the torch, shone it along the hallway.

All appeared unchanged. The hob's blue firelight glowed from the open galley door. The bunkroom and the forward radio room doors were both closed. Dreading each step, she approached the radio room, the water sound louder. She grasped the doorknob. Stopped.

'Oh, get on with it.'

And wrenched it open.

The burned radio equipment in the boat's prow was gone. In its place, surrounded by smashed wooden sections of hull and stanchion ends, a striated grey-white wall of ice glittered in the torchlight. Water gushed up in front of it to slosh near her feet.

Her mind made frantic calculations. The water was pouring into the bilges to join the ice already there where the keel had previously sheared off. The berg had effectively pinned the *Carrick* to the shingle bank, and dragged the prow fully below sea level. Would it now lean ever more heavily until it crushed the boat? Or would it be pulled away by what must have been a rising tide, and leave the *Carrick* to fill with water and sink?

Either way, her decision had been made for her. They were leaving. Now.

She went out, shutting the door against the awful presence of that ice wall. Back in the main cabin, she kneeled beside the unconscious man.

'Bastien,' she said. 'I'm here. I'm here.'

His breath came in tiny staccato gasps, a catch on each in-breath as if of pain. She had to heave him back into his bunk somehow. But first she hurried on deck.

The new moon's sliver glimmered in the south. Above her head, the aluminium mast lay almost level with the deck. The jib arm bent out at a crazy angle over the side. One of the berg's huge, sharp spines, twenty feet long, hung right over what remained of the prow. The rest of the berg plunged down into the broken sea ice. The north wind had grown so that the water where the berg had cut its path was already freezing over; greasy ice coalesced into paler crystalline needles to form gently bobbing patches.

The berg itself made no sound now, even with the gale and tide. She hoped that meant it had wedged itself securely to the shingle. Her throat and lungs frosted with each breath. She caught up the ropes she'd gathered earlier, threw them inside. Snapped steel cables flailed through the air, so she had to raise her arms either side of her head to protect herself. Then, abruptly, the wind died altogether. The tide itself seemed also to. Absolute silence fell down upon her. The remote stars glittered on, as if in confirmation of the universe's cold indifference.

She stood for a moment, appalled by her isolation. Then she ducked inside and pushed the door closed.

Ross

'What do you want, Ross?'

For a moment, Ross couldn't speak, the phone receiver cold against his ear.

'I'm Coast Guard, that the idea?' Don Escamilla said. 'I can talk to my people. Get a search going.'

'That's about it, yes.'

'She's dead, Ross! Grady, Lightsy, Leavitt are dead. They're all dead. I'm not going play the whining dork making demands.'

'I've got a map coordinate. We just need...'

'The whole world hates you, buddy. This some PR crap you're pulling?'

'I'm not doing it for publicity.'

'Then what?'

'I want to do the right thing,' Ross said.

'The *right thing*?' There was such incredulity in the man's voice that Ross quailed.

The line went dead.

Escamilla was right. What *was* he doing? Trying to atone? As if finding Carrie would make up for his culpability in the accident, in the death of so many men and women. Nearly a month had passed already. If she hadn't died immediately, she'd be dead by now.

But it wasn't certain. Nothing was certain.

He scrubbed his fingers through his hair. Paperwork towered on his desk. Pentada memoranda gathered for governmental action; his legal defence lawyer's preparatory documentation – already at over three thousand pages, however likely it now seemed that he'd dodge the bullet; the entire working records of every person who'd died on the *Belyy Medved*; documentation from PentOil's US insolvency lawyers. Willetts had declared bankruptcy after his loan had been called in. He was trying to push the blame back onto his creditors, who were busy folding Ross into the story.

A separate stack of papers on the floor related to Lokgas. He was learning just how hard it was to make a Russian company – okay, an Azerbaijani company–accountable. The *Belyy Medved*'s Chinese-flag registration showed complex legal discrepancies. Ross faced financial liability for the drillship's hulk salvage.

Responsibility for shutting down the well had been taken from him by the federal government, although he was still cc-ed into everything. They'd had to scupper the notion of landing a submersible on the pack ice, dropping it down through a hole. Though the ice had proven too thick for the *Raven*, it was nonetheless also too raftered and unsafe for a fixed-wing aircraft to land on the pack.

And still the well spewed oil.

His phone rang.

'Ross?'

'Lieutenant Escamilla.'

'I'll be in Tuk in twelve hours. You say you got map coordinates?'

'I have.'

'Just do me a favour. Keep your mouth shut about this, would you?'

—

The helicopter lurched into the air, nose rising and falling alarmingly. Then it yawed sideways. The whole machine vibrated as if it were about to fall to pieces. Ross could hear the interior fittings, few though they were, hammering against the hull. As Escamilla spoke a few words to the Tuk control tower, Ross noticed the instrumentation in front of him resembled something from a museum, all nineteen-fifties switches and dials. Ross clutched the armrests. He was going to die trying to find a dead woman with the ex-husband she hated.

'What is this, anyway?'

'Russian Mil Mi-8. Transport chopper. Ex-Iraqi military.'

'Where'd you dig it up?'

'Friend of mine. He supplies lumber companies in northern BC. It's averse to lifting off, even empty.'

They shuddered and clanked into the air, then headed north across the shore ice.

'Where we going?' Escamilla said. He sounded almost jaunty. Ross gave him the coordinates. Escamilla had an electronic GPS strapped to the controls beside him. He punched them in.

'That even work?' Ross said. 'You know, the magnetic compass...ah...the arctic...you know.'

Escamilla shrugged. 'We'll follow the Banks Island coastline, then go from there.'

'Why'd you change your mind?' he said.

The pilot didn't answer at first. Then he said, 'She tell you why we split up?'

'Something about an affair?' Ross said cautiously.

'She screwed someone else, right? She was a slut; she did me wrong. Everyone knew.'

'Something like that.'

'Well, she didn't.'

The helicopter hit turbulence. Ross was thrown hard against his belt straps. 'She didn't...?'

'Didn't have an affair. Least, not far as I know. We were arguing. We had a thousand rows. But that night, she wouldn't lay
off. She could drink, you know.'

'I do know.'

'Normally, she was much the same drunk as sober. Same
kind of hard-ass...'

'Oh yes.'

Escamilla glanced over at him, his gaze hostile. 'We were
at a bar in Victoria. All kinds of Coast Guard people there, cele-
brating someone's retirement. She's bored, she tells me. Bored
by it all. By Canada. By Canucks. Bored of me.'

'I'm sorry to hear that.'

'No, she was right. I was boring,' Escamilla said. 'I am boring. Not that I knew it till I met Carrie. I screwed it all up for
her, really. She was this hotshot rescue specialist. But she mar-
ries me, moves to Canada. Thought I'd land her the same role
out here. I promised. But they wouldn't give her the gig. Different skill sets, different regs, usual bullshit. About her being a
woman, seemed to me. And me, I'm just your simple, all-Cana-
dian boy. I love to fly. I drink beer, watch ice hockey, go kaya-
king. Carrie? She was smart. Smarter than she let on, even to
herself.' His voice had become so filled with pain, Ross almost
reached over to pat him on the arm.

'So, what happened that night at the bar?'

'We were arguing. I was in a temper. I'd had enough. She
tells me she's going to the washroom. Instead, she grabs hold of
this random guy, kisses him. Right there in front of our whole
crew. Then she leads him out the door. I'm telling everyone,
bitch can do what she wants. Everyone's bad-mouthing her,
backing me up. Holding me back when I'm heading out the
door after them. But through the window I see Carrie walking

away from the man, and she's flipping him the bird, laughing. He's standing there, stumped.'

Ross looked over at him. 'What did you do?'

'I didn't say anything.'

'She'd packed her bag and moved out by the time I got home that night. And all this time, I just let the lie play out, let it fester in everyone's minds.'

The Banks Island coastline passed by on their right. Ross could see it only by the exposed rock here and there, and the indistinct outlines of braided river mouths beneath the snow cover. Then they came to an area where open water was visible, a black pencil line a mile from the shore, blurry and indistinct.

'Here it is,' said Escamilla.

'What?' Ross was still thinking about relationships. About cruelty. Carrie had embarrassed her husband that night. He'd sure paid her back.

'The Banks Island polynya.' Escamilla pointed forwards. 'Polynyas are open stretches of water. You can track Banks Islands' polynyas right up the coast between the shore and sea ice. Comes and goes, apparently.'

'Why's it not frozen?'

'Tides. The Beaufort gyre. Pack ice rubbing against the shore. Shit, I don't know. Google it.'

'So you never told anyone about that night?'

Escamilla glanced over at Ross, held his gaze. 'Not till I told you.'

'And here we both are,' said Ross.

Escamilla didn't answer.

Carrie

Carrie covered the sores on Bastien's lower back with the last of the bandages. She rolled him flat, propped pillows. The hollow eye sockets were crow black. His flesh sagged as if draped over the skeleton of a far smaller man. His breath stank. Fever raged but there was nothing she could do.

After the berg hit, she'd heaved him off the floor and onto his bunk. She hadn't known if she was going to kill him doing it. It didn't matter either way. Death lurked just a few feet away. They were surely going to sink, or the berg would crush them to splinters. No one was coming, that was clear enough.

'The Arctic is home to the Antichrist,' he whispered, 'if you believe the early Christians. It's where the devil himself placed his throne.'

She waved her hand in front of her face, cleared the frosted breath that hung in the air. The galley hob had gone out.

She stared at Bastien. 'What a ray of sunshine you are,' she croaked.

'Perhaps He's come. He's here.'

His head above its neck brace had slumped slightly sideways so his stricken face sagged in her direction. Black spittle had drizzled and frozen across his chin. His crusted lips were a mass of ravine-like cracks. She looked away.

'Is it so bad?' he said. There was a soft, level clarity to his whispered voice now, a disinterested tone that spoke more accurately than any visual sign to his physical predicament.

'You're dying,' she told him.

'"Life's but a walking shadow." We are all dying.'

'But you're going first. Like, tomorrow.'

The skin around his eyes contracted.

'I'm an arse,' Carrie said. 'I'm sorry, Bastien.'

'No one is coming.'

'They think we're dead.'

'And you will wait until the heavens have blazed forth for me.'

'Something like that.'

'You need to go. You'll run out of provisions.'

'How terribly, *terribly* brave of you.'

'You'll starve.'

'I'll use the four bullets your bad planning left me.'

'Not so easy. Not in the night.'

She took up his limp hand, sweaty with heat. Patted it awkwardly.

'I believe I've lived my life usefully,' he said.

'Hey, you blew shit up.' What was it with her?

'Our moral position...is all we have.'

'The Pearly Gates aren't going to swing open on that logic.'

He smiled faintly.

She felt the bones and knuckle joints of his hands as clearly as if his skin was merely silk.

'I wanted to know my son was safe,' he whispered.

She pointed at the PentOil dossier on the table. 'He made this dossier useless. It's going to die with us.'

'No.' He paused to breathe. 'You, Carrie: you live. To tell everyone.'

'I don't exactly trust you, Bastien. All these half-truths. These coincidences.'

His eyes were open, but they did not blink, didn't move, did not seem to see. If she couldn't still hear the gurgle in his lungs and throat, see the dilation of his nostrils, she'd imagine him dead already. She had no comfort to offer.

At last, his eyes, laced through with little blood worms,

gazed out of that dead face with something resembling passion. But he spoke with the same level, whispering tone: 'I killed him, Carrie.'

Her hand was crushing his. 'Who?'

'Frederic.'

'The mate?'

'My deathbed confession. And you the priest.'

'You got to do better than that.'

'He was Willetts' man. A spy.'

'Oh, please.'

'He was decent enough, really. But twenty-two. You can't hold such a secret on a two-man boat. Not at that age. His attempts to learn my passwords, to access computer accounts. I saw through him inside a week.'

'So, what, you killed him?'

'He knew something was going on with Willetts' visit. He had a good idea I was communicating with the drillship. He couldn't be sure but he was going to warn Willetts.'

'So you're saying you murdered the mate, Bastien.'

'He sabotaged the comms that day. Started the fire. We fought it together. I sent him to shorten sail. The storm. I'd been silent about what I knew until then. Needed him. I thought knowing gave me control. But I came on deck, accused him. Every wave heeled us so far over; the engine, the automated systems: all gone. He swore at me. I was incensed, tormented about Jay. Terrified of what my son might do, of what might happen. I struck out with the emergency tiller arm I'd brought up from below. Just as we dropped into a wave trough. I struck him so hard, oh God! He was in the water. Not moving.'

'So you put the dinghy overboard to what, rescue him after a change of heart? Or to cover your tracks?' They were more statements than questions. 'Then you fell through the hatch.'

Bastien wept, trapped in the ruin of his body.

Ross

'Let's make this quick,' Escamilla said, snatching up a pair of binoculars. 'I shouldn't leave the engine too long in this cold.'

The rotors were still turning as they stepped out the doorway. The air made Ross recoil. It was many degrees lower than Tuk. His eyes felt harder in their sockets, his cheeks pinched. Pulling his parka hood tight about his face, he leaned heavily on his walking cane. Once the rotors came to a stop all they heard was the soft wheeze of the wind. Visibility had dimmed significantly down here at ground level, even with the aurora shimmering above.

There was no yacht. There was nothing at all.

'Let me see the picture,' Escamilla said.

'This is what I'm talking about,' said Ross, pointing to the image printout from the oil-spill drone. He showed him the little, rounded-off rectangle of heat, the vague double line to either side.

'You bought me all this way for that?'

'The lines to each side of the rectangle match each other exactly in length. It's too angular to be an animal.'

'But the whole image is a mess of blurs and lines.' Escamilla turned away, walked a few paces. 'Why in hell didn't I take a look at this before?'

'Because you have hope.'

'Hope?' Escamilla swept his hand round, taking everything in. 'We're nowhere! There's nothing for hundreds of miles. No one. Oh, goddamn it...' His voice tailed off, and he walked away down the snow slope towards what Ross took to be the shore.

Ross followed him. Along the shoreline, a couple of bergs had come in and beached in the shallows; strange sculptures.

He gazed seawards.

The ice near the shore was mostly flat. There seemed to be a line a few hundred yards out where ridges and shards stood up at crazy angles: the line between shore and sea ice.

Away to his left, he noticed one much larger berg. It rose like a miniature mountain. Along its base, at an angle of perhaps ten degrees, ran a dark line, so perfectly straight it drew one's gaze. He looked at it for a while, wondering what it could be. His eyes widened.

'Escamilla!' he called. 'See the berg, the one on its own out there?'

'I see it.' He stared through his binoculars, passed them to Ross. The line looked man-made.

Escamilla was already on the ice. Ross couldn't keep up. Oddly, the ice felt almost sticky, like sandpaper. It gripped the soles of his boots. But its irregularities had him relying ever more heavily on his cane. By the time he arrived, Escamilla was kneeling. Ross saw a metal tube about forty feet long. One end disappeared into the ice. Two little poles emerged above its midpoint. He saw eyelets here and there. It was plainly a mast.

'Oh my God,' he said.

Escamilla's hands rested on his knees. His head was lowered. Then abruptly, he began to paw at the ground where the mast entered the ice. Ross collapsed beside him. They cleared the looser ice and snow in moments. Saw the mast plunging down through the opaque surface.

'Wait here,' Escamilla said. He raced away towards the helicopter. Returned with an axe, shovel and a heavy torch. 'Get back,' he told Ross.

Ross watched him hacking at the ice. Great chunks of it flew up. He hit the mast itself on several occasions and the sound rang out dully, like a cracked ship's bell. Soon, he'd bored out a hole two feet deep. The ice was looser there. He took up the spade, powered it down, breaking and shovelling.

Finally, Escamilla cut through, the water splashing up around the shovel head. He beat the hole ever wider until it was some four feet long by a couple wide. Then he fell back, panting, hardly able to catch his breath. Ross put a hand on his shoulder, but he shrugged it off. He pulled a powerful torch over. When he switched it on, Ross's pupils shrank so fast the wider landscape about them disappeared into darkness. He kneeled beside Escamilla as he directed the torchlight into the water.

Ross saw only the surface reflecting back the light. Escamilla lowered the torch until its glass almost touched the water. They peered in.

Gradually, Ross made out the mast travelling down into the darkness for a few more feet. Then he saw where it joined something much bigger at an acute angle. This flat, pale surface was laid out almost horizontally below them at a depth of maybe four feet. His mind took a few moments to compute. Then he understood. The mast had buckled dramatically, but was still attached to a boat beneath the ice. A flap of canvas was visible near the mast base with some lettering on it. He made out the letters 'r r i c'.

'The yacht was the *Carrick*,' Ross said quietly.

'So,' Escamilla said. 'She's gone.'

Carrie

'Two twenty-five-pound tins of biscuit,' Bastien recited to Carrie. 'Two five-pound tins of sugar, a few pounds of coffee and cans of condensed milk. An oil stove and five one-gallon tins of oil. Matches, a hatchet, knives, a can opener, salt, needles, thread. A rifle with one hundred rounds of ammunition and a shotgun with fifty rounds. Twelve six-pound tins of pemmican.'

Carrie came up short in the braces, nearly thrown onto her back. Turning, she saw the stretcher snagged between two jagged splinters of ice. Caught again. She dropped the two walking poles she'd crafted, went down to one knee, gasping for breath, almost cried out in frustration. Behind her, she could see the *Carrick* in the dim, grey light, a frail, crumpled series of angles huddled in gloom against the sheer face of the giant floeberg.

'And the following medical supplies,' Bastien went on. 'Catgut and needles, gauze, tannic acid, quinine, plaster-surgical liniment, bandages and cotton, boracic acid, and dusting powder.'

'Put me down for a sack of dusting powder,' Carrie said.

'Those were Robert Peary's instructions for a well-stocked trip to the Pole.' 'How d'you even remember this stuff?'

But he didn't answer. Ignoring him, Carrie dragged herself back to the boat's emergency stretcher. She had tied on a couple of lengths of painter to haul with. Iced the base up, as per Bastien's instruction. One among many instructions he'd been offering up over the past weeks.

'You're a goldmine,' she told him. 'A one-man Arctic library.'

'I loved those books as a boy,' he said, 'I still do. Even Robert Peary's racist pomposity, his relentless arrogance and will. But more than anyone else, I admire Nansen: his poetic soul, even his patchy leadership. But, like Peary, that ruthless will! Norwegians: they're the ones for the North.'

'Men of steel, gazing at far horizons,' Carrie said. 'All that good ol' cock'n'balls stuff.' She spoke in a sing-song voice as she hauled the heavy stretcher-sled over the broken shore ice.

'Peary said that any man unable to live without silk stockings was not fit to attempt the North Pole.'

Carrie slipped, fell on her side, an ice ridge punching into ribs still painful from when she'd skippered the *Carrick* through the storm. She cursed the land, the dark, the stretcher. Cursed Bastien for never shutting up.

'Only men would want to stride about in this crappy place,' she told him. 'With or without silk stockings.'

'Carrie, you're more a man than any man I've known.'

She had to be off the water and over the pebble beach by now. The ice and snow made it difficult to be sure. But the sled felt like it was sliding across gravel, not ice. Gravel and glue. She leaned further into the braces, her breath fogging out before her, dug in the walking poles. It was a balmy minus twenty-two, but the sweat prickled on her skin inside the thermals, beneath her survival suit. Dangerous sweat – threatening.

'Which is why most of them can't handle me.'

'Your husband,' Bastien went on, 'was the wrong kind of man, maybe?'

'Guess so.'

'Will he lament your presumed demise?'

At last, she arrived at a place of open ground. Heavy pebbles and sharper rocks showed where the shore ended and the interior of Banks Island began. She stopped.

'Poor Donny,' she said. 'I was always testing him. It wasn't fair.' She heaved at the braces.

'You married him, Carrie.'

'I married a poster campaign.'

'You crossed an ocean for him.'

'I hear a song coming on. I gave up a career.'

'Though you found another one.'

'I was a rescue swimmer. You know how many women make the grade? A few, ever, anywhere. Now what am I? I didn't even spot your fanatic son.'

She plucked a pebble, big as her hand, veined with a darker mineral. She hurled it out. Skyward. Seaward. At her husband's head. At her own pettiness and failures. With Donny. With all of it.

'I deserved it. There's nothing wrong with Donny.' Is. Was? 'What did I expect?'

'What *did* you expect?'

Now that was a question.

She searched around, found an area clear of rocks and snow. The wind blew the snow so it drifted against low out-crops, leaving exposed areas of barren ground. Was it day or night? She hadn't checked the time when she left the boat.

She'd bought a pick and a shovel. 'You'll need the pick,' Bastien told her.

She drove it at the ground. It bounced, making no visible indentation. The impact shook her. She kept at it anyway. But let's not avoid the question, Carrie: what *did* she expect, marrying Donny? Was it as simple as love? Tiny frozen chips of earth flew up.

'Picture the scene,' she told Bastien. 'An aircraft hangar. North East Scotland. Two uniformed groups facing each other. A joint training exercise. Canada and the UK. The Canucks are just Coast Guard. We're Navy. Elites, at least in our own minds.

"Thought you all should meet," says our CO, "before we start throwing each other out of helicopters." Donny was four inches taller than anyone, white teeth, jawline jutting, the Latin skin tone. The kind of superhero-type you only get on this continent. And he was staring at me. Okay, I'm the only female there. So I'm scowling back. When we fall out, he struts over. Everyone's watching. "Lieutenant Carrie Essler," he says. "We heard about you, even in the Commonwealth."

'I know him too. He's the pilot saved the crew of the research vessel *Karluk*, in a fifty-knot gale off Ellesmere Island, after a journey needed two mid-air refuellings. I tell him, "Don't fuck it up, lumberjack, we'll get along fine." And every time I'm in and out the North Sea, somehow his cheese-eating grin's close by.'

Bastien's smiling too. 'Lust can be all about friction.'

'The night we wrap the exercise…He was so – confident.'

'Every strong woman wants a man who can make her feel like a little girl.'

She rolled her eyes at that. The ground where she'd been driving the pick remained virtually untouched. Somehow this failure was the worst thing. Carrie drove the pick again and again into a boulder instead, until the rock cracked cleanly in two. She hurled the pick away. Went over to the stretcher. Dragged it to the centre of the open space. Jerked at the straps.

Bastien said, 'The most difficult thing is to live without lies. At least, not to believe in your own lies.'

'And here you are, a murderer, telling me I'm a liar. It comes to this.'

And, indeed, "this" was exactly what it had come to.

She rolled Bastien's corpse onto the ground.

It was still stiff with rigor mortis, more than twenty-four hours after he'd died.

She wasn't sure how long she'd just sat there in the boat cabin beside him, this past day, the silence incandescent once his final soft breaths had faded away into nothing.

Now, she kneeled beside his body. For a time, stared at the haggard, already-frosted wasteland of his face. His voice, his words, continued to fill her mind. She kissed him on the lips. Kissed him as she would a lover. Then she unzipped her survival suit at the neck, scrabbled inside her clothing. She lifted the British Navy dog-tags over her head. She'd worn them ever since she came to Canada. She placed them on his chest. Truth was, she'd been embarrassed by their pathetic sentiment; she'd rather be free of them anyhow.

At last she stood, began to pile rocks and pebbles about the corpse. When Bastien's cairn was built, she sat atop it. Away south, the cloud was more broken. The sky was the colour of a lingering bruise. The faintest sliver of sunlight glowed on the horizon. It was as dark as old blood.

Ross

The eerie sense of this big boat, beneath the ice in the freezing darkness of the sea, felt like loss. Ross rolled away, lay on his back, shut his eyes.

For a time, neither spoke. But, amid the pain, something nagged at him.

He said, 'Wrong.'

Escamilla sighed heavily. 'What?'

'The drone sees temperature. If the boat was already submerged like this, it wouldn't have been visible. So, it must have sunk later.'

'If there was heat, someone was alive inside,' Escamilla said. He got up, shouted, his voice almost a shriek. 'Carrie! Carrie!'

He scrambled up the side of the berg. Ross left his walking stick, crawled up behind. Escamilla reached down and hauled him to the highest point, a narrow, sharply angled plane of about six feet diameter.

'Carrie!' Escamilla called.

Ross still had the binoculars round his neck. He gazed through them. Calm, he was thinking. Be calm now. He followed a slow arc, beginning seawards and then round along the shore. There was nothing. He went around again, even more slowly, as Escamilla continued to call. Then, Ross thought he caught a flicker of movement. He paused, went back. Saw nothing, just the mottled spots of black stone against the pale-grey snow.

There it was again. A furtive shadow beside a rock. Then, yes, it moved. Ross saw now it was a fox, its coat a subtly different white from its surroundings.

'Escamilla,' he said. 'Quiet for a moment, will you?' Ross watched the fox. He didn't know why. Perhaps because it was the only other thing alive here. Or that any movement in this vacuum must be considered some kind of portent.

'I have to start the engines,' Escamilla said, his voice oddly composed after the drama of his calling just before.

'Shh,' Ross said.

The fox crept forwards now, towards a low mound of rocks, half covered in snow. And Ross saw two black birds were sitting atop the mound. The fox was busy, busy doing something. Snuffling the ground. Its head shook. Shook as if it were...

'Escamilla, follow me.'

'Why? What?'

'There's...oh, just follow me. Keep quiet.'

They made their way back across the shore ice. Periodically, Ross trained the binoculars on the low mound. As they stepped up onto the beach, the fox skittered away. The two birds – big crows or ravens – remained.

'See the birds?'

'So what?'

'I saw a fox. And these two birds. Might mean...' He left it unsaid, but Escamilla nodded.

The two ravens only lifted away when the men got within twenty feet of the mound. Squawking angrily, they landed nearby on flat ground.

Escamilla and Ross stopped ten feet short, both feeling a terrible inevitability at what they were going to find.

'Let's do this,' Ross said.

The first things he noticed were textile shreds. Though frayed and filthy, their artificial colours – yellow, ochre red – stood out against the greyscale of the ground. Only then did he notice what they were attached to.

Ross hobbled over and slumped down on the mound of stones. Before him lay scattered what were clearly human remains. From a scored and chewed boot, the bones and shredded skin of a lower leg emerged. Segments of still-fresh but frozen meat clung to it down near the ankle. With a distant clarity, Ross realised the carcass would barely rot in the polar freezer. A rib-cage, many of the ribs staved in and broken, lay some metres away. Ross reached down and lifted one of the stones from the ground, placed it on the mound beside him.

'We have to...' Escamilla began. But he could not go on. He was still standing beside Ross. Now he stepped forwards, then back, uncertain where to go or what to do. He swore under his breath. He walked forwards, pushed with his foot at a tangle of bone and textile. Ross saw a zipper and what looked to be parts of a fleece.

Ross said, 'Shouldn't we, you know, leave everything untouched? Isn't it a crime scene?'

'I'm a Coast Guard officer, Ross. I'm investigating.' He laughed, a hysteric bark swiftly suppressed.

'Okay.' Ross spoke with as level a voice as he could manage. 'The, ah, footwear we're seeing here is too big to have been Carrie. Right?'

Escamilla stared at the boot. 'Right,' he said, sounding calmer.

'So, we search the area. Looks like animals either killed, or at least partially ate, this person.'

'I don't think they were killed. We'd see blood splatter.'

'Okay, they died, and animals fed on the carcass. You do the surrounds; I'll go through what's here.'

As he combed the ground, Ross felt a prick of surprise at his ability to remain so dispassionate. Believing this was not Carrie helped.

He almost missed it. He'd passed by the little coil of windbreaker material already. His bad knee almost crumpled under him, and he had to jam his cane behind him to keep his balance. Then he saw it, close by the cane's tip, a sliver of metal gleaming beneath the yellow windbreaker scrap. Slowly, groaning aloud in discomfort, he kneeled. Drew up what he recognised as military dog tags. He heard Escamilla exclaim, heard his feet running towards him. Heard him whisper 'No!' even as they both read what was on the tags: *Carrie Essler 4050781*.

Carrie

Amid that vast silence of her solitude, she heard an exhalation of breath, close by, huge. The polar bear stood fifteen yards away, between her and the shore. The same one, she knew immediately, from the long wound beside its nose that she'd inflicted. It rested one paw on a broken slab of ice, head low, swaying, then lifting to scent the air. Its gaze never left Carrie.

'Well, aren't you a sight for sore eyes,' she said.

It looked better, if still gaunt, its shoulder bones poking through its matted fur, still sheened with oil. It moved with more assurance now, without that dragging desperation she'd seen when it first attacked the *Carrick*. Or with the madness of its encounter with the spill.

Her rifle was on the stretcher, midway between herself and the bear. She picked a stone from the grave. Stood, slowly as she could. Weighed the stone in her hand. She felt like a baseball pitcher on a mound. Suppressed a cackle of laughter. She was going to chuck a rock at a polar bear?

Ah well, sod it. She hurled the stone. It struck the bear a glancing blow on the skull. The animal bit out sideways, as if it thought itself attacked from another quarter. As it took its gaze from Carrie, she leaped down, sprinted for the rifle. Straight at the bear. She committed, dived forwards, snatched the rifle, rolled, came up on one knee, butt to her shoulder. Aimed along the barrel, rather than through the sight.

But the bear hadn't moved. It looked, if anything, bemused. It coughed twice, two sharp barks. As if the bear were laughing at her. She stood.

'Go on,' she told it, raising her voice. 'Hit the road, yer bampot.'

But still it didn't move. She lifted her hands, held the rifle aloft, waved it about. Shouted some more. 'Raaahhh!' But the bear growled in return, a sibilance so low, deep and comprehensive it might have been the sound of the tundra itself become animate. It took several steps to its left, keeping front-on to Carrie. Its head and long neck dropped between its shoulders.

'Oh, don't stalk me, you idiot,' she told it.

'If a bear and a human meet, one must die.' Bastien at his most vainglorious.

Carrie took the equivalent steps in the opposite direction, so that she and the bear began to circle each other. She kept the rifle trained on it. The animal lifted its nose again. Sniffed. Its gaze left Carrie to look towards the cairn. They were separated by no more than twenty feet. It growled once more, glared at Carrie. She slid the safety off.

'I've only four rounds left. You don't get a warning shot.'

The bear reared up on its hind legs to twice Carrie's height. She stumbled backwards, almost tripped. It took all her resolve not to fire. But the bear fell back onto all fours, swung away from her. She was breathing so hard it clouded her vision. Then she saw what the bear was doing.

'No, no!'

Almost, she ran towards it. But the bear turned her way, snarled. Its big rubbery lips beat against the massive canines, the throaty noise so ferocious her belly shook. Then it went back to pawing the stones covering Bastien's corpse.

She lifted the rifle once more to her shoulder. Took aim. Head or heart?

'And is that not the pertinent question?' Bastien said.

Pebbles and larger rocks skittered away like gravel beneath the bear's massive paws. A raven dropped from the darkness, landed on the cairn. The bear glanced up, then ignored it. The raven glared at Carrie. It cawed, a sound as dead as the rock on which it stood. Settled in to wait.

Carrie lowered the rifle, slung it across her back. She

stooped, took hold of one of the stretcher's braces. Dragged the empty sled slowly away and then sat on it, thirty yards off.

The bear burrowed its nose into the mound. Twisted its head to get further in. Tugged. Stones cascaded over it. The raven lifted into the air, complaining, before settling once more. A second raven landed beside it. The bear dragged Bastien's body clear. Carrie could just make out the hollows of his face as the bear placed a paw on his torso and then wrenched most of one forearm away.

'I suppose you're happy now.' She wasn't certain who it was she spoke to.

Ross

As the helicopter lifted off, emotion finally struck Ross. A grief so profound, so bottomless it terrified him as much as it hurt. As they'd gathered the remains into a tarpaulin. Escamilla had been business-like, his face an emotionless mask. Now Ross saw tears on the pilot's cheeks. Ross put both his hands, palms together, before his eyes. Breathed slowly in and out. He wondered if he might finally sleep an untroubled sleep. Now it was done, over.

But still, there was something. Something else. What was it? He'd lifted that stone off the ground and placed it back onto the mound. 'Back' onto the mound? There'd been stones scattered all across the ground, amid the remains, hadn't there? As if...As if?

'Escamilla?'

'What?' The pilot's voice came through Ross' headphones, hostile and distant.

'You remember the pile of stones by the...?'

'I didn't see a pile of stones.'

'I was sitting on it.'

'So what?'

'Did it seem like it might have been made by hand?'

Escamilla looked over at him, dismissive, angry. 'What you talking about, Ross?'

'Is it possible the stones were a burial site? The body had been buried. Interred. By someone else?'

'Oh, chrissakes, Ross. My dead wife's corpse is in the hold. Ex-wife. Nearly.' He shook his head violently.

'I'm just wondering if...'

'Wondering what? Some other person's out there? After burying her, they just headed off into the wilderness on a hiking tour? She's dead. The guy she found on board had a broken neck – he's dead. All those men on board your damn drillship – the men you had responsibility for. They're dead. It's hard shit. But they're gone.'

The huge noise of the helicopter made it easy not to speak. Not even to think Strangely, Ross's grief had retreated with Escamilla's words. He couldn't stop thinking about that outsize boot they'd found, too big for Carrie. About the stones. About burial sites. About those dog-tags and what they might mean.

'I'll drop you back in Tuk,' Escamilla said at last.

'Where you going on to?'

'Inuvik. Coast Guard base. Police headquarters there. Give them the body.'

'What if it isn't her?'

'D'you ever stop? If it isn't, she's in the boat.'

'Will you go back, lift it out the water?'

'Not till the summer. They'll send a CG boat up, maybe. You worked out the riddle. Congratulations. You found her.'

'I'm coming with you to Inuvik,' Ross said

Carrie

It came again: a bone-deep moan that seemed to envelop the boat. So accustomed had she become to her relentlessly eerie surroundings, Carrie chose to ignore it. The ice doing whatever it was that ice did.

A day had passed since she'd buried Bastien. She sat in the sloping main cabin, wrapped in a sleeping bag, reading one of Bastien's documents. Signed by none other than Jim Ross himself. Something to do with a safety test on the blowout preventer. It was stapled to an internal email sequence between Ross and the Offshore Installation Manager, one Mikhail Babushkin. OIM: 'Obviously, my friend, this test not possible again. BOP four hundred metres below surface.' Reply from Ross: 'Third year running, I see, Mikhail.' The safety certificate was dated two days after the emails. Naughty Jim.

Dead Jim. Somehow, she couldn't see him hobbling his way out of the inferno she'd witnessed on the drillship. How had he gotten himself involved in this rubbish? This file full of corporate negligence. She knew he wasn't a bad guy. Christ, he was her only friend.

But she was fooling herself. Her newfound fascination with the dossier was all about stalling. And the lethargy that accompanied prevarication.

'It's not foolish to be frightened of the Arctic,' Bastien told her.

But she didn't want to hear it. She'd spent her whole life proving she wasn't afraid: product of a tough father and three older brothers. Didn't take Freud to work that one out.

The sound came again, a groan from all directions at once. This time, she felt a shiver in the boat itself. And there was no ignoring that. She placed the documents back in the big folder.

Zipped its watertight plastic cover closed, before tossing it onto the bench beside the dining table. It was bulky. She'd have to make sure she squeezed the air out of it in future. Then she shrugged into an oversized parka, went on deck.

A noise: that rifle shot of breaking ice she'd grown accustomed to. She stared along the channel between the low shingle banks – through which the *Carrick* and the berg had been directed towards their final resting place. The unseen sun lent the ice a rusty glow.

What was happening?

She had to blink a couple of times, but then she saw. The ice was moving, lifting and falling as if it were somehow breathing. And the breaths rolled in towards her. She understood: the water beneath the ice was restive. A high tide, or a weather pattern further out at sea.

Then the colossal, low moan came again. The deck trembled beneath her feet. She stared up at the berg. It tipped a fraction further above her. A scraping, gouging noise accompanied it. The *Carrick*'s stern lifted, just a little more, from the water.

For a moment, she stood immobile. More gunshots from the ice. The *Carrick*'s pressurised hull squealed. The ice-surface lifting and falling. Scudding clouds. The stars whispering behind. She had a sudden memory from an Asterix comic book. The chief of the tribe saying he only feared one thing: the sky falling on his head.

'Time to move on,' she said.

She dropped back into the cabin. Inside, the squealing hull was so loud, Carrie put her hands over her ears. Then, abruptly, the entire boat twisted along its axis. The floor tipped alarmingly forwards. The door to the smashed radio room buckled. Water gushed out around its frame.

Carrie dragged off her parka, pulled on two fleeces she'd laid out on a bench. Some quilted trousers, and then she pulled on her ungainly survival suit. Left it partly unzipped. She stepped into her boots. Outside, thunderous explosions. The boat shook ever more profoundly. She kneeled beside the open door to the stern stowage space. Began hauling out and throwing everything she'd prepared up the ladder into the cockpit. She thought: check it off! Be certain. Remembering her forgotten EPLT. But the cacophony of destruction rang out all around her. The boat dipped further by the prow. Lastly, she dragged out the two sections of the stretcher, manhandled them on deck.

The berg teetered to and fro – something the size of a building swaying like that, just above her head! It drove the *Carrick*'s prow down and hard against the shingle bank. She couldn't see more than a hundred yards. But the ice that covered the shingle bank to shoreward remained solid. She kicked the cabin door shut to stop everything rolling back inside. Frantically, she heaved all her provisions overboard onto the shingle bank.

A crack like a splitting tree reverberated from the prow. The stern dropped back suddenly onto what was now open water. Carrie was thrown down. Her head struck the pilot seat. A flash burst across her vision. She rolled on the floor, curled up, her hands to her head. Felt her hair wet across the side she'd struck.

Somehow, she came to her knees. A surge of nausea. She leaned over the side of the boat and threw up.

When she opened them, the sea's surface was close by her face. The boat was sharply heeled over to seaward, sinking fast.

On her knees, she shuffled across to the shoreward side of the cockpit. Tried to remember if she had everything she needed. Her mind could make no sense of anything. Somehow, she managed to hoist herself over the side, drop onto the ice and scramble away from the cacophony of the berg devouring the yacht.

For a time, she just squatted, clutched her head, tried to hold in the pain that threatened to burst her skull, fought the nausea. But she had to move, to get organised. And do it now. Her gear lay scattered like shipwreck jetsam. How long would this ice hold? She knew nothing of such things. Knew nothing about anything out here...

Come on, panic wasn't her thing.

So she breathed, took control of the pain, repressed her need to gag. She removed a glove and felt the wound carefully. Already the area had swollen. The cut seemed about three inches long across the left side of her scalp. It was bleeding heavily.

She looked around, saw the backpack. Pulled out the medical bag she'd prepared. Inside, she found the surgical stapler. She felt the cut more carefully. It went into the hairline, in fact. She'd risk stapling her filthy hair into the wound.

Just do it!

She fired the staples – one, two, three – into her head before she could think any more about it. She danced from foot to foot for some seconds, describing the pain in graphic detail to the world. Vertigo made her fall on her backside. And then she could only moan in agony.

The *Carrick* had settled with its deck almost level with the ice now. The berg bobbed and jigged, uneasy. Squinting against the throbbing and disorientation in her head, she gathered her equipment together. All the canned and dried foods that remained – so little, in fact, it only half-filled a shoulder bag. Bastien's old tent, sleeping bag, a pair of snowshoes. Several lengths of rope and some sailcloth. The backpack with the medical gear, knives, hatchet, extra clothing, temperature gauge, compass, map and sextant, saucepan, spoon, small lantern, torch and the few batteries left. Three thermoses for water. A little polar kerosene cooker and the only spare canister.

'An inventory means the difference between life and death,' Bastien said. She'd forgotten how pompous he could sound.

She fitted the stretcher together, loaded everything on. Didn't pull the sailcloth cover over, wanting to double check everything. She dragged her stretcher-sled as far away from the yacht as she thought safe. The broken sea ice's noise had diminished. But the berg cradling the *Carrick* took up again. It tipped then straightened, began to tip again. Once more the boat cried out, complaining. The broken mast waggled with the berg's grinding motions.

She'd forgotten something. What?

'The dossier's the only thing that can bring proper justice to this situation,' Bastien said.

Abruptly, she was stumbling back towards the *Carrick*.

The fucking dossier!

The *Carrick* bumped against the sea ice, already far lower in the water, mostly sunk. She paused. It was only a low jump over the side into the cockpit. But the cockpit was filled with water.

Give it up?

'All objects become valueless in the context of life itself,' Bastien lectured.

'Oh do piss off.' She leaped, splashed into the cockpit water. Her head rang with the impact of landing. The boat shuddered so badly she barely kept her feet. But she tugged open the cabin doors, heavy against the water's drag. The cabin was almost completely submerged, just a couple of feet of air space at the top. The water's surface shook, spray flying up like spitting oil from a hot pan. She peered in. The berg's striated surface was visible down the smashed hallway. It had entirely sheered away the prow. Only its pressure on the hull against the shingle bank kept the yacht afloat.

And now the berg-wall shifted, the vertical lines along its surface seeming to bend towards her. She glanced up, saw the whole berg toppling sideways. She stared back into the cabin. And now there it was! Bobbing at the far end: Bastien's dossier in its watertight bag.

She hesitated. If she was still in there when the berg hit the cabin, she'd die.

But that made her laugh out loud. Like she wasn't going to die anyway.

She zipped her suit tightly to her neck. Threw herself down the companionway ladder. She waded through the water, the ferocious crashing and squealing of the rotating berg all about her as it scoured the sinking yacht. She reached for the bag, but it bobbed out of reach, sucked by the shifting water into the hallway. She lunged, tried to catch it, but it rolled away towards the void that had been the prow. The water drew in that direction as the great berg swung around the boat.

'Please!' she called, but she had to turn away or be sucked into the maelstrom.

She fought her way back through the swirling water using her arms and legs, as it drew ever harder against her. She caught hold of the ladder with one hand. Her body was lifted horizontally. And now the ocean flooded in over the side, as the berg dragged the port gunwale below the waterline. It gushed into the cockpit, washed over Carrie.

The freezing, salt cold on her exposed, injured head almost made her black out. But somehow, she clung on. As the flow subsided, she reached up with her other hand and grasped the ladder. Then, rung by rung, she hauled herself up and out of the cabin door, feet scrabbling for a hold. The cockpit was entirely submerged. The berg picked up speed as it toppled. She had a glimpse of it, insanely vast to be flashing by so close.

She threw herself up and over the far side onto the ice. Then a wave of water spun her over and over across the surface.

She came to a halt on her back. The cold clamped her head. She thought she might faint. For a moment, maybe she did. Nausea boiled in her stomach and throat. Then she remembered her stretcher.

Somehow, it was still upright. The wave had pushed it on until it had come up against a low ridge of broken ice, where the shingle bank ended and the deeper water between it and the shore began.

For a moment, relief overcame the despair at losing the document bag. But only for a moment.

She sat up, ran her fingers through her hair, rubbed, trying to warm her skull. Then she hugged her knees. Watched the berg bouncing up and down, sending churning washes across the shingle ice surface, like waves on a beach. The *Carrick* had disappeared. Only its mast protruded from the water at an acute angle. Everything, everyone, all of it now was gone.

Slowly, she got to her feet. Lurched back towards the sunken yacht. The berg had, at last, come to a standstill. She saw the boat through the murk of the shifting ocean. It had been neatly pinioned between berg and shingle bank, about four feet down. Only four feet, but impossibly far away, even for such as her. Her survival suit visor was water resistant, not proof. And the stitched rent, where the polar bear ripped her suit, had already allowed a dribble of freezing water inside. It was hopeless.

She squatted there, by the ice edge. Part of her did feel relief, she realised. She'd been spared the necessity to choose. To choose what to show the world on her return. Whose side to take. Whether to betray Ross. Whether to lie. Nature had freed her of that burden.

The water foamed and shuddered around the berg's flanks. Slowly, it settled. And as it did, something bobbed up to bump against the ice, twenty feet away on Carrie's right. She raised her eyes to the sky.

'You're a real shitter, you know that?' Her voice was squeaky and brittle. Wearily, she stood, walked over, lifted Bastien's dossier bag from the water. Shook her head. Wished she hadn't. Then she trudged towards her sled.

Ross

'I have to say, it's a hell of a thing.' George Nares leaned back in his chair. He cricked his neck and stared at the ceiling. His jowls drooped like empty sacks. Ross thought he looked wrung through the mill.

They were sitting round a table at Inuvik's Coast Guard base. The fluorescent lights felt far too bright. Stink of sweat and stress. Black night out the windows. The photographs Ross took at the crash site before they left lay strewn across the conference table. Hathaway held Carrie's dog tags in her hand. She gazed at them, lost in thought.

'Hell of a thing, sure,' Ross said. 'And now we have to get back out there. Start a search.'

Nobody spoke. Ross took his walking cane, cracked its head on the table. Everyone jumped – Escamilla, Nares, Hathaway,

Oates, a couple of local CG personnel, the Inuvik police chief.

'Damn it,' said Ross. 'Why's this even a debate?'

'Essler was Coast Guard, one of us,' said Nares, slowly. 'One of four we lost that day, including the officer with oversight of the entire Arctic region.'

All of them killed on your rig, were the words left unspoken.

But Ross pressed on anyway. '*If* Carrie's lost. And you people are the ones sent her up here – in disgrace.'

Nobody replied, and Ross regretted his outburst. He was too tired, too fried by what he'd been through.

Escamilla said, quietly, 'Grady gave Carrie this job to get her away from me, from all the bad feeling. And to promote her. He was trying to help.'

Oh Carrie, Ross thought, you were so sure they'd been out to get you. Ross's brain clicked through another reality where Carrie had finished her few years up here and transferred back to the UK, but now experienced, a specialist, with years in the High Arctic. She'd surely have ended up as some sort of Navy head honcho.

'Franklin,' Hathaway said, looking at the police chief, 'when will we see the autopsy report?'

'Couple days,' he replied. 'We're sending them to Yellow-knife in the morning.'

'I recognise it's hardly my field of expertise,' Hathaway said, 'but any reallocation of limited resources interferes with our ongoing investigation into the *Belyy Medved* disaster. Everyone's working flat out as is. Here's how I see it. We know the yacht was not under control when first sighted. Essler – Carrie – told the pilot there was just one man, seriously injured. That was the last we heard. Although the support boat saw distress flares fired, it made the decision to turn back to the *Belyy Medved*.

'So,' she went on, 'alternatives. One: the dog tags mean the remains are Carrie's. She survives the crash, makes it to shore. Dies somehow – cold, injuries – and her body's eaten by animals. Two: the remains are this Bastien d'Urville, the environmentalist who owned the boat – and the father of our main suspect. He survives somehow and she doesn't. He takes her dog tags, for whatever reason, then suffers the same fate on shore.' She looked round. 'Does anyone have a further alternative?'

Nares said, 'Will the autopsy offer a date of death?'

'Unlikely,' said Franklin. 'Flesh doesn't decompose the same way in the cold.'

'What are we going to learn?'

'Age, gender. Dental records will ultimately show who it is, with a bit of luck and research. No fingerprints, of course.'

Ross had been growing more frustrated. 'How about this for an alternative? One of them dies, one lives. They take the body ashore. Bury it under a cairn of stones. Set off to try and save themselves.'

'This cairn of Ross's,' said Nares. 'Escamilla?'

'I'm sorry, Ross.' Escamilla lifted one of the pictures, peered at it. The flash photography made the images white, flat, bounded by darkness. The "cairn" barely registered: a random tumble of stones. 'I just didn't see it that way.'

'There were no other raised mounds,' Ross said.

'Which is why anyone who pulls theirself out the water is gonna make for it,' said an Inuvialuit senior Coast Guard officer named Freddy Schweig. 'Refuge, a wind break.'

'Ross.' Nares rested his elbows on the table, linked his fingers and propped his gloomy face on top. 'Even if someone had survived and tried to get out: first, weeks have gone by. They'd have made it to Sachs Harbour by now, or died in the attempt. Second, it's winter, it's dark, we don't have the assets to scour such a huge area, and in such conditions.' He rubbed his fingers down his face, and Ross saw that, of course, this hurt him a great deal as well. 'Third, wouldn't they have left a sign? A message of some sort?'

Exhaustion took hold of Ross. Something like despair.

Escamilla said, 'The odds just got stacked too high, even for her.'

'It's after midnight. Get some sleep, both of you,' said Nares, pushing himself laboriously to his feet. 'And Escamilla, come find me before you leave. I want a word about that piece of junk you got parked on the airstrip.' But he said it with the trace of a smile.

The conference broke up. Everyone left except Hathaway, Escamilla and Ross. Hathaway came round the table. She put both her hands on Escamilla's shoulders for a moment. Then she perched on the edge of the table beside Ross.

'You were close to her,' she said to him, 'maybe you loved her. Maybe you want her to live for all those who died. But we have history's worst oil-spill disaster unfolding.' She gazed at him kindly. 'You must decide, Mr Ross...Jim: do you want to be part of the cure or do you want to chase ghosts?' She patted him on the arm, stood and left.

Ross looked at Escamilla. 'I'm sorry,' he said.

Escamilla held up Carrie's dog-tags. 'Don't be.'

—

Ross stepped out of the police officer's truck, raised his hand in thanks for the lift. The 'O' in the red neon 'Hotel' sign above the porch flickered. He placed one careful foot after another, leaning unsteadily on his cane, barely able to lift his bad knee. He pushed blindly through the front doors. He didn't even have a toothbrush.

'Jim,' a voice said.

Ross stood blinking in the bright foyer light. Willetts was sitting at one of the tables scattered about with a bottle of bourbon and two glasses.

'I took the liberty,' Willetts said.

Ross sat and poured himself two fingers. He threw it back in a single slug, poured another. Then he regarded the man who was no longer his boss. The fearsome wound across Willetts' head still dominated. His face looked pale, thinner, older, his eye sockets hollowed out. But that sardonic air remained – in his posture, in the elevation of his chin, the way he looked just slightly down the narrow ridge of his nose at Ross.

'No crutches, I see,' Ross said.

Willetts held his palms upwards. 'I thank God above for even the smallest miracle. Did you dine already?' He pointed. On the table, an outsize bag of potato chips lay open. Ross read the flavour: 'moose jerky'. He put his hand inside.

'What are you doing here, anyway?' he said, crunching.

'I'm taking the flight to Yellowknife in the morning, then connections to Edmonton and home.'

'Feds took your private jet, did they?'

'I have relinquished the lease,' he said. He rummaged in his cashmere overcoat pocket. 'Here.' He pushed a key fob across the table. 'The concierge was on his way to bed.'

Ross leaned back, let his eyes close. He had no more energy left to be angry.

'I always saw you more as a Graham Greene character,' Willetts said, 'than one from a Jack London novel.'

Ross exhaled heavily, still with his eyes shut. 'You heard, then?'

'I was with Ms Hathaway when the call came through of your arrival. What did you find?'

'The trail's dead. She's dead.' The words came out flat.

'You did all you could.'

Ross opened his eyes, glared across at Willetts. 'Did I?' He leaned forwards in something that approximated anger. 'Did we?'

Willetts met his gaze impassively.

Ross said, 'The Christmas tree had a false safety-check history that's going to fool no one.'

'A machine part's safety-check history is hardly pertinent, Jim, when sixty-five tonnes of travelling block come crashing down on top of it. Come crashing down because of a maliciously-directed computer virus.'

'And that shouldn't have been possible, whatever systems shut down.'

Willetts made a dismissive sound. 'As a recent leader of our great country showed us: accusation, directed straight and true and noisily, *trumps* anything so inconvenient as mere fact.'

'What were you talking about with Hathaway?'

Willetts smiled, the faintest curl at the corners of his lips. 'You were always an insightful man, Jim.'

Ross said nothing.

'It appears the *Belyy Medved* database has been erased, including much of your data. Even the clouded materials. That same damn computer virus.'

Willetts gave a rueful shrug so beautifully crafted Ross would have clapped if he'd had the energy.

'I didn't see Hathaway as quite so crooked,' he said.

'Oh, she would be swift to proclaim her innocence.'

Willetts used the thumb and middle finger of his left hand to massage his forehead just above his eyebrows. 'There's no positive to be found in the events of these past weeks,' he said. 'The death toll is appalling, the impact on the natural world a catastrophe.' He sipped at his bourbon, glanced at the reception counter, then reached into an inner pocket and drew out a packet of cigarettes. He lit one with his vintage Zippo, put his head back and blew smoke at the ceiling. The fingers holding the cigarette were mustard-coloured with nicotine, his fingernails thicker than Ross remembered them, yellowing, an old man's nails.

'However,' Willetts went on, and his voice barely contained any of his usual drawl, 'the world requires energy. It requires plastics, tar for building roads, clothing. I need hardly lecture. There were times we balanced risk with progress perhaps…infelicitously. Still, the blame for this disaster lies elsewhere: in the actions of a terrorist. An environmental terrorist. Ms Hathaway and the Canadian government are most keen the world should understand this.' Willetts leaned forwards. He clamped hold of the edge of the table with his hand, so hard his skin whitened. 'I also am keen.'

He pointed at Ross with the two fingers of his hand that held the cigarette, as if aiming a pistol. 'How about you, Jim?' he said. 'What do you want the world to understand?'

—

Later, Ross lay on his bed, still in his clothes.

Willetts wanted his silence. Again. With the files either snaffled by the government or "erased by the virus", which was of course the most egregious bullshit. And if stories came out?

213

Bury the corporate negligence beneath a barrage of redirected blame directed at the dead activist Jay Skelton. Jay, whom Ross had watched hurl himself into the black ocean.

As clear an act of guilt as might be imagined. And, it might equally be argued, as clear a form of justice served.

And Jim Ross, what was *he* doing? People came to the Arctic, they worked in their machine environments. They stayed indoors, hated it, imagined nothing more than thousands of miles of grey, flat tundra. Ross could barely walk four hundred yards with his knee. Still, he thought of the small library of books on the Arctic he'd collected, all of them lined up in his Tuktoyaktuk bedroom, like a shelf full of salves to his weak conscience.

Hathaway was right, he'd been chasing ghosts. And he sure was tired. Weeks and weeks of tired. His eyes began to shut.

But that mound of stones: a cairn. It *was* a cairn. Animals had pulled it to pieces, but it made no sense as a natural feature.

And what if the boat hadn't crashed immediately? What if Carrie had spent time with the injured man? What if she grew to like him? She had a penchant for the doomed, after all. She'd proven that in becoming friends with Ross. What if...?

Oh, put it away. It was time to put it away. He lay down, shut his eyes deliberately now. Enough.

But what if...what if all Carrie had to offer the dead had been those dog tags? When she buried him. A token of whatever kinship they'd formed in adversity.

He knew what he had to do. The guy he'd need to persuade wouldn't like it. Not one bit.

And, with that, finally, Ross fell asleep.

—

Clinging to his old tweed trilby, Ross dragged his bag from the Twin Otter's hold, amid the scuffle of passengers hurrying to snatch their own. He scuttled, leaning heavily on his walking stick, towards the box-like airport building. *Welcome to Sachs Harbour, Banks Island* a battered sign read. He ducked through the door beneath.

Joe Amaruq was waiting for him.

—

'You more crazy even than all the other *qallunaats* come up here.' It was Joe Amaruq's brother speaking. Joe – uncharacteristically – laughed. He leaned forwards, swapped a leisurely high-five with his brother. But Ross noticed the brother wasn't smiling. Earlier, he'd offered Ross his name as Nootaikok, though Amaruq had grunted, as if that might have been a joke.

'Call it tidying up a loose end,' Ross said.

'Some kind of tidying,' said Nootaikok. He was bigger than Amaruq, bulky, tending to fat. His face was wide, lined in such a way he looked as if he were about to snarl. He wore traditional Inuvialuit clothing – as far as Ross imagined it to be – fur leggings, boots with the skin of an animal showing on the outside. Some kind of hide shirt.

They were sitting in the front room of Amaruq's single-storey, pre-fab house. The furniture was modern, designer; all low, sharp lines. A huge TV and accoutrements – speakers, a VR games console. Soft lighting. Two rather beautiful paintings on the wall, abstracts in soft tones, little vivid flecks of brighter colour here and there, suggestive of lost souls in vast polar landscapes. It was all rather unexpected and metropolitan. Ross had imagined – what? Vintage snowshoes, dried fish, polar bear skins and – oh, he didn't know, really. Stereotypes. Of course, given Amaruq's oil-business career, he had the money to ship in good furniture from the south, as many local people didn't.

'She's *your* loose end,' Amaruq said quietly, 'not mine. Woman accused me of being some sort of terrorist.'

'Terrorists come from south of the 60th parallel,' his brother said.

Amaruq snorted.

'It was just her job. She hated it.' Ross picked up his cup, swirled the greasy tea. Took another hesitant sip. Tasted fat, or seal blubber, or whatever. Maybe he was 'white-man crazy', after all. There'd been a call in the Canadian parliament that morning for any senior management still alive to face immediate prosecution – despite the terrorist angle. Ross's name had been mentioned. Eco-terror or not, someone in a suit had to take the rap, and Ross was still the face of corporate skulduggery. Actually, Ross had already done a deal with Hathaway for the ten million dollars of crude still stored on the *Belyy Medved* from the well test. It covered at least the initial costs of salvage.

In fact, there'd been plenty of other voices in parliament to defend business, even to defend Ross. They'd talked about risk, investment, the greater good. Still, he ought to be with his lawyers, preparing a defence.

'I'm not asking you to do it for free,' Ross said.

Nootaikok made a rude sound, looked pointedly away. Amaruq just stared at Ross, without visible emotion. He sprawled in a lounge chair, his feet in thick socks crossed on the coffee table between them. Ross could smell them, smell damp clothing, old sweat, and a more subtle undercurrent, an acrid aroma of something recently cooked.

The silence lengthened.

'I don't mean it like that, Joe. I'm sorry. Hellfire, you saved my life, more than once. I just...it was you told me about your family business – tundra tours, hunting. So how much does it take to mount an expedition?' He glanced at Joe's brother. 'And to make it worth your while.'

Nootaikok muttered something in his own language. Amaruq murmured a reply. The wind beat, abruptly savage, at the walls.

'You hear that?' Amaruq said. 'Wind's going to change. Trouble coming.'

'Way I remember it, you're not someone cares much about the weather.'

Joe smiled sparingly, then stood. He lifted his arms and stretched. 'You really found the boat, then?'

'I did.'

'Dead body?'

'We don't know yet it's Carrie. But I...'

'...just know it isn't. You said.'

'Even if it is, there could be someone else out there. But I reckon she put those dog-tags on the body when she buried it. Her way of, I don't know...'

'Travel on a hunch,' said Joe's brother. 'On a *qallunaat* hunch, hundreds of miles through the Dark Time.'

Amaruq smiled. 'My brother's an angry man,' he said.

Ross reached inside his gilet, drew out an envelope. 'I got six thousand dollars.'

'This what you sliced off the Pentada emergency fund?' Nootaikok leaned towards him, aggressive. 'Cheat the people out of what they owed.'

'It's my own money,' Ross said. He pulled a roll of notes

from his trouser pocket. 'In fact, I got six thousand seven hundred eighty dollars. Here.' He pushed the roll and envelope across the table towards Nootaikok. 'Take it all.'

Nootaikok stood the roll vertically, balanced the envelope on top. Turned it round and round with fingers that looked like they'd been cut from thick leather.

'You dig on this woman, huh?' he said.

Ross looked at Amaruq, who was staring into the electric fire that glowed in a false fireplace of weathered driftwood. 'What you think, Joe?'

Amaruq spoke quietly, 'If her own people don't buy it, you bring it to us?'

'Her own people don't want her found. She may have, I don't know, talked with Jay Skelton's father. Shared notes. She might know things. They've not got any incentive to do more than they have.' Ross tried to dial down his bitterness, to not sound so crazy white man. 'Coast Guard's got too much to think about. Autopsy's going to take a few more days. We only found bones, bits of skin.' He paused, remembering. 'But I know Carrie, Joe. She just wouldn't have...' He threw his arms in the air, aware of how pathetic he sounded.

'Two hundred miles and more up there,' Amaruq said. 'Same back. Winter's come. Dark Time's come. Weather's on the change.'

'It's been cold, right? Cold's good, so the ice is hard for travel. Isn't that right? She – whoever it is – will be coming south.'

Nootaikok made a contemptuous sound. 'There's why you *quallunaat* die up here. Like there's one sort of ice!'

'Which is why I need your help.'

'Going get warm,' Amaruq said. 'Melt the pack-ice. Break it up.'

218

Nootaikok mumbled something dismissive.

'Can't you go by land?'

'Too long. Too far. Too much trouble between.'

Nootaikok said, 'And if she gone out on the ice, she's dead anyhow.'

'Though if she's so clever,' Amaruq said, 'she sticks close by the shore.'

Nootaikok spoke angrily in his own language to his brother.

Ross broke in. 'Sounds like you guys know your stuff. We have to try. See what we can see. It's all I ask.'

'You're not going far as the end of the village.' Nootaikok pointed at Ross's walking cane.

Amaruq said something sharp. Then he and Nootaikok spoke together, Amaruq all the time staring at the fire.

'No,' Nootaikok said. And he made a dismissive gesture towards the money on the table, and towards Ross.

'Okay, no,' Joe Amaruq said. They continued to argue, but it seemed personal now.

Ross lay back on the sofa. He cricked his neck, his temples throbbing. He'd done everything he could. He'd gone all the way. There was nowhere else. Nothing else. No one else.

He'd failed.

WHITE ROAD

Carrie

Carrie lay on her stomach. Watching, waiting. A faint crackle sounded every time she blinked, the liquid from her eyes freezing on her eyelashes. She worried she'd freeze before the moment came.

'You need carbohydrates, proteins, fats, fibre, minerals, vitamins,' Bastien was telling her. 'Carbs should make up fifty percent of your diet. Fats twenty-five, proteins the same.'

'All I've got's the random rubbish from your boat.'

'Freddy and I were out here a long time.'

To protect herself from the wind, she lay to leeward of a mound of rubble ice, piled six feet high and fifteen yards across. Ice-particles like dust blew across her vision. When the wind gusted, they swirled in misty curtains, blocking her line of sight.

She'd camped half a mile south of the *Carrick* the first night, then the following day walked ten hours, despite the scalp wound from when the boat sank and the unending headache of her concussion. She'd pitched her tent beside a weathered, beach-bound floeberg the second night, walked six more hours so far today.

'Keep to the land and the shore ice,' Bastien advised her. 'The pack ice is suicide.' In fact, the land was so low, so broken into little bays and flat headlands that petered into islets, all of it now snow- and ice-covered, that often she could not entirely be sure where the land ended and the ice began.

'Where the pack grinds against the shore-ice, it rafters. Rubble and ridges form. Water-leads open and close. Polynyas. A dangerous region, although it's here you'll find wildlife.'

'I should've brought my camera.'

'Walrus have been known to erupt from the water by an

223

ice edge to kill the human walking there.' She listened to him wheeze as he laughed. 'Solitary, rogue males. Listen for their battle cry, "Oock, Oock, Oock". But they're gone by this time of year.'

Her breath gathered in frosted clumps like cotton candy. She had to brush her hand in front of her face periodically to continue her vigil.

Neither the stars nor the sun's afterglow had been the light by which she'd travelled. Instead, an aurora curled like vast, rippling, gossamer curtains, washing the sky with light. The air itself seemed to shimmer with rose pink and lime green, and the ice grew strange and magical, its textures reflecting in a million, tiny, distinct ways. She thought she could actually hear the aurora: a faint rustling, as if of fabrics moving against each other. At one point, it seemed to turn into the clatter of a distant helicopter. Still, when wonder became illusion, it was time to get back to the nitty gritty of making progress. And she had one task, and only one: to walk 200 miles through the polar night to Sachs Harbour and salvation.

Her stretcher-sled dragged as though it moved through concrete. She reckoned she'd made at best one mile an hour. So she'd covered maybe thirty miles so far. Three days of food left. Four rounds in the rifle.

So here she was, lying in the cold, waiting and watching.

'Vitamin C deficiency was the undoing of many early expeditions. A body can't produce its own minerals. Generally, that's also true of vitamins. So take the supplements.'

'Your cupboard was bare.'

'Ah, yes...If you're eating a lot of bear liver...'

'Who wouldn't?'

'If you do, be careful. You can overdose on Vitamin A.'

'How in all the seven hells am I expected to know when I've had too much bear liver?'

'Blurred vision. Pain deep in your bones, skin colour changes. It's too strong even for dogs. They go bald.'

'I'll have a quiet word with any owners of bald dogs I come across.'

'Still, bear fat makes a delicious alternative to butter for frying other foods.'

'All right, shut up. I'm trying to concentrate.'

Now, at last, she saw it again. Okay, not too fast, now, Carrie. But not too slow. She flexed the cold fingers of her right hand, clad only in an under-glove. She closed one eye.

The gunshot cracked with shocking violence. Carrie was up from behind the rubble ice and running even as the sound faded. The seal had almost exploded when the bullet struck. Now, it flopped and thrashed in its death throes. As she neared, it teetered on the edge of its breathing hole. Its tail slid back into the water. Carrie dived forwards, dropping the rifle. She skidded along the ice, caught hold of its head with both hands.

In its black, doleful eyes she saw, reflected, the aurora. For a second, she felt as though she understood something...something, but what? Then the seal's weight was too much. She cried out, dug her fingers deeper in behind its skull. Yet its body – as heavy as Carrie's – slid inexorably down the greasy edges of the breathing hole. She was drawn along with it, refusing to let go. Then, abruptly, it slipped through her fingers. She had to press her hands to the sides, almost following it in. Its dead face disappeared beneath the black water. Frost fog – where the water was exposed to the air – billowed about her. She struggled backwards, flopping like a seal herself.

She screamed her frustration.

'Of all Arctic proficiencies,' Bastien said, 'learning to give up your expectations is the most important.'

'Oh, please just die,' she told him.

She got to her feet. The ice was a mess of seal blood, black in the dimming light. She was covered in it too. Nothing to be done. She pulled her right mitten over her freezing hand, retrieved the rifle. Above, the aurora writhed, convulsed as if dying too.

Abruptly, the aurora disappeared. Heavy clouds rolled in from the north and west, a dense, black bloom across the sky. The sun-glow in the south was almost gone. She could hardly make out the mound of ice now. She hurried forwards. She had to get to the sled and then back to shore as soon as possible. Make camp before it became too dark.

Carrie jogged away from the seal hole towards the ice rubble mound.

'My expectation is to live,' she said. She had three bullets left.

—

Her eyes fixed on the sled, fifty yards away. But the last breaks in the cloud cover disappeared. The far distant southern horizon showed the very faintest of dim red glows. But it cast no ambient light. Instead, the darkness became so complete, she had to stop. The sled, the very ice-scape itself: everything had gone.

Isolation beyond anything she'd imagined possible engulfed her. She crouched as if she were being hunted. Not five minutes ago, the world had been a twilit space, visibility to a mile or more.

So stop, Carrie. Stay still. She'd been facing the sled. In crouching, she'd not twisted her head, had she? No. So, follow your nose, girl. And that wry thought calmed her. Plus, the faint line of red at the horizon was almost directly to her right. But not quite. Keep it there. She took a step.

Then stopped again. If she got it wrong, that would be it. Game over. How far had the sled been? Maybe fifty yards. Call it seventy paces. She counted aloud – 'sixteen, seventeen, eighteen' – her voice falling dead. She lost count in the early fifties, but forced herself to keep going, to approximate. 'Fifty-nine, sixty, sixty-one...'

'Seventy.' No sled. She squinted, peered around. She could just about see her hands close by her face. She thought of Dante's ninth level of hell, as Bastien had described it to her. Satan buried to his waist in the black ice.

The faint red horizon glow had veered forwards. She'd let it drift. Not paid enough attention. The sled was potentially... where? To her left. Yes, either level or slightly behind her – she should have walked right into it before she ran out of numbers.

Keep the horizon line where it is. Say seven steps left, three back, six right, three back, seven left and so on. What if she'd not reach it? She would have. Seventy steps. But distance was hard to judge in a flat landscape. Well, she was a sailor, she had to trust herself.

On her fifth step sideways, her leg hit the sled. She draped herself across it, hugged her belongings like lost children.

She said at last, 'Abject terror.'

Bastien chuckled knowingly.

She felt her way along the sled. Rummaged in the rucksack and drew out the torch. Turned it on. The wind gusted. Ice grit flew through the beam and beat against her body. She drew on her visor. She'd not noticed before, but the clear plastic was heavily scored. She closed her eyes, tried to make calculations. How far to land? She got into her sled harness, shone her torch on the ground until she found her footprints, already fast fading. She followed them back to the mound of rubble ice.

Leeward of the wind, she pulled out her tent. The cold crept through her suit. Her teeth chattered. She was parched with thirst, her tongue swollen, her movements jerky and inept. She hadn't eaten for several hours. A mistake. But that made her angry. She stamped the pegs into the ice, tying two guy ropes to the sled, which she'd jammed between big, broken chunks of floe ice. Inside the tent, with the lantern on and her little hob working, she sipped the last slushy water from a thermos.

The wind slapped the tent walls, played a desolate music on the guy ropes.

'One day in, and already you're lost on the sea ice.' Bastien sounded smug.

'Just getting the hang of things.'

'All alone. The ocean bare inches beneath. No one to save you.'

The gas hissed, the wind hissed. The fabrics surrounding her – tent canvas, sleeping bag, a variety of synthetic pieces of clothing – scrunched and scraped against each other. Her shoulders almost touched her ears. Tension. She stretched her neck, pulling with both hands at the base of her skull. Then she stirred the contents of the pan: macaroni and little nuggets of the ice she'd carved from the floe-berg that destroyed the *Carrick*.

'Salt can find no place in ice's crystalline structure. As time passes, the salt is leached away. You can wash in first year ice, cook with second year, make tea with third.' Dead guy wisdom.

The water was bubbling in the pan. She poured in half the final tin of kidney beans. She should have bought some salt. Oh, the irony.

'You need six thousand calories a day to keep up your strength,' Bastien said.

'Trying to fatten me up?'

'Otherwise,' he went on, ignoring her, as he often did, 'fatigue grows. Starvation of the muscles. Your body can no longer resist the cold.'

She turned the kidney bean can in her hands. Sighed.

'So is this suicide?' she said, sitting atop the pack ice, who knew how far from land.

Bastien made a non-committal sound. 'I'm here with you,' he said.

She hunched forwards, her forehead resting on her knees. She stayed that way until the pan overflowed, water hissing down its sides.

—

Carrie shrugged on her sled harness. Picked up her walking poles, hopped up and down a couple of times.

'My mission, should I choose to accept it,' she informed the world. 'Tramp the polar wastes clutching a load of conspiracy theory papers about some dodgy, coffin drillship. Papers every eco-crazy's going to wet their knickers over. Though they likely blew the bloody thing up anyway.'

Mission impossibly stupid.

Her compass directed itself toward anything metal – a zip, a nail, a clip, her watch – as readily as it showed magnetic north. She held it as far from her body as possible. It wavered, having a think. And magnetic north itself was currently somewhere beneath the Arctic Ocean heading for Siberia. Meaning it was, uh, northwest or west-northwest of her current position? Something vaguely like that.

Never mind, the wind had been out of the north-northwest. She'd made the camp to leeward of the wind beside this rubble mound. So...that way. Keep the crazily wavering compass needle pointing over her right shoulder.

The real problem – okay, the most immediate: it was ten a.m., but only a dim miasma of light filtered through the gunmetal cloud. And the light made of the ice-scape a blank, two-dimensional canvas, so undifferentiated that she could discern nothing at all. Her feet seemed to float in a pale, ashen fog. It was as good as a white-out. Call it a grey-out. When she'd been taking down the tent, packing the sled, her possessions' solid lines were points of focus. She hadn't noticed the absolute blank of what lay ahead. At each step, she could be putting her foot into a bank of snow or a lead covered only in mush ice. She was as good as blind.

She pondered for a few moments, then took a spare pair of red over-gloves from the sled. She peered at her wavering compass, then threw one of the gloves several yards ahead.

She set off towards it, trying and failing to make a Hansel and Gretel gag out of her predicament. The sled slipped along nicely, at least. She'd poured liquid water across the raised sections of its base, let the water freeze solid. Rubbed it smooth. After a few yards, she threw the other glove on beyond the first. Then she tripped over something, only just keeping her feet by digging in her walking poles.

She took out her torch, switched it on. A chunk of ice rubble the size and shape of a toaster. In the torchlight, she could make out others scattered across the striated surface.

'Going to be a long day,' she said.

The torchlight veered around as she clutched it in one hand along with a walking pole. Every few yards she had to stoop and throw a glove, checking the uncertain compass each time. There was no wind. After all these weeks of it hissing across the ice out of the north, the complete silence made this shadow world even more uncanny. The ocean, so close beneath the ice, felt like a hidden predator, Godzilla-huge. Bastien had told her how in the far north of the polar ocean lay the abyssal depths, in places nearly eighteen thousand feet deep. She kept wanting to swing round and shine the torch behind her. Catch whatever pale creeper lurked, waiting to pounce. When she did turn to look back, her breath formed a frost trail behind her, hanging weirdly static in the air.

'Fear'll kill ya soon as bears,' she said aloud, trying for a jaunty tone. But the silence seemed to prick up its ears, as though suddenly alerted to her presence.

And then, abruptly, a breeze started up. It blew right into her face, several degrees warmer. A wind from the south. She stopped, just allowing it to play across the bare skin of her face, the faint sensation – not of warmth, but of, well, 'less cold'.

'Blow the bloody clouds away, won't...' She was silenced by the sound of a gunshot.

Then three more of differing tones, followed by a weird twanging, like the thickest steel cables in the world, pulled taut and played by giants. The surface beneath her shivered. Still she could make out nothing at all through the grey-out. But she heard growling, muted agonized screeches. Her heart quickened. The ice must be moving with the temperature change.

'What is climate change?' Bastien was prone to the rhetorical. 'Diesel-driven cruise-ships full of tourists come to see the polar bears before the ice disappears and they all drown.'

'I'd give a lot for some fat Yank in Hawaiian shorts helping me aboard.'

She walked on, picking and throwing her gloves more quickly and further each time, not checking the compass now; haste beyond the reality of her failing food supply. A ridge of ice rose before her, its massive series of interlocked, flat-sided ice fragments, twenty-feet high, formed a disorderly miniature mountain range. Raftering ice, she realised. Two floes crashing into one another, forcing each other into the air, like time-lapse, tectonic-plate geology. The ridge stretched away as far as her torchlight could reach in either direction.

What did it mean?

The wind picked up. More thunderous reports, crackling grumbles, a noise like a shell beach sliding in a tide. She could see nothing. No obvious route over the ridge revealed itself. So, she turned left, east, shoreward...she guessed. The compass veered all over the place. It would begin to settle, then swing off just with the movement of her breath.

Still, it was just a little brighter now. She took a thermos from her sled, drank a few gulps of water. Helped herself to the penultimate square of chocolate. Sucked its frozen sweetness until she felt calmer.

She should have left a message at the crash site. Or on the burial mound. She'd got passive, relied on Bastien's advice, instead of her own judgement.

The torch began to turn yellow and then orange. Almost, she hurled it at the ice ridge beside her. She wanted to stamp it into a thousand tiny parts, grind the bulb glass into dust. Instead, she rummaged through her rucksack and pocketed the last set of batteries.

'Your expectations are what will not survive,' Bastien reminded her.

'Oh please piss off.'

She plodded forward, following the dim orange beam. Anger beat fear every time. Though anger was just about as useless in this frosted hell.

It felt warmer. Not just warmer. A lot warmer. Maybe fifteen degrees. Her infuriatingly uncomfortable survival suit suddenly felt like a sweat-box.

A cannon went off ahead.

More like warship artillery. Immediately after, there came an odd, deep, sibilant growl and accompanying gurgle, like the digestive system of some gargantuan beast. She shone the torch forward through the lightening grey as the sound grew louder. Whatever it was, it was coming her way.

Just as her mind understood what it must be, a black line in the surface came slicing toward her, faster than she could run. The whole ice floe was splitting apart.

Slipping, skidding on the ice, driving her poles in, hauling at the resistant sled, she threw herself to her left. The crack came rushing past. Water frothed and splashed. Fog boiled from the crack, as if it were filled with lava. She lost her footing, fell, twisted in her sled harness. Frantically, she struggled to her feet, dragged the harness over her head. The torch dropped to the ground. All around her came the booms and cracks of shattering ice.

And then the reality of her situation struck her – she was the wrong side of the lead. The north side. And with that thought, oddly enough, her panic left her. She had no time left. No food left. She *must* make progress.

She lifted the harness, hauled the sled round, back toward

the smoking, black water. Snatched up the torch. The crack was four feet wide already. Too wide. She shook her head at her own folly, even as she ran toward the lead. And leaped.

But her foot slipped at its edge. She toppled forward. Had time to reach out, just as her torso crashed into the far side. The torch skittered away to hit the base of the ice ridge she'd been following. It lay there, a little pool of light, as Carrie's legs dropped into the water. Fingers clawing the ice, her elbows digging into the surface, she tried to keep herself from sliding back. The fog swirled about her. She felt the harness slide down from her waist to her thighs. Heard the sled creaking on the lead's far lip.

It was going in, and she was going with it.

'I won't...' she cried out, heaving herself onto the points of her elbows, howling again with the effort. One arm whipped ahead a few inches. Dug in. She thought the muscles in her neck were going to snap. But she ground on. Her hips lifted from the water. She forced her thighs to press the harness into the ice edge, hold onto it. Then she moved one knee up onto the ice.

She swivelled like a spinning bottle, her legs coming fully out of the water, snatched the harness. She saw the sled teetering on the far edge. Already the crack had widened. Crazy now with terror, strong beyond reason, she stood, hauled on the harness, her feet sliding. Drew the front of the sled across, just above the water's surface. Its nose touched the near side. Not stopping, she pulled as if in a tug-of-war competition. The back of the sled dropped into the water. It dragged her back toward the water as it began to sink.

She shouted, a noise without meaning. Leaned back, pulled so hard she felt something pop in her mid-back.

An agonising flame roared up and down her spine. But still

she hauled and the sled came over and slid up onto the ice. She hauled it on toward the ridge. The ledge between the pressure ridge and the water lead was no wider than twelve feet. The ridge itself formed a series of miniature peaks and narrow gorges. She pulled the sled close by a steep little valley, maybe five feet across. She manhandled it into the narrow space until it jammed. Bared her teeth at the fire in her spine. Snatched up the torch, shone it out toward the lead as she collapsed.

Water churned; fog curled up from the surface. She lay against the sled, gasping. Out of the gloom all around came creaks and bangs and odd peals, as if huge, freezing bells were being struck or scraped with rasping hammers. She watched the black, smoking lead as it grew and grew until she could no longer see the far side.

—

She couldn't just sit here. Let the Arctic swallow her.

Somehow, she crawled to the top of the ice ridge. The grey-out had dispersed in the brightening twilight of the day. A half-moon glimmered between clouds, milky in the indigo sky. Its light revealed a rubbled, ridged, striated and bewildering desolation, utterly lacking in colour and life. Rubble ice lay scattered across the great, wind-scoured flats. The moonlight threw vast, black shadows from even the lowest mounds. Roiling blurs showed where miniature ice-storms were lifted by the wind. The breeze came even warmer.

The open lead behind her stretched as far as she could see in either direction, still smoking as the water met the air. Beyond the lead, the ice seemed flatter, somehow. But why was she seeing the moon to her left? Should it not be cutting a low arc across the *southern* sky?

'The moon can be an ally,' Bastien said. 'It won't set some-times for four or five days in a row. Stefansson wrote that at such times you could have three or four hours a day when you might read ordinary print quite clearly.'

Given that, she'd try to read her compass. She laid it down at arm's length on a flat section of ice. The red pointer swung through ever-narrowing arcs and then – still shivering, as if unsure – pointed generally away to her right and slightly ahead.

'Oh...' She blew an ironic kiss. The ridge did not travel from west to east, as she'd imagined, but from north to south. She'd been walking west, directly *away* from the land, before the ice broke up. Worse, when she'd leaped across the lead, she'd put herself on its seaward side.

She'd nearly died for nothing.

She dredged up every Navy curse she could remember. Cursed her ignorance of this savage place. She cursed it and herself and all those idiots, now likely dead, who'd led her here. And then she started to laugh. She made a Laurel and Hardy gesture with her hands. Another fine mess...her laughter bordering on the frantic. But the pain in her back soon stopped her laughter too.

She slipped excruciatingly off the ice spur, down and past the jammed sled, her feet hitting the ice heavily. Pain surged up her spine to clench the base of her skull. A herniated disc? Ligament tear? She stood, groaning, walked in little circles, fighting it. Then she lay on the ice, tried to think. Her mind felt dull, apathetic. The pain, she realised, was too much to bear. She couldn't haul her sled. She could hardly stand up. And where the hell was she anyway? The cold seeped up into her back. In fact, an ice pack was just what she'd needed. Not a bad call, lying down, after all. She quietened further. Actually, yes, a quick nap. Let it all go...

A sound jolted her awake. A splash of some kind.

'In the polar regions, cold plus sleep can often equal death.'

She thought of herself, back on board the *Carrick* in thick socks and a heavy sweater, drinking whiskey and saying 'Yeah, yeah,' as Bastien droned on.

So, 'Yeah, yeah,' she said, for the sake of form, rolled over, pushed herself up, moaned.

Out on the lead, two seals watched her with a taunting insolence. Carrie noticed they were making strange flicking motions, shutting their eyes and smacking their faces against the water. Again and again they did this, until suddenly they dropped below the surface and were gone.

There was something about the water's surface, some trick of the light, perhaps. Carefully, she approached the lead edge. She switched on her torch and shone it down. A rainbow glittered back at her. She kneeled, pulled her glove from her hand and let two fingers trail in the water, brought them to her nose. In that vast absence of aroma, her senses had become hyper-acute. They didn't need to be in this instance, however. She knew crude.

As she sniffed its sweet-sour smell, a profound change came over her, as if she'd snorted a drug. The undulating black waters of the lead had the rich, colour-shifting spectrum of treacle. Fracture lines zigzagged enthrallingly through the ice ridge's myriad geometries. The clearing sky had turned a teal blue so limpid and lovely she could hardly bear it. She stared, astonished, at the water mists drifting like quiet ghosts. The whole broken, complex icescape glowed like ivory in the moon's wash.

'Did you do this to me?' she asked Bastien.

'I'm dead,' he replied.

She kneeled beside the black lead. The oil floated on the water's surface like a virus seen through a microscope. That she might have played some part in bringing such corruption here...

Still breathing as if trying to calm herself after sex, Carrie walked back to the sled. She tugged at it. Her back spasmed. She moved round to one side, rested her hands against the ice wall, pushed against the sled with her back. It didn't irritate her spine quite as badly. She put one boot up and pushed again, but it wouldn't move. Cautiously, she clambered up beside the sled. When she was above it, she sat, put her feet to its upper edge, pushed with her legs.

The sled held a moment, then dropped away. It slid down onto the flat. And kept going – slithering on towards the lead. In a kind of slow-motion horror, Carrie could only watch as it approached the water. It slowed, slowed, reached the lead's edge. Its front end ran out over the surface. And then it came to a halt.

'Oh, fall in,' she said. 'Give me a quick end.'

But she didn't mean it.

On the lead's far side, she thought she saw a shadow moving. She squinted. There it was again. A movement, one darker shadow among others, a few hundred yards away, close by a larger chunk of floeberg. But then it was gone. She caught herself before saying, 'Bastien?'

—

She managed two hours, following the narrow shelf between the pressure ridge and lead. First, she pulled the sled while walking backwards. Once she'd fallen twenty times or so, and when the pain became too great, she walked sideways, then forwards, though that was almost beyond bearing. When she could stand none of it any longer, somehow she pitched her tent in a gap between ridge peaks.

She crawled in, got the sputtering gas ring going. Lay for a time on her back, the sleeping bag beneath her, trying to relax her body and calm the spasms. She made tea. As a sachet of vegetable rice boiled, she opened the medicine bag. Three 30mg tablets of codeine were all the painkillers left. Her hands shook so badly that she could hardly hold one of the tiny pills to her teeth to break it in half. She clutched the hot cup, rocked, breathed, eventually felt the slow rush of the drug. It barely took the edge off.

She cut the last two tinned sausages into the rice, the other half of the final can of kidney beans she'd opened at her last stop, seemingly a geological age ago. She ate, but her hunger remained.

'Actually, Stefansson thought we worry overly about starvation. "No one who has tried fasting can be induced to fear four or five days without food," as he put it.'

Perhaps from spite – against herself? against him? – she ate a chunk of pemmican. She'd only understood it was even food when Bastien directed her to fetch it from the *Carrick*'s galley. Dried meat powder, rendered fat and berries ground together, then pressed into bricks. She sucked each frozen chunk until it softened, grimacing.

'Men being men by eating the foulest crap they can invent,' she said.

'You must save yourself.' Bastien playing the martyr again.

'Though hauling your damn dossier means I'm saving you too, right? Saving your name: from murderous fanatic to martyr. They'll be hugging your tombstone. If I survive.'

But he never responded to that kind of logic.

She sipped her cold tea, hunched against the agony in her back. Argued with herself about taking the other codeine tablet half. Won. Or lost. Took it. Lay down. Wondered, as she'd tried not to do too often, if Donny and Jim had survived the drillship.

—

She woke to the tent walls cracking like sails in a storm. Muffled booms, rifle shots, that weird twanging.

'Oh, what now?'

Her voice sounded so weary she almost stayed where she was. Her back hurt atrociously, the muscles rigid along her spine. But then she realised that, in fact, she was warm. Too warm. So accustomed was she to waking in the icy cold, the huge effort to emerge from her bedding, that she hardly knew what to do. But then a louder twanging crack came almost directly outside. She scrambled from the bag, dragged her survival suit on. She'd been foolish removing it, but it had helped: she'd slept. She put her head out of the tent.

Little, stinging missiles hit her face. An ice-storm was blowing. She ducked back in, fitted her hood and visor. When she clambered out, the wind tried to drag her sideways alongside the ridge. She dug her fingers into cracks in the ridge wall, clung on, got her balance, looked around.

The moon painted silver lines on the clouds streaking past. But it was not where she expected it to be. It should have been to the right of her tent flap. Instead, it had moved almost ninety degrees. Where the lead ought to be, multiple broken ice-floe sheets swirled and grated against one another. The ridge itself shuddered beneath her hands. On three sides, she saw the black shadow of water.

Wincing beneath the jarring anguish in her spine, she clambered up the ridge to the top.

'Oh,' she said, and the sound lingered on. 'Ohhhhhh.'

On the far side, the landscape had become a splintered patchwork of ice, narrow black lead lines between, all moving in a slow dance, bumping, sliding, grinding against each other, as far as the eye could see. The wind lifted the water into moonlit, drifting fog banks. It was a sight more terrifying, yet at the same time more spectacular, than anything she had yet experienced. Perhaps she ought just to stop. To give in. Sit here and watch the world come to pieces around her. She had the best view in the house.

'You're resting *on* water, *over* water,' Bastien said.

When she looked to left and right, this ridge she'd been following all this time formed a vaguely semi-circular stretch of floe in the moonlight, its thicker structure holding together still, as everything else came to pieces. But it had sagged, become a long bend, a huge hunter's bow. And she was in the middle of the bend, which explained the change in perspective when she'd first emerged from the tent.

Now, the pressure ridge to the north began to disintegrate. Piece by jagged piece, it crumbled away. As if in surrender, a whole section collapsed. The black water churned, the massive ice sections rolling over and over. It hissed like some terrible animal at bay. This whole uneasy chunk of floe on which she rested was held to its southern neighbours only by the thicker, shuddering ice of the ridge. Its restlessness was so unnerving, she had to call aloud to herself to make sense of what she had to do.

'Strike the camp...Bind it tighter to the sled, you idiot... Don't lose anything... Harness on...Bust this joint.'

'I'm here,' said Bastien.

'Not now,' she told him, but she wondered why he'd say such a thing.

Clutching the walking poles, she leaned forwards to haul, but the pain was so bad she had to crouch down instead. She pressed her fists into her temples. She squeezed through the hood, trying somehow to reduce the agony. She needed focus. At any moment, this ice slab would break free of its mooring and she'd be marooned on a crumbling, free-floating berg on the ocean.

Crying out with each step, she slogged forwards over the ice ledge's dancing surface. Its shivering movement, the way it dropped and rose, meant her legs hardly knew what to do. Her knees gave way at the wrong moment. Her rump slammed down on her ankles. Her back exploded in anguish.

But now the ridge beside her began to come apart in earnest. Fragments of ice showered down on her. Looking up, she saw one giant piece, big as a pick-up truck, teetering one way and the other. Desperately, she picked up her pace, adrenalin numbing the physical anguish.

A tearing clamour, snaps, a series of bangs and then a sizzling rush. The weight of the sled against her harness suddenly vanished. Over her shoulder, she saw it lifted up on a wave of smashed ice and roiling water where the ridge had come down behind her. She had time to take another step before the sled whipped her legs away and she collapsed on top of it. She careered forwards amid the wave's roar. A ball of ice two feet thick whistled just past her head. The water and slush-ice gushed about her body. She was screaming.

At last, it stopped. She lay still, arched diagonally over the sled like a sacrifice across an altar. The water's confusion subsided. Carrie fidgeted the sled harness from her waist, dragged herself to her feet. The floe she'd just escaped was turning away like some stately liner leaving dock. A mass of smaller ice chunks still cascaded down the broken ridge-end into the frothing sea.

Her arms, her body, glimmered in subtly refracting colours. For a time, she just stared at herself in fascination. She was hallucinating. Then she understood. Where the water had washed over her, she was covered in a thin film of oil.

—

'All in all, I really am jolly keen to live,' she said aloud in a flippant, Victorian-adventurer's tone. Most of them came to ends as sticky as the ice had turned, of course.

'The Inuit have always placed great value on the long narrative line of their survival, their human relationships, with each other and with the Arctic.'

Carrie clutched at Bastien's voice, soft amid the polar cacophony. But, 'Given the situation, I don't care,' she told him.

'Our desire to seize and possess: it lacks intimacy, it can't see the subtle. The Inuit weren't nearly as impressed with white men as we imagine they were.'

She stopped, hands on her knees, panting, baring her teeth at the pain. 'So when the rape and plunder thing doesn't cut it, meditate in the wilderness instead. That your point?' She tried to imagine him shrugging, but she'd only known him paralysed.

And here, at last, there was nowhere left to go.

Ahead, the ice lip she'd been following just faded away into mush and water. She sat on the sled. Sipped water. The weather was so warm, it hadn't turned to slush in her thermos. She unzipped the front of her suit.

'So this is climate change?' she said.

He didn't answer. Bastien had barely discussed the bottom line: the raison d'être for all this. It was such a given nowadays, after all. But this crazy shift in temperature seemed beyond all sense.

She sucked the very last chunk of pemmican, fouler than dog-food, but hey.

'End of the line,' she said, and her jaunty tone surprised her.

'We'll see each other soon,' said Bastien.

—

Sometime later – she could not be sure how long, she'd been mesmerised by the swirling mass of mush and ice, the prismatic flicker of oil on the surface – sometime later, she noticed something moving with more purpose amid it all. She squinted. A smaller berg chunk, a few hundred yards away north, out in the middle of the lead. But it was dodging between obstacles.

A polar bear, swimming. Coming her way. It took almost her entire energy just to get up, scrabble among her belongings for the rifle. Then she sat once more, watched its progress, feeling only a sort of grim resignation.

It was about a hundred yards away now. But a shattered ice floe, forty yards long, swung across its path. The bear's forepaws lifted from the water, one after another, to grasp the ice surface. She was reminded of the bear trying to clamber aboard the *Carrick*, the thick hair, sodden and tight to its skin, giving its forelegs the look of heavily-muscled human arms. Carrie felt a sudden affection. But then it dragged its huge body up onto the ice. She remembered desperately jabbing with the *Carrick*'s boat hook. Those talons as they ripped across her suit.

'Bears never bother hiding.' Bastien was an admirer. 'They're cantankerous, wayward, impulsive. And they can run at twenty-five miles an hour. If they could eat you, why shouldn't they?'

The bear just lay spread-eagled, however, its legs pointing in four directions. Exhausted. Oily.

'That you, Bastien?' she said softly.

At that distance, she couldn't see whether this bear carried the scars she'd inflicted. The binoculars were in her rucksack. Three rounds in the rifle and a day's food. The floe turned slowly, the prostrate bear with it, comically clinging on for dear life.

At last, it pulled itself up to sit on its hind quarters. It pressed its nose and face up and down along its front legs. It cuffed itself with its forepaws, scraping, scratching, worrying its head. Then it pushed itself along, its head flat on the ice. As it did so, it became increasingly agitated. It swung round, trying to bite its own flanks. Round and round like a dog chasing its tail. She heard its deep, breathy growls even against the wind. Soon, it had worked up a passion, leaping, whirling about, snapping the air. It walked in circles as if drunk. Finally, it dropped once more to the ice, its mouth making biting motions, as if trying to catch flies buzzing about its face.

The oil: the oil driving it mad. She remembered the seal she'd shot. The glint of the aurora in its dying eyes. A sheen of oil.

As the bear lay there, exhausted, defeated by the oil – defeated: a polar bear! – rage like an adrenaline surge revived Carrie. Death meant failure, for herself, for Bastien, for...well, everything. For all this. Sitting here waiting to die. Defeated.

That was not a word she could accept.

—

With the blunt side of her hatchet Carrie had beaten the ends of her two walking poles into bent claws. The polar bear had given her the idea as it pulled itself up onto the floe.

Now, she waited, poised, on one knee, claws out, ready. She had to be patient. But already, the water lapped about her. The ice surface was soft, damp, slushy. The whole, melting pressure-ridge floeberg on which she was marooned, quivered. The wind had risen to a soughing whine that made her want to give up the entire enterprise, put her hands over her ears and sleep.

Instead, she reached out with her two poles, grabbed at a passing floe sheet, ten feet wide, turning in the soupy lead. One pole caught and she was almost dragged into the water. She had to stumble sideways, her back spasming, as she sought to pull the pole free. It came away, but her foot went through the mush to her thigh. She almost fell into the lead's maelstrom. Of course, such a chunk of ice must weigh many tons. It was hopeless.

Away north, the polar bear had gone. She searched the lead. Saw nothing that seemed to move with more purpose than the southward drifting morass.

But now the very floe on which the bear had been recuperating drifted closer. She grappled with the sled harness, pulled it loosely about her body, waited in the lee of the ever-more-crazily tilting ice-ridge pinnacles. The floe neared. She stood with her pole claws out over the water. The floe resembled a huge arrowhead with jagged edges. Its tip, rounded off and partly melted, headed directly for her.

'Ohhh shit,' Carrie had time to say, as the berg drove into the soft ice where she stood. She leaped but was brought up short by her sled harness. She dropped onto the arrowhead point. The two floes' impact sent fault lines speeding away across both

246

surfaces. The ice beneath her bunched and cracked, began to rafter. She scrambled forwards, the sled so heavy. She felt it slip sideways to her right, pulling her with it. She lost her balance; only just drove the bent poles into the floe to keep from falling into the melee of ice and water.

She grasped the sled's hand-grips, hustled it away from the disintegrating floe lip. She slipped and slid, kicking her way backwards across the wet ice from the destruction of the two bergs. Then she had to stop, dizzy with pain. She watched her new floe drive slowly deeper into the one from which she'd just escaped.

The floe's tail – the arrowhead's wider end – swung round, the embedded nose acting as a fulcrum. Then, with a colossal crack and groan, it tore itself in half. As the berg-section came free, it turned slow circles, out into the frothing lead. She was left on a sort of irregular pentagon, fifteen yards across at its widest point. The black melt-pools on its surface glowered.

And then it began to rain.

'You've got to be kidding me,' Carrie said.

It was late November in the polar winter at seventy-four degrees north. The rain came in sheets, as if hurled from massive buckets by a demented god.

'Acid rain falling,' Bastien said. 'The Arctic's a sink for airborne mercury and sulphur from the mines in the south.'

'Be quiet, Bastien,' she begged him. She wasn't sure she could bear it. Oil in the water, acid in the air.

He said, 'I'm nearly done.'

Grimacing with pain, she stood. She was sweating heavily inside her suit. The visor misted. She unzipped it. The cold rain beat at her face. It hissed like a leaking gas main as it impacted the surface. She was right out in the middle of the lead now.

Still, the pressure ridge was coming apart, huge raftered slabs sagging, tumbling, crashing down into the water. Through the gaps, she saw the ocean's ice-crust stretching away towards the horizon, all of it warping and crumbling in the warm air and rain.

A sharp white line showed the more secure landfast ice, maybe three hundred yards away. It might as well have been three hundred miles.

Ahead, the lead kinked east, towards the shore before swinging away southwest. As debris would on a river bend, the mush-ice had gathered on the kink's inside corner, the water rushing faster round the wider side. It formed a porridge, lifting and popping like lava.

An idea came to her. So outrageous was it that, at first, she just shook her head, the rainwater flying from her hood in all directions. But her floe was melting, cracks meandering in every direction.

'Die or die trying.'

—

Carrie's floeberg reached the thick belt of mushed ice.

This was it.

'Ready, ready, ready,' she was saying. 'I'm ready, I'm ready.'

Calm. Wait. Watch for the exact moment.

Instead of driving into the kink-corner mush, her berg – so soft itself that it hardly held together – rolled along the mush's outer boundary furthest from land.

Ungainly, she tried to take some sideways steps, the sled harnessed to her. But she immediately fell over.

It was extraordinarily difficult to get up. She looked at her feet. The snowshoes she'd just put on were shaped like the body of a fish. She'd always imagined they'd look like tennis rackets, but clearly that was obsolete.

She rolled on her side, pulled herself up with the help of her walking poles. They sunk deep into the floe's surface. She shuffled around the floe edge as it continued to slide along the bank of mush ice.

She heard a gravelly grating from behind. Saw the entire berg being torn to pieces by the lead's fierce current. It just seemed to fizzle away into the swift-flowing water.

Now or never.

She put one snow-shoed foot out over the mush ice, pressed it down. The shoe's rear end immediately slipped under. She nearly lost her balance again, trying to remove it. She breathed in rapid little gasps, the rain coming through her open hood face, trickling cold down her neck. The sled grew abruptly heavier against her harness. Just hesitated a moment more on the edge.

'Oh, for God's sake: die or die trying, Carrie.'

And she stepped out onto the mush.

She kept the snowshoe as flat as possible. Felt it beginning to sink. Quickly, she took a second step. Her foot sank in...Another step. Another. Quick enough that her feet could not slide beneath the surface. She hardly lifted each shoe an inch above the surface. Just shuffled forwards. And then the sled slithered onto the mush surface.

But she was prepared for it. She took the sled's weight. Shuffled. Felt it glide across the surface, its weight better distributed than her own. It held, as long as she kept moving, didn't stop for even a second. Kept the pace exactly as it was, not faster, not slower. How far to go? No idea. She didn't dare even to look up for fear of losing her balance.

Little swells formed round the edges of her snowshoes, glistening in the moonlight from the south, where the clouds remained broken. They rippled away as she moved. Forwards... forwards.

She was like Jesus walking on the water. Or on a Slush Puppy.

Then the moonlight disappeared.

In the darkness, rain in her eyes, she faltered. The sled dragged at its harness, threatening to pull her back and down. But her foot lifted, shuffled forwards, placed itself down. The other foot followed. Muscles in her torso tightened yet further to take the sled's weight into themselves, not translate it into any downward force. But the agony was in some other body, not her own. One foot forwards. Then the other. A gliding motion.

But now the mush came softer still. Her feet sank deeper, whatever she might do. So she ran. Low-footed, the muscles in her calves and ankles locked solid: hydraulic pistons, refusing the drag of the slush. Five, six, seven steps, the harness sucking her back until she couldn't go on. Her feet immediately went in to the ankles, the snowshoes caught. But one final, enormous heave, crying out. A last frantic step. And her foot jarred against a harder surface.

She struggled to hold her balance. Her rear foot sunk deeper. She went to one knee. Her hands scrabbled, fingers clawing on the harder ice. But she was toppling back.

Then she caught hold of the walking poles – still hanging loose in their thongs about her wrist – swivelled one round and thumped its claw end into the surface, like a horizontal ice climber. Then the other claw. She clung on. Heaved herself forwards. Quick now. The sled!

She swung round, scrabbling for grip on the surface, the snowshoes hopeless as she hauled at the sled. It was half under. Howling now, she drew the sled up and up...and on to the harder ice.

She lay there on her back, groaning with the torment through her spine, and the horror of the past minutes. Stars appeared and disappeared. But the rain continued to pour down on her face. Now she laughed – so hard she coughed. Spluttering, she rolled on her side, away from the weather. Curled into a ball. But it was all right, she was on the shore ice once more.

—

Without thought, she crunched both the remaining codeine tablets. But she was so thirsty, she couldn't swallow, the medicine burning acid in her throat. She pulled a water thermos out, sucked down half its contents. Then she lay curled up with her back to the wind, her face buried beneath the sled tarpaulin. The agony in her spine took away all thought. She could only try to resist, to cope, to wait for the codeine's relief.

When it came, swiftly passing through her empty stomach into her blood, she sighed like she'd just eaten a great meal. The muscles in her neck released. Her back unclenched. Her mind drifted into opioid hallucination.

She is a bear. She raises her nose to the air: that air through which only the very faintest aromas will come in the cold. Something. Saliva floods her mouth.

'In the polar winter, even the mind retreats into itself. How far do you want to go, Carrie?'

She was not a bear. Just a woman lying on the wet ice, dying. Gingerly, she used the sled to push herself to her feet. She rocked, woozy with the codeine.

'I'm all mushed up,' she said. But she'd run near dry of wit.

She aimed herself east-ish. Anyway, away from the lead. She wondered if she'd actually know when she reached the land. In fact, the rain and wind had cleared stretches of the shingle beach. It rose from the ice surface in a gentle sweep that stretched diagonally away south. As her feet crunched onto the wet, black pebbles, she had to gulp down tears. She allowed herself one huge inhalation of breath. Walking along the curving beach, she could hardly keep her balance, the wind came so ferociously out of the south-west. The sled dragged, stuck. She fished out her torch. The sleet flashed through its beam, frighteningly fast.

'Banks Island,' Bastien said, his voice a comfort, whatever words he chose to speak.

'I thought you were done.'

'Nearly,' he said.

She trudged on for how long she couldn't tell, bent almost double as the beach swung round in something like a bay, until she was walking directly into the wind. She came down off the top of the beach. And, shortly, some larger something rose up, black against the darkening evening. She shone her torch. A big, grounded berg. Somehow, it had fallen forwards, or else an upper section had broken as it wedged itself into the shingle. She could see here that the beach dropped off more steeply. Like a stubby thumb ten feet high, the berg lay there, its leeward wall translucent in the torchlight.

She hauled her sled up beside it. For a moment, she just sank to her haunches and rested, free at last from the full force of the wind and sleet.

But Bastien said, 'No one survives sleeping in the open.'

She nodded her head wearily. Accepting. The painkiller was

only going to last so long. As swiftly as possible, she drew out the tent. She drove guy rope stays into the berg ice with the blunt end of her hatchet. Groaned with each blow, the pain-killers already wearing off. She threw her sleeping bag, ruck-sack, the last of the food and the cooking equipment into the tiny tent, trying to avoid sending the weather in with it. She filled the sled with heavy stones and tied the other guy ropes off to it. Then, as quickly as possible, she peeled off her sodden survival suit – that wretched, sagging lifesaver – and collapsed in through the tent flap.

She lay, gasping, unable even to seal the tent closed. It felt colder again. The sleet blew like an avalanche of stones. It was hardening into snow.

She could hear her own breathing, light and fast. She put her fingers to her head wound. The skin bulged around the three staples, puffy with infection. Her back was beginning to spasm once more. But, oh, she was done with it, with all of it.

She thought about Jim, irritating and ridiculous, her friend. Donny and his comedically lantern jaw, his fuck-me smile.

'How much *is* enough?' Bastien asked. She had no answer.

A shower of ice blew in. She struggled to a sitting posi-tion, scrabbled to catch the tent flap stays with her stiff gloves. Through the cascading sleet, she thought she caught a move-ment. Some vague outline moving against the flow, like a con-gealing of the storm itself. She watched it from the most pro-found space of torpor. The outline coalesced, grew, as if some-thing were approaching. A black, shiny point moved at its cen-tre, probing, searching.

Bastien said, 'I'm leaving now.'

And the form fused into the bear.

Joe Amaruq

Joe Amaruq was smiling. Not that anyone would see it. Not behind the heavy goggles, the deep, fur-lined hood, the balaclava with little air holes for his nostrils and mouth. And he preferred to keep it private, anyhow. His brother, Nootaikok, would not approve. Even a day and a night and a morning into their journey, Nootaikok was still sulking. Maybe that wasn't fair. It wasn't sulking, exactly; more the testiness that dealing with white people always gave him. Ironic, given he ran their family's sport hunting business. Or perhaps a fairer way to put it would be to suggest it was precisely for that reason that he'd grown so moody.

Anyhow, now was a time to be glad. Their two snowmobiles raced across the shore-ice. In the moonlight, the surface showed flat, hard and unbroken for miles. It was minus thirty. A lot lower with their speed. Yes, the cold found every seam line in his clothing, every narrow gap. Yes, his throat was raw with breathing, even protected as he was. Yes, it was a damn fool errand. But they were being paid well by Ross. And it was – say it! – an adventure. Just he and his brother, off adventuring. Something they'd not done for a very long time; not since Amaruq had left to study and then to work in the south.

Yesterday, they'd bumped and crawled overland, the sled Nootaikok's snowmobile towed slowing them down even more. They'd followed old trapline trails north and west through the low mountains behind Cape Kellett. Amaruq had argued the shore ice near the Kellett cliffs was as reliable as anywhere, given how cold it was. But Nootaikok hadn't trusted it; historically it had never proven trustworthy. And for sure, not after that crazy rain storm and thaw a couple days back.

'Weather's not healthy anymore,' his brother had said. 'Don't make sense from day to day, even. I won't be on the ice anywhere I can't make a quick run back to land.' Nootaikok had spoken with that flat voice he used when he wasn't going to debate the issue, and certainly not with his kid brother. So that had been that.

It had been tortuous going through the maze of valleys and clefts, even with his brother's near-as-dammit complete knowledge of the region. Cold air off the sea turned to fog in the mountains. It filled the narrow precipices, already black where the twilight and the moon couldn't reach. The headlights were all but useless. Amaruq had actually driven into an icy cliff wall at one point, denting but otherwise not damaging his snowmobile. Only his pride. Still, he'd suffered his brother's mockery with good grace, caught up in the joy of the journey.

But here now, on the ice at last, they followed the west coast's low shoreline of bays and spits. They'd seen almost no sign of fracturing or tide cracks. The cold had returned, bizarrely sudden, in this winter that made no sense.

'We'd been due a cold one,' their uncle had said before they left. 'Don't care how much the weather's been wrecked. Sometimes the old frost just wants to show itself again.'

Above, no clouds at all were visible. The stars glittered like the stony eyes of the dead. But the dead didn't bother Amaruq. What did they care about anything down here? Polaris pointed them on their way. Here was clarity, Amaruq thought. The simple flow of life.

Nootaikok reduced speed and Amaruq came alongside. They trundled along for a couple of minutes, then slowed to a halt. Amaruq's brother pulled his hood back, lifted his googles. He wore a scarf with a skull design about his jaw and mouth. He tugged it down and he was grinning, too, after all.

'Why don't you give up that garbage career of yours?' he said.

'I might.'

'Save the Arctic, rah rah rah,' Nootaikok chanted, pumping his fist like a protester.

'You got that right.'

Nootaikok pointed ahead. 'We gonna come into some weather,' he said.

Amaruq saw a darker line hazing the lowest stars in the north. 'Wind and ice dust, I reckon.'

'Yep.'

'Where are we?' Amaruq fiddled for his GPS reader and map, stashed in the little bag tucked under his windshield.

His brother looked on disdainfully. He pointed off right. 'Land's curving east into Storkerson Bay. We follow it in and round. Keep to the close shore ice.'

'Nervous in your old age, brother?'

'Not dying this trip. Not searching for some long-dead *qallunaat*. Let's eat. Move on. Want to get close, by the end of the day's journeying. Even take a look at this boat wreck.'

They sat together on a muskox skin, shoulders and legs touching. Chewed dried char and seal blubber. Sipped the tepid tea they'd made that morning, carefully stowed, buried deep in their gear.

'Too cold to smoke,' Nootaikok said.

'It'll kill you.'

Nootaikok passed his brother a piece of chocolate, said, 'What we gonna find?'

Amaruq blew air. 'Something, nothing.'

'You met her. She the kind of white girl might still be out here?'

The moonlight cast a soft, milky light that seemed to caress the surface of the world. An aurora coalesced into being. Long pale sheets of pink and emerald curled down out of the heavens, undulating, bitingly beautiful, even to Amaruq's experienced eyes.

'She jumps out of helicopters.' He shrugged. 'All I know.'

Nootaikok pointed to the aurora. 'The spirits have lit the path to the other side for someone,' he said.

'You're past your prime.' And grinned at his older brother.

Nootaikok pushed himself to his feet. 'Not me,' he said.

As they curved round the bay, travelling fast now, they soon came to the weather. Wind and ice dust, as Amaruq had suggested. The wind blew from the north-east. A cold wind. Hard and unforgiving. A wind that could mean trouble, or mean nothing at all. It lifted the speckling ice dust from the land, threw it with casual ferocity across the flats and into Amaruq's body. He watched it flash past his goggles. Had to lean into the wind, angle the snowmobile's steering skis that way or be dragged left.

It wasn't a white-out, exactly. If he kept ten yards or so behind his brother's snowmobile and sled, he could see him clearly enough. And looking up, he could make out still a tinge of auroral colours. Lighting the way from this world to the next. Great: just the sort of omen they needed. And the storm threatened to grow. You could miss stuff. Miss a person easy as glancing the wrong way.

It was what it was.

—

Three hours later, Amaruq's body felt as if it had been beaten with sticks. He hunched beneath his windshield, kept his brother directly ahead. The temperature had dropped considerably.

Even Amaruq found it hard to breathe. He had to turn his head out of the wind to catch each breath. How far had they come? Nothing like as far as they'd wanted, for sure. Anyway, how the hell was Nootaikok steering? Sure, they were heading pretty much in the right direction. But how straight was straight in the middle of this? What had he been thinking? It was a disaster. He leaned into the wind, praying for his brother to stop. Oh man, soft indeed. Nootaikok was right. The *qallunaat* world was absolutely, lay your dollars down, ruining him.

The ice storm came more in gusts now. It meant he could see farther, off and on. He caught sight of the broken black and white of a snow-blown shingle shoreline to his right. Maybe a hundred yards away. He had to hand it to his brother. High-class navigating.

He was remembering a trip fifteen years back, out to the ice edge, south of Kellett. A late October twilight, and the last really cold year when the ice had come properly. He and Nootaikok. Seal hunting, it was supposed to be. Didn't get any. What an embarrassment coming back. But they'd been out for the caper, really. The two of them sat for hours round a seal hole, and not a single head showed itself, until at precisely the same moment, the two of them had leaped up, cursing every swimming beast in the entire ocean down there. They'd got blind drunk with a bottle of bad vodka. Then the two of them built the worst damn igloo ever. Wrong floe ice, wrong shape ice bricks. Wrong everything. Even funnier.

Now, suddenly, Nootaikok braked hard. His sled jackknifed up behind him as he skidded to a halt. Amaruq frantically hit his own brakes. Too late. He jammed the handlebars right, slid sideways across the ice and crunched into the sled. Not too hard, but enough to throw him off the snowmobile and onto the tarpaulined stack of provisions. His ribs crunched painfully into the row of jerrycans. He slid slowly off onto the ice, groaning.

'What...?' he managed.

But Nootaikok made an urgent sound, pointing forwards. Amaruq came to his feet, rubbing his side. He peered through the flurrying haze. Pulled off his goggles. Saw nothing. But Nootaikok scrambled backwards off his machine. He kneeled behind it, scrabbled for the rifle secured beside the saddle in its thick case.

Amaruq was about to do the same when he caught sight of what it was his brother had seen. For only a second, he saw it. A wisp. He was a boy again, sitting on the floor in his auntie's house. She was working a smoking gas ring, boiling something. Telling tall tales in the long winter dark. Frightening tales. Stories about being far out on the ice. The lost spirits who wandered there.

Nootaikok already had his gun out. He crouched behind his snowmobile, scrabbling in his haste to work the rifle's mechanism.

Amaruq called out, 'Hey, brother, still scared of ghosts?'

Nootaikok paused. He stared at the gun in his hands for a time. Then his head inside its hood sagged. Slowly, he got to his feet. He looked round at Amaruq. Pulled down his scarf, looked sheepish, shook his head.

Together, the two of them walked forwards. Ice-spicules swirled thickly about them so they could hardly see ten feet. Neither spoke.

Abruptly, a few paces away, the spirit emerged once more from the fog. Shapeless, coloured an eerie, dull orange, it seemed oddly twisted, as if it to escape some heavy blow. It staggered, step by blundering step, towards them.

Amaruq called out, 'Hey.'

The figure stopped, lifted its head. An unnatural, scarred, flat surface where a face should be. Nootaikok jerked back. But Amaruq grinned. He walked forwards, took hold of the figure's clawed hands, where they clutched two bent metal tubes.

It dropped to its knees. Amaruq stooped as well. He pushed back his own hood, rolled up his balaclava onto his head. Then he reached up and opened the visor from the figure's ruined survival suit hood – the kind of suit he'd worn himself a hundred times before.

Her face was grey, puffy. Dark chasms spread out from her eyes and mouth. Black frostbite on her cheeks. A scraggle of hair hung, solid and frozen, down each side. An evil looking wound snaked out of her hairline, the pus that rose from it frozen solid. But her eyes viewed him keenly enough. Even, he thought, with a trace of humour.

'Carrie,' he told her. 'We've come to get you.'

He noticed only now that she was dragging some sort of sled. On it, Amaruq saw sections of a polar bear's bloody, frozen body, secured with ties. Its head and part of its back fur rested on top, appallingly badly flensed. A distinctive scar ran alongside its nose.

'She got one of our bears,' Nootaikok said.

Carrie noticed what they were looking at. 'I didn't want to do it.' Her voice breaking. 'Now I can't hear him anymore.'

She sank fully to the ground. 'Got...anything for pain?' she croaked.

He nodded. He said, 'We met before.'

She gave him a thin smile. 'Not a terrorist, after all.'

'Guess not,' he said.

THE DOSSIER

Ross

Ross stepped out of the taxi. It was snowing so heavily he'd not seen much of Yellowknife on the drive from the airport. But what he had seen felt completely alien. After all that had happened this past couple of months – after the north – he couldn't compute the hustle of even so small a city, even one in the midst of a snowstorm. And it was much more properly daylight down here as well. Tuk's otherworldly blue twilight had been replaced by a straightforwardly grey winter's day.

A few TV news media vans were still parked up outside. He plodded between them and into Stanton Territorial Hospital's foyer. He kept his hood up as he passed the huddle of reporters inside. He didn't want to talk publicly about anything. Particularly, he didn't want it broadcast that he'd had anything to do with Carrie's rescue. When the RCMP constable had knocked on his door in Tuk to tell him they'd found her, when the young man had said, 'Well done, sir,' Ross's first emotion had been embarrassment.

Speaking Carrie's name as quietly as possible to the receptionist, he told them who he was. She ran her finger down a list, nodded, gave him directions. He took the lift to the second floor, spoke to the young woman at the nurses' station.

'Tell the officer who you are,' she told him, pointing down the corridor. 'We've had a few journalists trying to get in.' A policeman was sitting in a chair outside a door at the far end.

'I'm Ross, Carrie's...Ms Essler's friend,' he said. The policeman just gestured to the door, bored.

Ross faltered. Hathaway had been right: Ross's obsession with finding Carrie had always been suspect. Bound up with atonement. All those men and women dead. He knew the depth of his own guilt, even if the world had shifted its focus on to eco-terrorism these past days. Willetts pontificating on any news channel who'd have him about the horrors of extremism.

But Carrie! She was alive. He knocked and walked straight in.

She was propped up in bed, but looked as if she'd been strapped to a pole against which she now slumped. Thick bandages covered her cheeks. Others were wrapped about her forehead and ears. Her lips were cracked, black, split into chasms horribly wide, her skin grey, deathly. With her eyes closed, she barely seemed alive. He hesitated, aghast at her condition.

'You going come in, or just stand there goggling?' A female nurse with huge hips and a bigger smile fiddled with a drip feed. Ross limped over to the other side of the bed.

'Oh God,' he muttered. He lifted a hand but dropped it back to his side.

'Don't you fret,' said the nurse, finishing off and heading out the door. 'That lady tougher'n a wrecking ball.'

Carrie's eyes opened. And there she was: that cynical gaze, more a glare, burning from the ruin of her face. Her lips formed the beginnings of a smile.

'Thank you,' she croaked.

He shook his head, made a nothing sound, looked away. 'Joe Amaruq and his brother...'

But she reached out and took his hand. 'Thank you,' she said again.

He searched for words. 'You killed a polar bear.'

She shrugged faintly. 'Girl's got to eat.'

'Still the hard-ass.'

'Joe's brother says he'll claim for it. Inuit have quotas. I stole one off them, so he says. Fee's ten thousand bucks.'

'How are you?' Ross still held her hand.

'Not dead. Which is plenty.'

'Way everyone's telling it, you dragged yourself and that stretcher of gear a hundred miles across breaking ice. And with a herniated disc so bad your surgeon wants to write a paper on it.'

For a time, Ross and Carrie just looked at each other.

'I heard,' Carrie said.

'About the *Belyy Medved*?'

'Joe said you fought pretty hard to stop the spill.'

'And failed.'

'Where you at with it now?'

'Our tug got a submersible down there, when the ice started breaking up for a day or two. It's...'

'Bad?'

'Oh, Christ.' He sat in the chair beside the bed. 'Everything's...We're going to try to get a rig over the relief well. But now it's cold again. The ice's so thick...' His words faded into silence.

After a time, Carrie said carefully, 'So they're pinning it on the tree huggers?' She stared at him intently.

He sighed, pulled off his coat and sat in the armchair by the bed. Hanging his cane on the bed's sidebars, he kneaded his bad leg. He couldn't find words. Perhaps he didn't know how to start. He lifted off his trilby and placed it on the bedside table.

'Always dug that hat,' she said. 'Bloody silly up here.' She regarded him with such fondness he had to look away. He remembered that last evening they'd spent in each other's company. The Tuk bar, the night before it all happened. He'd come close to telling her the truth.

Carrie pointed across the room, said, 'Get my bag, would you?'

Ross turned. What he saw first was Don Escamilla, sprawled across an armchair in his pilot's uniform. He looked bedraggled, exhausted. He regarded Ross without expression, but nodded in greeting. By his feet, a colourless old rucksack lay on the floor, so battered it hardly held itself together.

Ross went over, stood in front of Don, said quietly, 'How you doing?' Don's mouth made a movement as if he were about to speak, but then he just shrugged faintly. Ross picked up the bag.

'There's a Ziploc inside,' Carrie said.

Ross pulled it out, a thick plastic document sack, as beaten up as the rucksack, the plastic yellowed and almost opaque.

'Donny, could you give us a few minutes?' Carrie's croaking voice sounded softer when she spoke to him.

Escamilla pushed himself up from the armchair, made to step past Ross. But then he put his hand on Ross's shoulder for a moment, squeezed.

'I didn't believe you,' he said and went out.

'Open it,' Carrie told Ross.

He sat beside her again, pulled out a thick dossier folder, two USB sticks. Opening the folder, he saw email chain printouts, rig safety documents. Saw his signature. Saw his signature everywhere. Eventually, he allowed the pages to just filter through his fingers.

'How...?' he said.

She explained. 'There's a whole lot more on the USB sticks.'

When he looked up at her, Carrie's eyes were filled with tears. She reached out and he took her hand. Her fingernails were black, broken, her skin like an old woman's.

'What should I do?' she whispered.

Ross exhaled. He felt as if he could just keep breathing out and out. Like a vise had been unclamped from his chest.

'You should do the right thing,' he said.

'They'll string you up. Willetts too.'

He found himself holding his breath yet nodding. She was right. And so it wouldn't just be Jay Skelton, eco-terrorist. It would be all of them: the Russian-Azerbaijani drillship owners, the lax Canadian regulators. Willetts, the corner-cutting American and, yes, Ross and his shell company. They'd all be in the crosshairs. But he wouldn't be the solitary scapegoat, not this time. Carrie was right. Ross and Willetts would both be going to jail.

Ross found he could keep breathing out and out and out, until the only thing left inside was...

'It's all right,' he told Carrie. 'It's just the truth.'

Deliverance will not come from the rushing noisy centres of civilization. It will come from the lonely places.

Fridtjof Nansen, Farthest North

Glossary

Blowout
The uncontrolled release of crude oil or gas from a well. A blowout can be extremely dangerous. A single spark can ignite the escaping hydrocarbons creating a catastrophic fire.

Blowout Preventer [BOP]
A device fitted to a wellhead to prevent a blowout. Subsea BOPs can be massive machines, four storeys high and weighing over two hundred and eighty tonnes. The BOP is made up of annulars and shears, which can seal off the well, either temporarily or, in more dramatic instances, by severing the pipes and disengaging the riser from the well completely.

Derrick
The structure that supports all the equipment used for drilling a well. Most often a tall tower of steel girders, it houses a variety of machines for lifting and turning the drill-stem, and sending drilling fluids (or mud) down the well to cool the drill-bit as it bites into the earth.

Drill Floor
Directly beneath the derrick, this is the area where most of the work of drilling is done, from attaching the pipes that go down the well, fixing the drill-bit, and so on. It sits directly above the wellhead. On an offshore rig, the wellhead, of course, may be thousands of feet below, at the bottom of the ocean.

Drill Shack   *The drill-floor control centre, where the driller and others control all equipment for the drilling operation.*

Well Test   *A procedure to determine a hydrocarbon reservoir's capacity, its pressure, porousness, scale and more. After a series of protective measures are put in place, the well is allowed to flow for a period that can last an hour or up to several days. This is an important moment for the drilling company, as it offers the key evidence about a reservoir's financial viability.*

Dynamic Positioning System (DPS)   *A series of thrusters on an oil rig or drillship that keep it exactly in position over the wellhead on the seabed. The DPS uses a variety of measuring and directional systems to judge its exact position and keep it there. The DPS is operated from the bridge by Dynamic Positioning Officers.*

Emergency Disconnect System (EDS)   *A piece of equipment used on offshore rigs and drillships that can be activated in an emergency to swiftly disconnect from the wellhead, sealing both the well and the riser to avoid oil and mud spilling into the sea.*

Flare Boom   *A device on an oil rig used to burn off unwanted gas from the well. The boom stretches high and away to avoid the flames affecting the rig itself.*

Inuvialuit or Inuit?	*This story is set in the Inuvialuit Settlement Region of Canada's Western Arctic, the home of the Inuvialuit people. The Inuvialuit are 'Inuit', a term that describes culturally and historically similar groups of indigenous peoples who inhabit the sub-Arctic and Arctic regions of North America and parts of Russia. While some of my characters use the word 'Inuit' in their dialogue, this reflects their own ignorance of the distinction rather than, hopefully, the author's.*
Moonpool	*An opening in the bottom of a drillship's hull, that offers direct access to the sea. The moonpool sits directly beneath the drill-floor, and the riser and all drill-stem equipment drop down through it to the wellhead on the seabed.*
Mud	*The drilling fluids that are sent down the drill hole for a variety of purposes, from keeping the well pressure balanced (to avoid a blowout) to ensuring the revolving drill-bit that bores the hole does not overheat. The name 'mud' belies the expense and complexity of the fluid itself, which contains all kinds of suspended solids, emulsified water or oil, uniquely designed for the peculiarities of each well hole. Mud worth several million dollars may be down a well hole at one time, and it is carefully delivered and extracted for re-use.*

Offshore Installation Manager (OIM)	*The most senior manager in charge of drilling operations on an oil rig or drillship.*
Offshore Support Vessel (OSV)	*A cargo ship designed to support oil rigs by delivering supplies and equipment to and from shore. Often with a prow shaped like a giant cheese wedge and a long low open tail, on which cargo is positioned.*
(Proven) Reserves Statement	*A document produced by a Reserves Engineer stating the capacity and viability of a hydrocarbon reservoir, after a drill-stem test. This statement determines whether the reservoir will proceed to production (i.e. the hydrocarbons will be extracted from the reservoir).*
Reserves Engineer	*An independent professional brought in during a drill-stem (or well) test to assess a hydrocarbon reservoir's capacity and viability.*
Riser (& Riser Stack)	*A wide pipe connecting the blowout preventer to the oil rig or drillship on the surface, down through which the drill-stem itself passes. Its main function is to take mud back to the surface, although it has a variety of secondary safety functions as well.*

Submersible (often called an ROV, a Remotely Operated Vessel	*An unmanned submersible that is controlled from the surface. The ROV is used for a variety of purposes, from inspecting subsea structures, to overseeing subsea operations like lowering and raising the blowout preventer, building the wellhead and so on. The ROV has manipulable arms with which it can, for instance, turn valves.*
Travelling Block	*The freely moving section of the block and tackle in a derrick that lifts and lowers heavy machinery.*
Top Drive	*Suspended beneath the travelling block in a derrick, the top drive provides the torque that turns the drill pipe and drills the well.*
Wellhead	*The machinery at the surface of a well (on the seabed, offshore) that maintains the structure and controls pressure.*
Well Test Tree (sometimes called the "Christmas Tree")	*An assemblage of valves and other fittings that regulate the flow of oil and gas coming out of a well during a well/drill-stem test.*

Acknowledgements

To my draft readers, Martin Stannard, George Green and David Wharton, plus Alex Goldsmith and Jamie Isbester for casting a salty eye over my poor seamanship. Gordon M and Pete O, oil industry experts, for so generously offering their experience to a polar bear hugger like me; Gordon, particularly, for giving me a steer on how I might blow up an oil rig. All errors, of course, my own. To Katie, Alex and Ines at Claret for marvellous editorialising and support, and Petya for a wonderful cover. To Isobel Dixon, my literary agent, who has somehow never yet rolled her eyes in my presence as she's supported me all these years. To the British Library's Eccles Centre for a 'Literary Fellowship in North American Studies' to get part of my research done. To the University of Leicester and my colleagues there for writing time and forbearance. To Nila and Brân as tiny tots for driving all the way to Aberdeen through January blizzards so I could see where Carrie grew up. To Anita, who it's all for and all because of, in the end.

You can find more information about the research
that went into *White Road* on my blogsite here:

harrydwhitehead.blogspot.com